THE CONFIRMATION

THE CONFIRMATION

L G DICKSON

Matador
9 Priory Business Park,
Wistow Road, Kibworth Beauchamp,
Leicestershire. LE8 0RX
Tel: 0116 279 2299
Email: books@troubador.co.uk
Web: www.troubador.co.uk/matador
Twitter: @matadorbooks

ISBN 978 1788035 736

British Library Cataloguing in Publication Data.
A catalogue record for this book is available from the British Library.

Printed and bound by CPI Group (UK) Ltd, Croydon, CR0 4YY
Typeset in 11pt Minion Pro by Troubador Publishing Ltd, Leicester, UK

Matador is an imprint of Troubador Publishing Ltd

For John, Phyllis, Hilary and Jonathan

ACKNOWLEDGMENTS

I would like to thank Andy Wightman MSP, whose book 'The Poor Had No Lawyers' informed James's political ambitions, particularly his passion for land reform.

I am indebted to Skriva Writing School and my tutor Sophie Cooke who has both taught and inspired me. To my writing buddies particularly Helen, Mary Anne and Gavin – it has been a joy to share this journey with you.

Finally, to those closest to me, for your love, support and unwavering confidence in me – thank you.

The Confirmation

Yes, yours, my love, is the right human face.
I in my mind had waited for this long,
Seeing the false and searching for the true,
Then found you as a traveller finds a place
Of welcome suddenly amid the wrong
Valleys and rocks and twisting roads. But you,
What shall I call you? A fountain in a waste,
A well of water in a country dry,
Or anything that's honest and good, an eye
That makes the whole world bright. Your open heart,
Simple with giving, gives the primal deed,
The first good world, the blossom, the blowing seed,
The hearth, the steadfast land, the wandering sea,
Not beautiful or rare in every part,
But like yourself, as they were meant to be.

EDWIN MUIR

CHAPTER 1

Books were stacked in all four corners of the lounge – segregated into fiction and non. Endless reference books on submarine warfare and Arctic exploration sat next to derring-do stories of wartime adventure and revolutionary exploits. She knew exactly the books that would fire his imagination and hold him engrossed for hours – his attention diverted away from her. She loved the feeling of knowing that hours of searching neglected corners of Edinburgh's secondhand bookshops had turned up another little gem – one he accepted with thanks and love. Following an almighty embrace that threatened to crush vertebrae, he would smile lovingly at her, settle down and disappear off into another space and time. She looked at them now from across the room – a mixture of pristine and faded covers, torn spines and exposed binder tape. What did he want her to do with them? Had he said? She wasn't sure that he had so it was probably best to leave things as they were. He'd let her know in good time. All in good time.

A tumbled pile of soft brushed cotton shirts sat heaped upon the leather chair opposite. They would need ironing but she really needed a new ironing board cover. She'd mentioned that to him before. Not that she'd expected him to do anything about it. The thought prompted her to mentally list the domestic tasks that needed attention. Tasks which, for now, would have to wait. All she really wanted to do was press her face into the familiar fabric of those well-worn shirts.

She ignored the dull drone of her mobile phone switched to silent, and slowly stood up. Suddenly the shrill ringing of the landline shook her, making her feel dizzy and unsteady on her feet. She was forced back down. After three loud rings came the orderly click of the answer machine. It was Kirsty.

'Look, it's just me – again. We don't want to be a pain, honestly. We just want to come round and help. Get you back on your feet. Just ring – let us know you're okay.' There was a short pause. 'Well, that was all really. Love you. Love you lots.' And then she was gone.

She couldn't think about Kirsty. She couldn't think about any of them. Her head felt heavy, far too heavy and so she let the weight fall back into the soft cushion behind and closed her eyes. Something else could take the strain.

The phones had stopped now and her head began to fill with thoughts and images of other times and places. None of it made any sense. After a while, she forced herself to stand up and made her way through to the kitchen to pour the first wine of the night.

*

Fifteen years earlier, on an almost oppressively warm August night, Annie walked briskly towards her destination in Great King Street. Oppressively warm was not a description normally afforded to Edinburgh weather, even at the height of summer. Sunshine-filled days were too often accompanied by the chilled haar that rolled and tumbled down the city's thoroughfares from the North Sea but Annie could only feel warm air against her skin and no trace of a cooling breeze. She quickened her stride and turned into a street that, in its nineteenth-century hey day, had housed some of the most distinguished professional men and their families of Edinburgh. These handsome residences welcomed a more diverse mix of inhabitants in 1990 while still playing host to a smattering of top-end lawyers – her good friends Duncan and Kirsty Drummond among them.

Annie arrived at No. 92, somewhat out of breath and feeling slightly clammy. Her new salmon silk blouse was sticking to her and small patches of sweat were beginning to appear under her arms and more annoyingly under her bust where too-tight underwire was pressing into too-hot flesh. *Why did I think this was a good choice of outfit?* she thought to herself as she pulled the brass bell pull for the Drummond residence. It was, after all, only a regular Friday night get-together with her old university crowd and there really was no need to impress. For some unfathomable reason Annie had felt the urge to make a bit of an effort. And now here she was standing, hair sticking to face and with small droplets of sweat beginning to appear on her top lip.

Kirsty Drummond opened the door and enthusiastically flung her arms around her bedraggled friend. 'Oh my god, look at you. What the hell have you been doing?'

Annie attempted to explain work deadlines, protracted telephone calls from Mother and her kitten's predilection for ripping wallpaper, all of which had made her late and slightly bedraggled.

Kirsty ignored all of this, admiring her friend's new sweat-stained top, and drew Annie closer to her. 'Donald's disappeared down to Coniston this weekend, gorge walking I think,' she explained. 'Duncan came up with the genius idea of inviting our new neighbour in to make up the numbers. Hope you don't mind but I've been dying to check him out for weeks now. Keeps himself very much to himself,' she whispered loudly into Annie's ear.

'Great, fine,' Annie replied, rummaging in her bag for a clean hankie and paying little attention to her friend.

Donald was Kirsty's younger brother and was often drafted in to make up the numbers. Annie had known him since he was a boy and had watched him grow from a gawky youngster into a confident outdoorsy type. He really had very little in common with his sister's friends but was always pleasant company. As Annie dabbed her face with the paper hankie, trying not to leave any pieces of tissue on her still clammy face, she faced the dawning realisation that she was going to have to make conversation with a complete stranger. Her heart sank. Meeting new people required effort.

Kirsty forcefully guided Annie through the welcoming light and airy hall, and just as they were about to enter the large bay-windowed lounge, pulled Annie to one side. 'Of course, without Donald here to keep Duncan entertained, I'm afraid he's started a bit earlier than usual in the kitchen.'

Annie just smiled and squeezed her friend's hand.

4

This was not the time to offer up any views on Duncan Drummond's excesses.

'That's right,' said Kirsty looking relieved. 'No point worrying about that now.'

Annie entered the gathering and immediately saw the stranger slumped into a burst and tattered armchair in the corner of the room – one of Kirsty's so-called great finds in the furniture rooms on Leith Walk. Annie smiled to herself – this was the first time the incumbent truly had matched the chair. He caught her eye, smiled gently and proceeded to haul himself out of the sunken seat, protruding foam and fabric springing back to life as he stood to his feet. At this point, Annie wished she'd diverted off to the bathroom to attempt some running repairs, however, she had been late arriving and Kirsty had been keen to make introductions.

He was not an unhandsome man. His face, like the chair, was a tad worn and leathery but it merely accentuated his beautifully pale blue eyes. His beige linen suit was crumpled, soft cotton shirt unironed and frayed tie slightly askew. His brogues, however, were so highly polished Annie wondered what on earth prompted a man to take so much effort on his size tens and leave the rest of the ensemble to look so neglected. He towered over her *(at least six foot five, she thought)* and just as she was completing her assessment of his overall dimensions, she felt someone grab her by the elbow and thrust her clumsily towards his outstretched hand. Of course it was Kirsty. The poor man was here to make up numbers at the dinner table and satisfy the curiosity of the hostess. If things worked out well, Annie might also find herself with an interesting companion for any future dining emergencies. Whether or not either party desired this potential match-up was of no concern to Kirsty. There was an immediate logistical problem to overcome. Dinner tables should, whenever possible, comprise matching partners and compatibility really didn't come into the equation.

Annie's dinner companion, who had introduced himself as James, was, according to Duncan, a high-ranking civil servant who had just moved in across the landing. As the others wandered into the dining room it was Duncan this time who grabbed her by the elbow. 'I've heard he's quite big in land management, rural stuff, that kind of thing – seems to have the ear of the politicians anyway.'

Annie knew she was supposed to be impressed but all she wanted to do was move her now painful elbow out of Duncan's grasp and her face away from his already gin-infused breath.

They were all used to Duncan's excesses but as they took their seats at the dinner table everyone seemed to feel the need to throw apologetic glances from time to time in the direction of the stranger from across the hall. Kirsty's eyes fixed on Duncan, his behaviour becoming more erratic as he refilled his wine glass to the brim during each trip back to the kitchen.

Annie tried smiling across the table at Kirsty to see if that might reduce the tension but she just looked even more embarrassed. Duncan always cooked at dinner parties and his food was sublime but the constant topping up of his wine glass from a hidden stash in the kitchen often resulted in his being asleep before the main course was over, leaving everyone else to savour his latest creation and exchange complimentary noises. The introduction of a stranger to the dinner table did not give rise to a change in the group's behaviour. Annie knew that by the end of the meal everyone else would be carrying on a normal conversation and eating at a relaxed pace with mine host sat slumped and snoring at the head of the table.

The other dining companions, Gordon and Virginia, always reminded Annie of the devoted couple from an eighties sitcom that she could never quite remember the name of. They didn't quite extend to matching knitwear but more often than not appeared in almost identical outfits. It wasn't clear how they managed it, as their wardrobe was almost entirely acquired from Stockbridge's vast array of upmarket charity shops. Gordon worked in corporate social responsibility and Virginia was reading for a PhD in 'renewable energy from land-based resources'. Not the most scintillating of dinner companions but they were simply the kindest and most well-intentioned friends she had ever had.

James said very little during that first encounter. The Edinburgh Festivals had just drawn to a close, the natives were rediscovering their natural habitat and the artistically minded middle classes were either extolling the virtues or giving damning critiques of various performances, films and readings. This end of August, Saturday night gathering was no different. Duncan was still conscious at this stage in the evening and had decided to interrogate James on the extent of his engagement with the various festivals, but James appeared reluctant to join this earnest band of amateur critics. The rest of the group chatted about the

Leningrad Philharmonic Orchestra and Virginia, who herself had guzzled a few more glasses than usual, waxed lyrical about the Sir William Gillies retrospective at the Scottish Gallery.

Annie decided to push him. She told herself it was just to help the conversation flow but there was a spark of attraction – she knew there was.

'Well, James, what about your highlights? Anything interesting?'

'Not particularly. I didn't get to that much this year but from the reviews there seemed to be a lot that the tourists liked.'

Undeterred she continued. 'Not even on the music front? What about the Usher Hall's music programme? Did you get to any of that?'

'Yes, I did actually. Some of it anyway,' he replied, vaguely, before plunging his fork into Duncan's perfectly constructed tian of crab and avocado.

It was going to be a long evening. After numerous failed attempts at meaningful conversation she turned towards Virginia and they struck up a conversation on how a farmers' food market – 'they seem to be springing up all over the country' – would be a great addition to the area's culinary landscape while the prospect of any further retail developments in their lovely little 'village' was a complete abomination and must be resisted at all costs. Annie noticed James out of the corner of her eye, smirking and, almost imperceptibly, shaking his head.

'Sorry, James, did you say something?' she asked perhaps a bit too earnestly.

'No nothing.'

Then just as she was about to turn back to Virginia he muttered something about the well heeled of Stockbridge venting their anger at potential retail expansion when the big issues of the day like the implications of Yugoslavia falling apart were just passing them by.

Annie decided to pretend she hadn't heard him. She was trying to make conversation, have a good time with her friends and any superficial attraction she might have felt really wasn't going to compensate, even if it was accompanied by something resembling a political conscience. But then, just as she dropped her head to resume eating, Virginia suddenly stretched her hand out across the table and placed it on top of James's.

'Of course, you're absolutely right,' she cried out.

James merely looked startled and said nothing for the rest of the meal. Annie resisted the temptation to smile.

True to form, Duncan was in a deep slumber by the time everyone had finished the delicious paella and it was left to everyone else to clear the table around him and serve up their own portion of dessert. The assembled throng had done this so many times they were really quite adept at being able to converse, tidy up, eat and drink, leaving Duncan oblivious to all going on around him. James just looked uncomfortable, unsure whether to try to converse with his host or at least rouse him before the group retired back through to the lounge. Before he could do anything, Kirsty had slipped her arm through his and marched him off.

Suddenly James stopped her in the hall. 'Sorry, Kirsty, I've got a very early start in the morning and really need to be heading off. Thanks, really though, it was a lovely meal.'

He reached for the door but not before turning to say goodbye to the others. As he turned, his eyes fell upon Annie and he smiled the faintest, sweetest smile. She smiled back and in that instant felt an odd almost indescribable connection to this vaguely awkward and slightly irascible man. Perhaps it wouldn't be so terrible after all, if she got to know Mr James Kerr just a little bit better.

*

The following morning, Annie lay in a supine position on top of the bed, hands clasped across her chest and with a cold wet flannel pressed to her forehead. It wasn't the worst hangover in the world but she had attempted to rise two hours earlier and merely made it to the bathroom for flannel and painkillers. Setting aside the dull, throbbing headache it was the fact of drinking to excess that shocked her most. Mornings lost to overindulgence were a thing of the past – mostly consigned to student and early working years and more or less now reserved for birthdays and other festivities. Friday night dinner with the usual suspects did not normally lead her to drink to excess. There was so much to do on a Saturday. A thirty-minute run followed by shower, fresh morning rolls from the baker's and then the lists. She lived her life by lists, adding to them, ticking items off and creating new ones but perhaps that was it – last night hadn't just been the usual suspects.

Annie tried to piece together what had happened after James left and why she had seemingly abandoned her normal state of cautious reserve. She remembered plonking herself down next to Duncan, nudging him to stay awake and chat. Unused to anyone trying desperately to keep him up and socialising, Duncan had discovered an energetic second wind and had gone off to open his favourite late-bottled vintage port. The others saw this as a great opportunity to make their excuses and depart, even his own wife, who looked across to Annie, then turned to look at her beckoning bedroom door and turned back with a smile that suggested both relief and gratitude.

As she lay contemplating a second attempt at rising to face the day, Annie tried desperately to remember what they had been talking about all night but realised that was less important than the fact that she had just wanted to talk and not go home to sleep. All her senses seemed to have been heightened by her encounter with the stranger from across the hall and she had felt ready to witter on about anything and everything. Eventually exhausted by his new-found drinking chum, Duncan had suggested it was time to call a taxi and he too had looked longingly towards his bedroom door.

As Annie lay trying not to move her head, the kitten managed to scramble up the side of the mahogany sleigh bed, leaving, as she discovered later, tiny scratches on the side of the frame. He pulled the flannel off with his tiny claws and sat on her face licking at the cold wet residue on her forehead. It was now definitely time to get up and face what was left of the day. She managed a quick shower – all thoughts of a brisk jog around Inverleith Park had receded long ago – and then made herself some tea and toast. As she was beginning to return to normality the phone rang. The phone only ever rang on a Saturday morning if the caller was offering compensation for some five-year-old accident she'd forgotten all about, was offering to supply and fit new windows for any room in the house – or it was Annie's mother.

Helen Anderson lived in a stunning penthouse apartment in the West End of Edinburgh having moved there the year after Annie's father died. It was a rational, unsentimental move and made eminent sense to Annie that her mother should leave the rambling five-bedroomed home for somewhere smaller and easier to keep – less room for memories.

A family home needed to be filled with school uniforms, rugby kit and hockey sticks, Helen had proclaimed. The rooms should echo to the sound of children's laughter. Annie struggled with the rationale, given that her father had, for various reasons, rarely been at home during his working life. She was an only child and as such it was really only mother and daughter who rattled around the vast rooms and extensive gardens during her adolescence. Neither laughter nor the detritus of school sporting activities were much in evidence at 'Forth View' as Annie was growing up. On the occasions when her father did appear she broke free from her mother's regime of strict rules and orders and clung on to him – both physically and to his every word.

Annie picked up the phone and before she could utter any word of greeting her mother's voice boomed down the line.

'Annie dear, it's your mother. What are you doing tomorrow?'

That was it – short and to the point. If Annie's mental

faculties had been operating at even half normal capacity she would have thought of something. It might not have been entirely plausible but it would have allowed her a bit of thinking space.

'Nothing, Mother, why?' She heard herself say the words but it was too late to pull back.

'That's lovely, dear. The McHargs have tickets to some Hebrides thing at the Queen's Hall. There really is no one else I could think of to ask. It's just not everyone's cup of tea.'

'Hebrides what, Mother?' Annie asked. 'I don't know what that means and I don't know what on earth makes you think I would enjoy it, whatever it is.'

'Oh, sorry, dear,' Helen replied sounding a bit crestfallen. 'Of course you don't have to. I think it might be some kind of chamber group but really, don't worry about it. I'll just let the McHargs know it's really not for us.'

Annie recoiled. We are not an 'us' she felt like screaming but then feeling that familiar combination of duty, guilt and daughterly love she said, 'It's fine, Mother, we'll go. I just hadn't heard of them, that's all.'

'Okay, lovely, darling, I'll speak to you later to make arrangements.' Annie said her goodbyes and as she made her way wearily into the kitchen to feed the kitten the phone rang again. It was Kirsty.

'Thank goodness you're in. I really just wanted to apologise for inflicting Mr Kerr on you. What a difficult dinner guest and just so *rude*. All very disappointing really.'

'No, really, he wasn't that bad.' Annie felt an odd need to defend the man. 'Okay, he was a little bit rude but for whatever reason he obviously feels quite strongly about the big issues of the day. We're just not used to it on a Friday night, Kirst.'

'Duncan's worried that you were so hacked off that you decided to blot out the experience by throwing yourself into a full-on session with his nibs,' Kirsty went on, regardless.

'No, honestly, it was fine,' Annie protested. She really couldn't take any more difficult conversations today. 'How is Duncan anyway?' she asked, changing tack.

'Oh, I don't know,' Kirsty sighed. 'Fine I think – he's sloped off back to bed. So funny though, this morning when he woke he said he'd decided to call our neighbour JFK. Not in a good way though – James "Fucking" Kerr! Hilarious, I thought. Anyway must dash. Want to get down to Armstrong's and see if they've any red mullet left.'

And with that she was off.

The remainder of Saturday passed by in a bit of a blur. True to form Annie managed to tick off most things on her list – all achieved at a slightly more sedate pace than normal. Sunday morning dawned and she felt a lot more like her old self. It still felt unseasonably warm for the beginning of September in Edinburgh. She enjoyed her run round the park and made her way down to the boating pond, drinking in the views of the imposing Edinburgh skyline silhouetted against the clear blue sky. She bought the large cellophane-wrapped package that comprised *The Sunday Times* from the newsvendor at the corner of Portgower Place, a takeaway coffee from the café on Raeburn Place and skipped down the stairs to her basement flat in Dean Terrace.

Annie felt a strange sense of wellbeing. She caught

up with housework, some emails and generally pottered around the flat. As she was enjoying the second coffee of the day, with the kitten asleep in her lap, she realised that the man who had caused such upset two days before had been in her thoughts ever since. Not always up front and centre – sometimes lurking in the dark recesses but there nonetheless. *Well, this is an interesting development*, she thought, smiling to herself. The likelihood of meeting him again in any kind of social setting seemed remote but she decided she would probe Kirsty later in the week for a bit more of his backstory.

Finally it was time to get ready to meet Mother. They had arranged to meet at the entrance to the Queen's Hall. Converted from a church sometime in the seventies, the Hall was home to the Scottish Chamber Orchestra and a venue for visiting folk and jazz bands, particularly during festival season. As Annie crossed Clerk Street she noticed from the billboards at the front of the building that the 'Hebrides thing' was in fact the Hebrides Ensemble, a collective of world-class musicians based in Scotland performing a wide range of styles in chamber music, opera etc.

This might actually be quite good.

Mother was already there, dressed up to the nines.

'My, Mother, you look lovely,' Annie exclaimed, at the same time thinking she wouldn't be out of place at Covent Garden Opera House.

'You too, darling,' Helen replied. 'Jean and Alasdair are already in the bar.'

Helen, a vision in faux fur, marched off in front of Annie straight to the McHargs standing holding their warm gin and tonics. Annie noticed how her mother, after the requisite number of air kisses, essentially ignored Jean and focused all her attention on Captain McHarg. Scots Guards, you know. Well groomed, highly polished and an authority on every subject matter under the sun. Annie found him slightly nauseating but her mother literally fawned over the man. He was nothing like her father, nothing at all. As Annie approached her mother's friends she suddenly noticed the particularly tall gentleman in the far corner of the room whose head seemed to hover above all other patrons crammed into the bar area. Her heart skipped a beat. The Captain was talking to her but she wasn't listening. There he was, same linen suit, same piercing blue eyes, engaged in earnest conversation with… who? Annie couldn't quite make out if his companion was a man or woman. *Well, the art of sustained conversation clearly isn't completely beyond him,* she thought to herself. As she strained to get a better view, Annie felt the tug of her mother's hand on the sleeve of her camel coat.

Annie, Helen and the McHargs took their seats plumb in the middle of the upper gallery with wonderful views of the whole stage. The music, a new piece from Peter Maxwell Davies, was lively and interesting and Annie determined to relax and let the music flow through her. She closed her eyes but as she did so his face filled the space she had intended to leave for purely meditative thoughts. She began to wonder where he might be seated and scoured the central and side galleries for any sign but to no avail. She decided that he must be sitting downstairs and proceeded to give herself over to the enchanting sounds of cello, violin and flute. After two hours, the thoroughly enjoyable concert drew to a close; the group took their bows to the sound of rapturous applause and the patrons made their way to the exits. The McHargs kindly offered lifts to both Anderson ladies but as they lived on the other side of the city, Annie politely declined the offer.

'Plenty of black cabs at this time of night,' she insisted and began to follow her mother outside.

As the McHargs departed, Annie felt a hand press softly onto her shoulder. She knew immediately it was James and turned to see him smiling, eyes glinting in the dim evening twilight.

'I thought it was you,' he exclaimed. 'Lovely to bump into you like this.'

Annie's mother turned, eyebrows raised, staring over her glasses at the tall stranger.

'Oh, Mother, this is James, Kirsty and Duncan's new neighbour,' she said quickly, aware she was sounding a bit flustered.

James and Helen smiled politely at each other but he quickly returned his gaze to Annie. She wanted to usher her mother away but at the same time felt an inexplicable desire to remain firmly rooted to the spot.

'Look, you may just want to tell me to take a hike but I really would like us to start again.' He looked at her, almost pleading. 'I understand if you think I was being a bit obnoxious the other night but...'

'Come on, dear, we're going to let all the taxis go at this rate.' Annie heard her mother from over her shoulder.

'Okay. Let's arrange coffee or something.'

'Lovely,' he replied. 'Why don't you just give me a buzz at work, whatever works for you really.' He too was beginning to sound a bit flustered as he desperately looked for a pen from the inside of his jacket. He quickly scribbled down a number on the back of the concert programme before shoving the crumpled paper into Annie's hand and holding on as he did so.

'You'd better run,' he whispered gently. She didn't want to move. His voice sounded so much softer than it had during that awkward dinner and she just wanted to stay there in that moment holding his hand and listening to his unexpectedly soothing voice. Helen, however, was growing more and more impatient. Annie turned briefly to see that one of her trademark glowers was beginning to take shape.

'Okay, bye then.' Reluctantly she drew her hand away, all the while smiling back at him.

Annie turned, grabbed Helen by the arm, and practically dragged her off down Clerk Street.

'Okay, dear. Slow down for your old mother now,' Helen protested. 'And where did you say you met that man?' she asked.

Annie wasn't quite ready for the big interrogation so gave a very brief résumé of the dinner from hell, missing out on the more interesting moments. Before she knew what was happening, Helen had been bundled into the next available cab and Annie spent the duration of the taxi ride asking questions about the McHargs' children, the quality of service provided by the new cleaners in her mother's apartment complex and then rounded everything off by enquiring after the health of assorted friends and relatives. Helen was in her element and soon forgot all about the new man.

18

Annie didn't sleep at all well that night, even after administering a few drops of Rescue Remedy in the early hours. She tossed and turned, trying to make sense of the last forty-eight hours. He clearly was an attractive man, physically – well, to her anyway – and she had felt some kind of connection. Niggling away, however, was the thought that he was probably quite difficult. Then again, given their limited contact, she couldn't be sure how difficult. Facts were he could be abrupt and rude but then it probably wasn't fair to come to any fixed view on the basis of one of Kirsty and Duncan's slightly chaotic dinner parties. But why invest in any of it? What was to be gained?

Eventually she put the light on and tried to read her book but her mind drifted from the page in front of her. He was clearly a few years older than her, which probably meant emotional baggage. There would be a number of good reasons why it wouldn't work as a *proper* relationship. Not for the long haul anyway and if you weren't in it for the long haul what on earth was the point? Not that she'd ever let anything get close to being long term or permanent. She'd never had her heart broken; slightly bruised perhaps, but nothing too dramatic. Only one really serious relationship when she thought about it and really it wasn't anyone's fault. He'd had to go away with work. A young doctor volunteering with Médecins Sans Frontières. Utterly admirable, that's what everyone else thought. And of course they were right but it just wouldn't have worked. Not with the distance and the time spent apart. Best just to end it before anyone got really hurt.

And she was fine with that. Didn't really do the 'overwrought emotion' thing. It had just seemed such a waste of time and energy. No locking yourself away from friends and family for days on end, crying yourself to sleep, finding solace in a bottle of gin. No, these things happened to other people and she, Annie, reassuringly calm and rational, just got on with her life. No one would have noticed any real difference but Annie knew. She knew that another impenetrable layer had covered her heart and there was no earthly reason to think that it would be breached this time.

Annie closed her book, switched off the light and finally fell asleep.

She woke to the sound of the alarm with that familiar feeling of heavy exhaustion experienced after a night of broken sleep. It wasn't unusual for her to feel this way on a Monday morning but normally her head was full of preparation for the week ahead. Reading over witness depositions, preparing for employment tribunals, checking over settlement agreements. This morning really felt like a duvet day but it wasn't going to happen. She hauled herself out of bed, stood under the shower willing herself awake and finally emerged from the bathroom to pull on her cream silk blouse and tailored black trouser suit – all big pockets, big pleats but not too big shoulder pads. Annie could never face breakfast first thing in the morning so poured a glass of orange juice and made a quick cup of coffee. After the kitten was fed and litter tray cleaned, she took the brand new Nike Air Max trainers out of their box, the almost fluorescent white shoe and bright blue swoosh making her head throb, slipped her feet in and felt an immediate sense of cosy, cushioning comfort. Papers were filed back into the briefcase from whence they had come. Nothing had been reviewed, checked or annotated but Annie felt at least some satisfaction that papers had made it out of the office and, indeed, out of the briefcase for a weekend break.

The walk to work was all uphill but she liked to stretch her legs and feel her heart pumping, energised by the time she got to the front door of Saunders and MacKay in Moray Place. She really stretched out going up Gloucester Lane, feeling her new dazzling trainers slip slightly on the dewy cobbles. Temperatures had fallen quite dramatically overnight and there was a chill feel to the air, another sign that the festival city was returning to normality. Annie ignored the lactic acid build-up in her calf muscles and strode out impressively all the way to the top of the hill, collected herself during the more sedate amble along Queen Street and finally entered the noble elegance of Moray Place. Annie never tired of the nineteenth-century grand classical porticos and pillars that greeted her as she faced the twentieth-century world of commerce and litigation.

She entered the ground floor offices at No. 31. 'Anyone mind if I open a window?'

'Not at all,' a few voices murmured, less than enthusiastically.

'Okay, just for a minute.'

Annie noticed that Bryce's office was empty, muttered something about a quick private phone call and went in, quietly shutting the door behind her. *Well, obviously I am going to call him*, she thought to herself and pulled the crumpled programme from her bag. Her heart was racing as she made the call. 'James Kerr's phone' was the polite feminine greeting at the end of the line. Her heart sank and she replaced the receiver, saying nothing. *Well, that's that*, she thought. *There's tons to do so just get him out of your head and press on with McMurray v Lothian Regional Council.* She returned to her desk feeling just a bit deflated but got on with the business of the day.

Mid-morning, the office clerk Simon announced he was going for scones and Annie placed her usual order for cheese with lots of butter. Jolted out of witness statements and copies of faded invoices she suddenly got up and marched straight back into Bryce's office. The number was now imprinted in her memory and she quickly hit the keypad.

'James Kerr.'

'Well, that's short and to the point.'

'Annie? Lovely to hear from you. Ah yes, my business voice – not too off-putting, I hope.'

'No, no,' she stuttered. 'Just wondered about that cup of coffee sometime. Maybe later in the week or next week perhaps? Thought we could maybe just cross-check schedules, see where we are, that kind of thing.' She was rambling now.

'Yes, what about lunch today? Could you make Hendersons for one?'

'Oh yes, fine. Good. One it is.' She replaced the receiver. Her heart was in her mouth now. *Okay, that was a bit unexpected but perfectly manageable*, she thought to herself.

At twelve thirty she was in the ladies' reapplying lipstick and sorting her hair. Black patent court shoes were shoved into her bag and the still gleaming white trainers were back on her feet. *I'll change footwear just as I get to Hanover Street,* she decided.

As she approached the corner of Queen Street and Hanover Street she saw him coming from the opposite direction. *He's bound to say something about my choice of footwear,* she thought to herself but when they met he merely smiled and said he hoped the restaurant wouldn't be too busy. Hendersons, an Edinburgh institution, was a vegetarian heaven and had been a favourite lunch venue of Annie's for years.

'You're not vegetarian, are you?' asked Annie.

'No, not at all,' he replied. 'I just love the place. Serves unpretentious, good food and it's "so Edinburgh".' There was a sarcastic hint of Morningside in that final intonation, Annie thought.

They found a table for two in a cosy corner and then queued up for the light lunch option of soup and two salad portions. As they sat down again, Annie wondered whether she should try to wrestle the stilettos out of her bag but decided against. The state of her footwear clearly hadn't registered at all with him.

'Do you remember the Laigh Coffee House opposite?' he asked lifting a spoonful of tomato and basil soup to his mouth. It was a nice mouth, she thought.

'Oh gosh yes – Moultrie Kelsall!' she exclaimed. As he brought the spoon back down his face creased gently into a smile.

'I'd forgotten all about that place,' she went on. 'When I was young, every time we passed by – in the car, on the bus, walking along the street – my parents would point and say, "owned by Moultrie Kelsall, famous actor". I had no idea who he was, still don't, but I absolutely loved the name. Used to wait for them to say it every time and then I would turn it over and over in my head. I mean to say, what kind of a name is that? Moultrie Kelsall – I ask you!' A name from her childhood, signalling shared laughter and knowing smiles, had suddenly been brought back through the memory of her father's voice.

'He was my father's best friend,' James said quietly tucking into his potato salad.

'So he was real and you actually knew him?' Annie looked shocked.

'Yes, Father and he grew up together and kept in touch pretty much throughout their lives, even when Moultrie was in London.'

'Really. So where did they grow up? In fact where did you grow up?'

'Bearsden. Glasgow.'

'Glasgow, really?' A touch of incredulity had crept into her voice so she tried to recover the position. 'It's just that you don't have much of an accent.'

'I see. Are all Glaswegians synonymous with Rab C. Nesbitt?'

'Oh no, not at all. Truth be told I really don't know that many people from Glasgow.'

She looked up at him and they both laughed at how ridiculous that sounded. His 'so Edinburgh' comment was suddenly vindicated.

James ordered coffee for them both and they moved effortlessly into pleasant everyday conversation: parents and their famous acquaintances, respective careers,

24

walking in the Pentlands, the joy of having the Botanics right on their doorstep.

Annie could feel herself relax back into her pine chair and decided now was the time to gently probe the suddenly more malleable surface of Mr Kerr's persona.

'Well, I can't be the first woman you've tapped on the shoulder after a chamber concert, so what's the position with regard to significant others in the life of Mr James Kerr?' She'd jumped too soon. Far too soon.

He dropped his eyes, wrapped both hands round his coffee cup and stared into the frothy cappuccino. 'There haven't really been any, well, not for some time anyway. Just not sure I'm very good at it – relationships, I mean.'

'No, me neither.' It suddenly occurred to Annie that they might be kindred spirits, but not in a good way. She shook off all such thoughts and tried to move the conversation on.

'Well, there's more to life and all that. What sort of thing do you like to get up to, away from work?'

'That's the thing though. I'm really not very good with people. I think I just get too caught up with work, politics. Probably boring for most people but I guess it's stuff that really matters to me. Then I look at people like the Drummonds and think they really do have everything but choose to waste their lives on trying to impress, indulging in iniquitous gossip or idle tittle-tattle. I don't even know them really but what I've seen, what I've heard, just frustrates and annoys me. It wasn't just the dinner party. I've had the misfortune of bumping into them a few times now.'

Annie withdrew her hand and bristled slightly. 'Well,

they are my friends, James, and no, you don't know them. You have no idea about their lives, what makes them the people they are. I do and they're very dear to me.'

He looked up and could see the disappointment in her face. 'Sorry, yes I can see that. Perhaps I should just get the bill.'

Annie insisted on splitting the cost and the next few minutes passed in uncomfortable silence as they exchanged notes and divvied up change. As they emerged from the basement restaurant into the afternoon light, Annie looked up at him.

'You really don't make it easy.'

'No, I don't.' He looked shattered. 'Thank you for lunch – it was lovely. I'm just sorry I spoiled things.'

He put his hand on her shoulder and kissed her gently on the cheek. Annie stood motionless, unwilling to reciprocate, unwilling to display any hint of emotion.

As he turned to make his way back down Hanover Street, Annie felt a tightening knot in the pit of her stomach. *How desperately sad he looks*, she thought to herself.

Annie turned to walk back to the office. As she ambled along the busy thoroughfare that connected the east of the city to the west she felt nothing but a sense of crushing disappointment. If one of the busy residents or office workers rushing back to their desks after lunch had merely brushed her arm or a dog had barked at her from a window she would have crumpled. Suddenly she stopped and, with no clear idea of what she intended or expected, Annie turned and began to march back along Queen Street. Ignoring pedestrian crossings, she broke into a run, the trainers coming into their own, and caught up with James outside the Royal College of Physicians. Aesculapius, the Greek god of medicine and healing, looked down from on high.

She grabbed his arm, forcing him to turn round.

'You are not doing this. I won't let you do this. You can't be angry with people you don't know and you can't be so bloody prejudiced about everything. It must be obvious to you that I want to get to know you better. I know there's an attraction between us but, honestly, you're making it impossible.'

Quite unexpectedly, tears began to fall. She was aware that she had her hand on the lapel of his tweed jacket and was pressing into the soft cotton of his shirt. Somehow, and she was not yet clear about the how or why, he had managed to pierce a slight tear in that protective covering. He had got through and she couldn't let him do that and just walk away.

He pulled her to him and gently kissed the top of her head.

'Can we start again? Please?' he whispered. 'Everything will be fine. I know it will be.'

CHAPTER 2

In the beginning they spent nearly all their time together at the flat in Dean Terrace. She withdrew from many planned social gatherings but steadfastly kept up motherly visits and outings lest suspicion of a new romance should fall upon her. She knew the risks, the very real possibility that this was just not going to work but, in spite of that, she'd made a conscious decision to invest in this man and that was going to involve some dedicated time and effort.

She found herself one Saturday afternoon in Grays of George Street, ironmongers to Edinburgh's more gentrified types, including the Queen when she was staying at her modest little palace at the bottom of the Royal Mile. Annie's mother was looking for a new set of casserole dishes.

'Jean McHarg was asking about that new man we bumped into at the Queen's Hall.' Helen was inspecting the bottom of a large microwaveable dish and spoke in a low, dull tone in an unconvincing attempt to convey indifference.

'Oh yes, James. We've met for coffee, that's all. As I said, he's just a neighbour of the Drummonds.' Annie walked away to the other side of the shop, conscious of her less than truthful response and randomly picked up a packet of curtain hooks.

'Do you need curtain hooks, dear?'

Her escape was shortlived. 'No, not really.'

'Anyway, I said to Jean, "I think he's just a friend, colleague that kind of thing. Annie's far too sensible to get all embroiled at her age", I said. She's a successful businesswoman, after all. She can stand on her own two feet.'

Annie's heart sank. Standing on your own two feet. That was the important thing and if you could do that you really didn't need to be burdened with any kind of significant other in your life. No one at all.

*

One beautiful autumnal Saturday morning, James had gone for croissants from the Home Bakery and Annie was making a large pot of Italian deli coffee. In the space of eight weeks they had cocooned themselves away inside a cosy domestic world, choosing their restaurants and coffee houses carefully and being sure to amble along parts of the Water of Leith walkway that she knew her friends did not frequent.

She poured some orange juice and set out the butter and jam on the round dining table that looked out onto the small terrace. A rich cloak of autumnal colour already covered the communal garden at the back and the ancient Habitat patio table was covered with the detritus of a particularly stormy night – golden-red leaves, small twigs and pieces of bark, unable to resist the force of the wind, had broken off and scattered themselves to look like a small child's nature tray.

The door opened and in he came with bags full of croissants, Scotch pies and Viennese whirls.

'Oh my god, why do you do that?' Annie feigned exasperation.

He held her tightly to him. 'It's okay, you don't have to eat them all at once. We'll have the Viennese things later on this afternoon. Coffee ready? Oh and we can freeze the pies. Although I might have one right now – they're still hot. Look, take a bite – best pies in Edinburgh.'

'James, I told you I was meeting Kirsty and Virginia. Haven't seen them for ages and they're beginning to think I've left the country.'

'Well, I guess if you have to. Let's go out tonight then, shall we? How about the Loon Fung?'

'Yes, alright – that would be lovely.' Annie snuggled into his new red and green check Barbour shirt that she'd bought in Jenners' sale. Tucked into his faded green cords he seemed to match the room and the colours outside the window perfectly. She smiled to herself. What a ridiculous thing to think.

After breakfast they tidied up and James suggested driving down to Cramond to walk along by the River Almond.

There were so many parts of Edinburgh that Annie loved but Cramond village and the foreshore at the Firth of Forth held special meaning for her. When her father made his intermittent forays home he very often cajoled her into donning too many warm clothes and took her down to the promenade at Silverknowes. They would walk along the beach, till they got to the sailboats moored at the mouth of the Almond. The sound of clanking masts told her she

30

was approaching the small warm café where she would sit down excitedly to hot chocolate and marshmallows, her face getting redder as her tightly wound scarf and snug woolly hat turned from wind-chill blockers to thermal conductors.

Warm memories enveloped Annie as they parked the car and walked down to the promenade. They stopped outside the Cramond Galley Bistro and looked out at the boats bobbing gently in the calm waters, seagulls screeching overhead.

'Shall we ring for the ferryman?' James asked. The ferry ran between Cramond and the Dalmeny Estate, owned by the Earl and Countess of Rosebery. The ringing of a large ship's bell would summon the estate worker from his small cottage at the edge of the river and he would traverse the short stretch of water in his rowing boat to pick up ramblers and tourists who wanted to continue their walk through the estate to South Queensferry.

Annie looked up at him. 'James, you know we don't have time. I thought we were just going for a walk along the Almond.'

'Well, to be precise, *you* don't really have time,' he replied, frowning.

'That's absolutely correct.' She started to walk back to the car disregarding the plan to pop into the Bistro for a plate of soup.

They drove back to the flat in silence. Once through the front door, she took off her jacket, hung it on the coat hook and turned to him as he came in behind her.

'What's wrong? You can't possibly think I'm going to just abandon my friends and spend every waking moment with you. Do you know how emotionally immature that sounds? You're ten years older than me for God's sake.'

'It's just that we've been having such a nice time together and, well, it was such a nice day, that was all,' he replied, stroking her face.

Annie gently removed his hand from her face.

'Well, yes, we have and yes, it is a nice day but look, this is new – for both of us. I liked my life before you came along and I think I might like it even better with you in it but please, you have to let me – I don't know – just live my life.' And with that she walked off to the bathroom. She felt a small knot begin to form in her stomach as she wondered how he might react to her minor outburst. After a moment she began the ritual of cleansing and moisturising and followed the same subtle makeup regime she had used since her teens. Annie emerged feeling bright and refreshed.

'Okay, darling. This is what's going to happen. I am heading off to Café Florentine. Kirsty and Virginia will ask me where I've been hiding the past few weeks and I'm going to tell them I've been seeing the nightmare neighbour from next door. I'll tell them a bit about how we met again and explain that you're not always comfortable in social gatherings with people you don't really know; hence the slightly uncomfortable dinner party a few weeks back. However, I've got to know you very well over the last two months and discovered a shy but kind, warm and interesting character. They'll express surprise while muttering something about only ever wanting good things for me. I will then finish by suggesting that all six of us, yes that's right, three couples, get together very soon. Thoughts?'

She stood with her hands on her hips staring down at him sitting on the sofa. He was lounging comfortably with slippered feet up on the faded tartan-clad footstool that had remained fixed in the same position for years so as not to show the patch of badly worn carpet underneath. This month's copy of the *National Geographic* was set to one side and he looked at her quizzically over the top of his reading glasses. He looked as if he too had occupied that same part of the lounge for years, she thought.

'Why on earth do you want to do that?'

'Because I think it would be good for us. Good for you, to be honest.' She was disappointed in his response and couldn't hide it. 'I'm sorry but it can't be just you and me. I can't live like that. We're going to have to rejoin the human race at some point and I really would like you to get to know my friends. *Then* you can decide you don't like them.'

She sat down beside him and placed her hand on his thigh, grabbing at the thick cord trousers. He looked into her slightly sorrowful eyes, smiled gently and began to kiss her, softly at first and then with a passionate intensity that she loved and readily succumbed to. She felt the now familiar charge racing through her body, slid her hand up his chest, round to the back of his head and pulled him even closer. They sat, entwined, lost in each other, for what seemed like an eternity. When Annie pulled herself away her lips were numb.

'I take it that's a yes?' Her hand was on his cheek now, gently caressing him.

'Okay, my dear, I'll give it a go.'

Emboldened by his loving response and energised by the first flushes of new romance, Annie kissed him sweetly but firmly on the forehead.

'I wont be too long, promise.' He held her close one final time before she jumped from the sofa, grabbed her coat and bag and headed out the door.

The afternoon had dulled as Annie made her way up the hill to the café. It was a popular haunt with the slightly more bohemian Stockbridge residents, of which Virginia was one. Annie saw her sitting at a corner table through the back of the café, head buried in a Doris Lessing paperback.

'Hi, Gin.'

Virginia looked startled. 'Gosh, didn't see you there. Completely absorbed. Have you read any Lessing? Amazing woman.'

Virginia put the book down and broke into a wide smile. She stood up and wrapped her arms around Annie.

'Goodness, there I am prattling on about a silly book when I haven't seen you for ages.'

'Oh I know, I'm really sorry, Gin. I'll tell you all about it when Kirsty gets here. You look fab though.'

Virginia was as Virginia always was. She wore a pale blue blouse tucked into a purple velvet elasticated skirt topped off by a pair of shabby knee-high black boots. Her hair was resolutely scored down the middle, frizzy grey hair emerging from either side of the parting. She wore her premature greying with pride, embracing the natural production of what looked suspiciously like a length of fine wire wool.

Annie felt as though she had just emerged from a period of self-imposed isolation. It had been a very pleasant, comfortable confinement, but confinement nonetheless. Virginia was subjected to a quick-fire round of questions, with Annie leaning over and listening intently to her every reply. She was not accustomed to anyone being that interested in her everyday life and after giving Annie the lowdown on the first meeting of the Stockbridge Arts and Crafts Group, Virginia placed her hand atop Annie's before the next phase of interrogation commenced.

'Okay, darling. I know none of this is of any real interest to you. What on earth's been going on?'

'I'm just so pleased to see you. Honestly, I feel as though I haven't seen you for such a long time and it just struck me, as we were sitting here, how much I miss you. I don't know, Gin, maybe we just take each other for granted. You are such a good friend and yet I don't really know half of what goes on in your life.'

'Well, I do try to tell you and the others for that matter. No one ever seems that interested but that's absolutely fine.' Virginia smiled and tightened her grip on Annie's hand. 'The rest of you have such interesting lives, I'm more than happy to hear all about the latest big "case" you're all working on or how the skiing holiday went. You're all far more adventurous than me, or Gordon for that matter.'

There wasn't a hint of bitterness or resentment in her voice, Annie thought. It was more than she could bear. She got up, walked round to the other side of the table and hugged her friend from on high. Virginia stayed resolutely in her seat; Annie noticed how utterly perplexed she looked.

'Oh, Gin, I'm sorry. I think we're just all so wrapped up in our own wee worlds. If nothing else, the last couple of months have shown me that we really need to slow down and appreciate each other more. It's not whether Lothian Regional Council prosecutes some poor clerical worker at the Sports Centre for falsifying invoices that's important. I mean, obviously it's wrong, even if the poor woman was struggling to pay off her husband's gambling debts, but what's important, I mean really important – well, it's the people in our lives, the relationships we have. Don't you think? I mean, it takes time and effort to build and keep friendships, love even…'

The rambling monologue tailed off and Virginia looked desperately at the door of the café.

Right on cue, the door opened and in rushed Kirsty in a pink neon top and black spandex leggings tucked into woolly slouch socks.

'Sorry, girls, yoga started late today. Our instructor had been out on a bit of bender last night. Don't really think that's the sort of thing yoga instructors should be doing, mind you!' She dropped her Adidas holdall loudly onto the floor and collapsed into the vacant chair next to Virginia.

Kirsty had abandoned her Cindy Crawford body workout video some weeks previously, protesting that exercising in the Californian sunshine just didn't transfer to the confines of a Georgian drawing room. Yoga was the 'in thing' now and Kirsty had thrown herself into the new phenomenon with her usual enthusiasm, acquiring all the requisite clothing and signing up to twice-weekly classes. She radiated a kind of post-exercise high.

'I probably don't need the added stimulation but let's have coffee and cake!'

Coffees were ordered but Annie was ravenous, having missed out on the promised lunch at Cramond, and so went for the hot quiche option with salad and thick-cut bread.

'Gosh, did you miss lunch?' Kirsty enquired. Annie nodded but said nothing. She couldn't think how to begin the conversation she needed to have.

Annie sensed Virginia staring at her, waiting for the big reveal, but she wasn't yet ready to tell all. Kirsty jumped in to fill the void. Fuelled by a mixture of caffeine and endorphins, she dominated the next thirty minutes. She recounted her search for good quality winter curtains, Duncan's all-nighter following his first century for Dunedin Cricket Club, students in the attic flat who were not pulling their weight on the communal stair-cleaning front and finally, the apparent and most welcome disappearance of the nightmare neighbour, Mr JFK himself.

Annie had allowed herself to relax into the company, enjoying Kirsty's stories and the familiar feeling of not having to make an effort with good friends. Kirsty's final proclamation, however, jolted Annie from her composed state. Muscles tensed in her neck and she could feel the blood pulsate up to her cheeks. She couldn't bring herself to look up and remained focused on the warm broccoli and stilton quiche.

'Anyway, enough from me. What have you been up to, Miss Annie?'

Annie decided this was the moment to tell all even if it wasn't quite how she had envisaged breaking the news. She had thought to frame the announcement by describing a new relationship that had started slowly and was building into something very special. As she rehearsed it over in her head she couldn't help but think Kirsty and Duncan's opinion of James, which appeared to have remained resolutely negative, could only diminish all the warm, positive feelings she had been living with over the last few weeks. It would have been so easy to say nothing and return to her state of blissful exile.

'Actually, I've been seeing someone.' She said it quietly, not sure how to move to the next sentence.

'Well, there's a turn up for the books. What brought that on? I thought you were happy as you were?' Kirsty exclaimed. Virginia just looked anxious, her eyes darting back and forth between her two friends.

'Well, it's not always brilliant, Kirst. You know I love being with you lot but then I go home by myself and, well – it's fine most of the time but sometimes I think it would be nice to have someone around to talk to other than the cat. Anyway, it's early days but we've been having a really lovely time. I wouldn't say he's the easiest man to get to know but once you do you can see what a good and caring soul he really is. I don't know what it is but I can just be myself with him. He doesn't need me to be anything else – he just makes me feel safe and loved and to be honest I can't really remember what that feels like. Don't know if I ever did.'

Annie finally looked up and smiled at them both, tears inexplicably filling her eyes.

Virginia looked across sympathetically, her facial muscles visibly relaxing.

'Well, that's just wonderful, darling.'

It appeared to Annie that Virginia really required no further details. She had again placed her hand on Annie's and looked both genuinely happy for her dear friend and completely relieved that nothing bad had happened.

Kirsty simply looked aghast.

'I did wonder, even though I thought that notion had left you long ago when you reacted so badly to young Alex going off to Mozambique or wherever it was. I said to Duncan the other day, "I think she's landed herself a man". Of, course he was completely dismissive, you know what men are like. "Don't be daft", he said. "She's probably snowed under at work and then of course there's her mother…". Kirsty stopped in her tracks. 'Anyway enough of all that, tell us all about him.'

Kirsty too reached across and briefly held Annie's hand. However, it was more of an encouraging squeeze to spill the beans in contrast to Virginia's comforting touch.

Annie drew her hand away, wiped her mouth with her napkin, gathered herself and looked straight across at Kirsty.

'Actually, it's your neighbour, James Kerr.'

Kirsty's mouth fell open and stayed like that for what seemed an interminable period of time. Virginia's eyes widened and she proceeded to suck in her entire bottom lip. Annie looked at each of them in turn.

'Okay. Is anyone going to actually say something?'

'But he was such an arse,' Kirsty finally erupted.

'I think that's a bit of an exaggeration, Kirst,' Virginia retorted.

Annie felt that Virginia would have been more suited to a career in family mediation rather than pursuing a path which involved becoming inordinately passionate about sources of fuel.

'Anyway, as I said earlier, he's really nice once you get

to know him. He's interesting, he makes me laugh and even though it's early days I really think he cares for me. You just caught him on a bad day, that's all.'

'Well, that's all that matters.' Virginia smiled and then with a hint of annoyance in her expression turned to look at Kirsty.

'Well, of course it is,' Kirsty chimed in. 'It's just, well, I thought we'd all agreed he was a bit of a rude dinner guest and I think he and Duncan have had a few frosty exchanges since then.'

'Yes, well, it isn't all that matters. Not really. I want us all to start again. If he's going to be part of my life then I really want him to be part of your lives too.'

'Of course we can all start again.' Virginia appeared to adopt the role of spokesperson for the group. 'Why don't we all meet up for a drink? A pub's kind of neutral territory, isn't it?'

'That sounds great.' Annie was thankful for her friend's suggestion.

Kirsty nodded and smiled. Annie knew she was dying to break the news to Duncan.

'But, sorry, can we just rewind a bit. I mean, where did this all happen and how?'

Kirsty needed to know far more than Virginia did.

Annie described their meeting at the Queen's Hall and lunch date at Hendersons without going into any of the more dramatic details. Kirsty finally looked satisfied but Annie knew she was struggling to make sense of it all.

Well, that makes two of us, Annie thought to herself.

They moved the conversation on but Annie could sense

an undercurrent of tension. It was left to Virginia to organise the unlikely get-together and they left to get on with the rest of their Saturday. Virginia would follow her normal weekend routine of scouring the vintage shops in St Stephen Street and Kirsty announced she was making a beeline for Bower's the butchers to see what sort of game they had left.

'Found a leg of hare in the freezer. If I can get hold of some pheasant I've got the makings of a rather tasty terrine!'

Annie just wanted to get back to the sanctuary of her flat. She knew Gordon and Virginia would go out their way to make James feel welcome but she just had no idea how Kirsty and Duncan, particularly Duncan, would behave. Then again she had no real idea how James would behave either.

As she turned the key to her front door, Annie heard Ludovic meowing in the hall. He arched his back and rubbed up against her leg as she stepped inside. He liked to make sure his scent overwhelmed any rivals that she might have encountered on her foray into the world beyond the railings; beyond his territory. Satisfied that he had reclaimed her, the cream cat slunk back towards the lounge, long tail quivering.

Annie entered the lounge to find James in pretty much the same position she had left him. This time, however, he was fast asleep, chin down into his chest and glasses balanced unevenly on the tip of his nose.

How completely adorable he looks, she thought. Almost like a little boy; not that she knew what he had looked like as a little boy. After that initial conversation in Hendersons when James seemed to be at ease talking about his father, he had rarely mentioned his parents since. He seemed reluctant to speak about his upbringing and despite Annie asking to see photographs from childhood, none had been forthcoming. Very little had been forthcoming, she reflected.

She sat beside him on the couch and Ludovic jumped up, settling back into James's lap – the comfortable lair he had been forced to abandon to greet his mistress. Annie noticed that a rather battered-looking library book, identified by its coded spine label, had replaced the glossy periodical. The large hardback entitled *Gardens of Northern Italy* lay open across his chest, the plastic cover slipping ever downwards towards Ludovic's head.

James woke, looking startled, unsure for a moment where he was. As he turned and saw Annie's face he smiled.

'Ah, you're back. How was it? Did you tell all? Come close, I need to feel you close to me.'

As she snuggled in, the book finally lost its precarious grip on James's chest, gently sliding down the front of his shirt till it came to rest squarely on the cat's head. Ludovic could take no more encroachment onto his sleeping platform and with a short sharp meow, jumped down and sloped off towards the kitchen.

'Yes, well, they were obviously a bit surprised given how things had gone at the dinner. Once I told them what a nice time we'd been having, they seemed absolutely fine and really looking forward to meeting you again.' Annie was aware she was painting a far rosier scene than the one she'd just left but desperately wanted him to approach the next encounter in a positive frame of mind.

'In fact Virginia is going to organise a night out at the pub.'

'What pub?'

'I don't know. Probably in Stockbridge – the Baillie, the St Vincent, somewhere like that.'

'I like the St Vincent. Not that keen on the Baillie.'

'Well, I don't know, let's wait and see.'

'Will he be there?'

'Will who be there?'

'Mr Drummond.'

'Well, of course he will. He's Kirsty's husband and they are both my friends. And please stop calling him Mr Drummond. His name is Duncan.'

'Duncan Drummond.'

'Yes, Duncan Drummond. Good grief, James, stop being so deliberately obtuse. Can we now please change the subject? What is that you are reading?'

'Have you ever been to Italy?'

'Yes.' She hesitated. 'The year after my father died I took Mother to Florence. It was just lovely. I think I could go back there time and time again and never get bored. I've never been anywhere like it. Quite overwhelming really; so much culture and history in one place. I think it also really suited the two of us. There was just so much to see and do, no space or time for us to stop and revisit...'

'Revisit what?'

'Oh, just a lot had happened with my father the previous twelve months.'

'Tell me.' His voice, his look were all so reassuring she knew that for the first time ever she was about to disclose the full unabridged story. Not just edited highlights and no reimagined versions of the truth.

CHAPTER 3

She sat up, keeping her hand on the security blanket that was his soft textured shirt and found herself journeying back to her childhood.

Annie's early memories all seemed to centre around her father. His made-up stories, building things, making furniture for dolls' houses. It seemed to her that he had been the one who helped shape her little world. Yet most time was spent with her mother. He worked hard – evenings, weekends too while her mother stayed at home. Looking back it seemed odd that such a firm bond should form so early on between father and daughter but it did and, despite some testing times, it had endured right up to his death.

Hugh Anderson had been a lawyer working for one of the big banks initially. If you worked for the bank, you stayed with the bank and of course that was where their social lives centred. The same people moving round the same drinks parties. The men in sports jackets and brown suede shoes; the women wafting around in their Laura Ashley skirts, sipping at their Bacardi and Cokes or Scotch and water.

The more she described it to James, the more she realised how stifling it must have been. If they weren't doing the rounds of colleagues' cocktail parties, Saturday nights were devoted to badminton at the Church Hall, just with all the same people. The inane conversations, the mind-numbing gossip and petty suburban jealousies. It all seemed so normal then but it must have been absolute torture for her father. It just wasn't him.

Annie spoke of his interest in travel, other countries, other cultures, none of which interested her mother, unfortunately. Then one day, just after Annie's fourteenth birthday, both parents sat her down and made the monumental announcement. Daddy had been offered a position with a pharmaceutical company based in Geneva. They had a small research facility just outside Edinburgh but most of his time would be spent on the continent. The plan was that Mummy and her would stay put and Daddy would visit whenever he could. It was a great opportunity for Daddy but really far too much upheaval to drag her out of school. She had found herself staring at them both, trying to take in the enormity of what they were telling her. He was leaving. That's what she heard. That's what she knew. And even now, looking back, it seemed so at odds with their behaviour in the years that followed, to present the proposal with such confidence, certainty and unity.

Much later, Annie learned that her father was desperate for them all to move to Geneva but Helen wouldn't entertain the idea for a second. After he moved away, her mother inexplicably began to ooze resentment. The whole thing was completely perplexing to Annie, given that she'd appeared to go along with the move in the beginning. It was something she would never quite understand – the whole abandoned wife thing.

'Never mind abandoned wife, Annie, what about abandoned child?'

'I tried not to think of it like that. It was just his work. Well, that's what I kept telling myself.' As she spoke the pain returned. It was the almost indescribable feeling of panic and fear that had overwhelmed her as she tried to fathom what her life could possibly look like with her father gone. They told her she was overreacting but as far as Annie had been concerned they were ignoring the blatantly obvious truth. Her father could exist perfectly happily, somewhere else in the world and without her. Annie pulled herself back from the brink. She didn't want to go back to a world of hurt and humiliation. And all because she hadn't mattered quite as much as she thought she had. She pushed the dismal thoughts away, composed herself and continued.

She spoke of regrouping and establishing a new family norm. It had been strained but Annie and her mother rubbed along well enough for a few years. Helen clearly resented Hugh upsetting their safe, structured suburban life and Annie resented him for leaving her to deal with all the fallout. She hadn't been allowed to visit him, not even in the holidays, and was entirely dependent on her father's forays home.

'God, you were only a child, Annie. Being abandoned like that by your father and then your mother's reaction. None of that is fair, none of it. Losing a parent is horrendous. I know he didn't die or anything but somehow this seems almost as cruel. He's gone but he comes back occasionally and you don't know when you're going to see him. I'm sorry but it's just cruel.'

He spoke with such feeling, such anger at her pain that it made her want him all the more. He was on her side. Someone was on her side.

She spoke of her father's visits home becoming increasingly tense. The parents barely tolerating each other and Annie spending less time hanging on to his every word and more time trying to avoid his attempts at offloading. Her mother was being completely unreasonable, all he had ever wanted was to support his family as best he could, blah, blah. He'd suggested that all he wanted was for his family to be with him and that Helen had no intention of supporting him and his career. He even discussed Annie leaving Edinburgh and living with him permanently in Geneva.

But for all Helen's coldness towards him, Annie just couldn't bring herself to side with him against her.

She was sure she must have been making it sound worse than it was. Yes, it was bad but lots of kids go through that kind of thing. You just have to get on with it. Try to see both sides, equalise the love, don't cause upset. But whatever she did, it didn't seem to matter. Her parents' contempt for each other only grew and Annie was just grateful to escape to university.

A few years later, and with Hugh's visits home becoming more and more infrequent, Helen announced that her father had fallen for a young Swiss research scientist – name of Céline. The name sounded so smart, so sophisticated. But what was happening wasn't terribly sophisticated – it was betrayal, plain and simple. Annie let the news gnaw away at her for a while until finally she felt able to climb out and away from the twisted and tortured morass of half-truths, downright lies and character assassinations. For years and with no logical basis for believing it, she had thought her parents would somehow find a way back to each other, eventually. But now… now she was reconciled to the fact that the only hope, for everyone's sanity, was that Helen and Hugh might finally untangle themselves from this ugly mess of a marriage.

The weight had gradually lifted until all that was left was the burden of her mother's humiliation. The move to Geneva had been hard enough for her to explain to her social circle but now Helen had to suffer the indignity of an extra-marital relationship – the final degradation being Annie's decision to visit her father and Céline. It wasn't easy but Annie felt the need to at least try to be adult about the whole thing and go some way to acknowledging his new relationship.

'He was still your father, I guess. Still loved you.'

James could see it from her side. She had never really escaped trying to manage each of her parents' expectations but at that age, as a young student, she had matured enough to know she needed to make this new situation work, however flawed the people concerned and however difficult they might make her life. Forgiving him, forgiving both of them was another matter but she had had to put all that to one side. For her own sanity she had to forget about her fourteen-year-old self, just forget about her. It wasn't going to be the same, it would never be the same but she needed her father in her life. She would always need him in her life.

And then as fate would have it, Céline turned out

to be incredibly sweet and welcoming. She was so very pretty, perhaps more striking than pretty. Her hair was long, straight and dark with a funny little fringe that curled under halfway down her forehead which made her look even younger than she was. She was quite petite and altogether very different from Helen.

Hugh and Céline lived in an amazing house, beautifully designed by Céline but even early on it had seemed to Annie that her father wasn't entirely happy. They were clearly very comfortable with each other but there was a veil of despondency that seemed to hover over him. He laughed and smiled at all the right moments, he was attentive and affectionate towards both Annie and Céline but it was his eyes. They had just looked so sad, yearning even, as though something very precious was disappearing from his grasp and there was absolutely nothing he could do about it.

Then as Annie began to tell James about her father's illness she felt the dragging sadness return.

'You don't have to do this, Annie. Not now, not if you don't want to.'

But she carried on. There was no point stopping now. Her father had always smoked, cigars mostly, but he seemed to smoke a lot more after his move to Switzerland. And so came the almost inevitable lung cancer diagnosis. Oddly enough, Céline had been part of a team looking into the development of a vaccine that might treat lung cancer; something designed to boost the body's immune response against the cancer cells.

Annie recalled being at the hospital with her father, trying to make sense of it all. Why it was that cancer seemed to be the thing that put up the biggest resistance in our fight against ill health and death. Any sign of insurgence from the white blood cells and cancer just knocked them for six and, of course, here was Céline – right at the cutting edge of that research and yet powerless to help.

The company he worked for had been great. He had access to the best specialists, new treatments and latest drug trials. Annie recalled feeling strangely proud that they really had seemed to value him. He'd steered the company through a very difficult merger and, unlike many of his colleagues, had stayed loyal. He didn't look to jump ship to competitors who paid more money. He just wanted to do a good job and help the company to succeed.

She remembered the endless round of debilitating treatments, the strain of waiting for test results, life being put on hold. It was difficult for her but it just got too much for Hugh and Céline. The foundations of their relationship weren't strong enough to cope with such a brutal impact, and although Annie never doubted that they loved each other, it had been a love rooted in their life as was. They had enjoyed the finer things and Céline was so much younger, ambitious and used to living life at a hundred miles an hour.

Annie had watched from the periphery, dealing with her own emotions, wanting to help but not sure how to. Her father had grown frailer and she watched them both struggle with failing health and failing love. And then, without warning and with little associated drama, her father came to a decision. It felt to Annie as though he wanted to salvage what was good so he could remember that Céline had made him really very happy in ways he never had been with Helen. But just as importantly and perhaps more so, he didn't want her to feel any guilt for being unable to cope when he needed her most. And so he left.

Annie explained that the company owned a few properties in the centre of Geneva that they used for visiting clients and so Hugh moved into one of them. From a practical point of view it had been ideal. Everything was on the same level, a housekeeper cooked and cleaned, shopped.

Annie had told her mother everything and of her decision to visit her father, regularly. There was no room for debate. She might be losing him for good now and needed to cling on for as long as possible. Helen had accepted the position – whether it was with good grace or not was hard for Annie to tell. She just didn't say anything at all but then after one of Annie's trips over to Geneva, Helen had rung and asked to meet. Annie assumed she was just to go round to the house and so felt slightly unnerved when Helen suggested meeting in the lounge of the Roxburgh Hotel. She'd only just started her legal traineeship and it felt as though she was being asked to go along and give a deposition to her mother.

Helen had wanted details. What had happened, how it had happened and when it had happened. She didn't want any extraneous nonsense, nothing about Céline understandably and so Annie presented the facts of the case, as she knew them.

When Annie had finished, her mother began to drink her coffee. Must have been stone cold by then but Annie remembered how she just kept looking at her over the rim of the cup.

'Will Daddy stay in Geneva?' Annie hadn't heard her call him that for years but she merely shook her head. She had no idea what his plans were. It was when they got up to leave that her mother stumbled slightly and then turned, her face drawn, anxious looking.

'Would you mind asking Daddy if he might call me?'

Annie hadn't really known what her father's response might be but she just didn't hesitate. 'Of course I wouldn't mind,' she'd said.

She recalled at that moment taking her mother's arm to walk out of the hotel and feeling quite suddenly that whatever the future held for them they were all meant to face it together. The Anderson family, the three of them, would deal with all of it – the light and the dark.

And so her father had come home. Annie was never terribly sure how it happened. She had been down in Cumbria with the gang for a long weekend, came back and he was home; it was as if he'd never been away. Annie went round the following weekend for Sunday lunch. She found him gaunt and frail and eating only puréed food but he looked content, settled. It wasn't as though her mother fussed over him; she just saw to him. She seemed to anticipate what he needed and when he needed it. He, in turn, seemed to appreciate the little kindnesses; imperceptible to most people but clear as day to Annie.

'I don't know, James, it was just meant. I can't really explain what happened between them but it was just right that they were together at the end. They didn't suddenly become different people; they had the same flaws, the same frailties. In that last year, they just found each other again.'

The tears fell. James gently wiped them away with his thumb and kissed each still damp cheek.

'People do find each other when they need to, you know,' he said.

'Yes, I think they do.' Annie looked up, smiled, and then burrowed back into his shirt.

*

Kirsty and Duncan walked hand in hand down the cobbled street to the St Vincent bar. The cobbles were sleek and shiny after days of persistent drizzle and Kirsty's shoes were slipping on the wet surface.

'Hold on, Duncan, not so fast. I'm likely to go arse over tit at this rate.'

Duncan laughed and put a protective arm around his wife's waist.

'Wonder if JFK is going to be any more sociable now that he's been under our Annie's influence the past couple of months. At the very least I would hope he's learned some manners!'

'Oh, Duncan, don't. He must have qualities we just haven't seen yet. Annie wouldn't be attracted to a complete moron so let's just be civil and enjoy a good night.'

'Anything for you, darling. God, I'm gasping for a pint.'

They entered the narrow doorway into the small, cosy pub and squeezed past the regulars standing at the bar. Virginia and Gordon were tucked away into the corner at the far side of the dimly lit lounge area.

'Bloody hell, Gordon, what have you been up to? You look like you've just finished a bout of boxing and Gin here has just unlaced and pulled off the gloves like the good corner man she is!'

'I'm a what?' Virginia looked perplexed.

'Ah yes. Was reading some papers heading back down to the office and tripped over a broken paving stone. Went headfirst, papers flew up in the air and I held my arms out to break the fall. Ended up badly spraining both wrists.'

Gordon held both arms up for them to see. Bandages had been wound tightly round each hand, ending halfway up his arm.

'His hands were very badly swollen so when he got back to the office Guy from the Sustainability Team drove him straight to A&E. Nothing was broken, thank goodness; I've had to do literally everything for him. Haven't I, Gordon?' Virginia looked at her husband tenderly.

'Yes, you have, dear.'

'Not everything, surely!' Duncan guffawed.

'Right, that's enough of that!' Kirsty interjected. 'You poor darling. Now let's get some drinks in.'

'I'll go; you get the seats sorted out, Kirsty, and then help me back with the drinks. Mike Tyson there isn't much use. You'll have to lift his pint for him, Gin! Then we can talk about preparing a lawsuit against the council.'

Just as Duncan turned towards the bar the doors pushed open and Annie and James walked in.

'Great timing, you two,' Duncan bellowed. 'Must have been peering in through the door waiting for me to get up to the bar. What will it be then? Usual G&T, Annie? What about you, James?'

'Pint of IPA for me, Duncan, thank you. I'll help you

54

with the drinks.' James smiled but Annie could tell it was ever so slightly forced. She joined the others arranging tables and chairs, listened to the story about Gordon's mishap, all the while glancing back to see how the two men were getting along. All seemed well, she thought. As well as could be expected.

As they brought the drinks back, Annie shuffled along the green leather bench set against the wall to make room for James. He sat down and she immediately placed a reassuring hand on his leg. James turned and smiled, raised his glass and called 'Cheers'. The rest of the company echoed his good wishes and they settled down to drink and chat.

'Following the Test match, James?' Duncan asked.

'No, I've never really been interested in cricket. Not that interested in sport, to be honest.'

Duncan ignored both statements and went on to describe the latest England performance against the West Indies.

'What gets me is they talk about the middle order suffering a batting collapse; like they were subjected to some kind of terrible ordeal. Nobody did it to them, James. You know what I mean? They did it to themselves.'

'Well, yes, but surely the opposition bowlers must have just been too good for them at the end of the day.'

'Well, they're proficient enough, I'll grant you, but the batsmen just fell apart. You need to stand up to that kind of fast pace, James. Stand up straight and step into the ball.' Duncan stood up and proceeded to demonstrate the perfect cover drive, finishing off with a flourish of his imaginary cricket bat.

'Maybe it was a combination of good bowling and poor batting.'

'Yes, yes. Probably a bit of both.' Duncan remained standing, imaginary cricket bat held aloft. A couple of the old regulars propping up the bar, faces ravaged by years of steady alcohol and nicotine intake, looked on incredulously.

Annie turned and smiled at James. *He really is trying his best*, she thought, as she gently squeezed his leg.

Virginia leaned across the table towards James. 'So you work in St Andrew's House? That must be exciting being right at the heart of things.'

'"St Andrew's House" and "exciting" aren't often found in the same sentence, I must say. It's not really very exciting when all the big decisions are taken down at Westminster. We just "tartanise" them up here.'

'Oh, what a funny expression.' Virginia took a sip of her red wine. 'I probably don't like his politics very much but I do like the look of our Secretary of State. Ian Lang, isn't it? He's quite a handsome chap.'

'Oh, for God's sake, Virginia.' Gordon looked embarrassed.

'Well, I'm pretty apolitical myself, Virginia.' James smiled across at her. 'It's just that my interests lie in improving land management and it's difficult to make sensible decisions about such things remotely. I'm really interested in the people on the ground, who manage and tend the land; are its custodians for future generations. They're the people who need to be able to make the right decisions that suit their circumstances. Anyway, that's maybe all a bit heavy for a Saturday night!'

'Oh no, not at all. You're quite right, obviously.'

'Sounds like you're leaning towards communism there, James,' Duncan interjected, and then swiftly downed the remains of his pint.

'I don't think you can equate advancing crofters' rights to state communism.'

Annie could see James's hackles were starting to rise.

'Another round for everybody? James and I will get these in.' Annie lifted his arm and took him off to the bar.

'God, he really is a prat, Annie.'

'Yes, well, we'll discuss that later.'

*

'I thought that went rather well, didn't you? James was actually quite good company. A few crackpot ideas but much more civil now Annie's got a grip of him.' Duncan poured himself a large Scotch and slumped into the tattered old leather armchair.

'Yes, well, I'm not sure how much he enjoyed your cricket sermon but all in all it was a very nice evening; and Annie seems happy, which is the main thing. Aren't you coming to bed?' Kirsty asked forlornly.

'No, no. Early Fleetwood Mac concert on BBC2 shortly then I'll be right in.'

Kirsty knew that was a precursor to an all-nighter in the armchair, most of the Laphroaig consumed and her wakening up to whisky breath at four in the morning. She headed off for a bath, wishing her life were just a little bit different.

*

James threw his coat on to the old pew chair in the hall. 'I'm going to have a large glass of red. Anything for you?'

'Same, thanks. That and a hot bath should reduce the tension in my neck and shoulder muscles!'

'Really? I thought the evening went okay. Take Mr Drummond out of the equation and it would have been almost pleasant.'

'Oh, James. We really must get to the point when meeting my friends doesn't rate as some kind of endurance test.'

'Sorry, I just find it difficult to understand how you could have cultivated any kind of meaningful friendship with that man over the years. I think I'm getting to know you quite well and, for the life of me, I can't see how you can be bothered to give him the time of day – unless of course it's just to appease Kirsty who, despite appearing to be a bit of an upper class twit, seems pretty harmless.'

'I tell you what, James, why don't I meet some of your morally upstanding, perfectly mannered friends who no doubt belong to the "right" social class, whatever that may be? Come to think of it, I haven't heard you mention any friends. Could it be you're just a bit too quick to judge? Just a bit too good at picking up on any *hint* of human frailty?'

They stared at each other, saying nothing. Annie wanted to say more but she was exhausted.

'I'm going to run a bath.' She took the glass of wine out of his hand and headed to the sanctuary of the bathroom where she undressed quickly and wrapped herself up in her soft towelling robe. As the bath filled she quickly downed the wine. The hot vapours from the bath and the sudden downing of warm Merlot made her feel drowsy. She slid under the water, allowing it to lap gently over her body, her skin tingling with the heat. Her head was semi-immersed, as she closed her eyes in an attempt to insulate her mind from the senseless arguments that existed beyond the bathroom door. How much simpler life had been before James, and yet the thought that he was waiting for her to emerge, sitting on the couch or warming up the bed, made her happier than she'd been in a very long time. Annie could only hope that the nourishing body soak generously poured into the bath would make good on its promise to leave her mind renewed and soul soothed.

*

'I'm going to tell you something about Duncan. I don't expect you to comment; I'm just going to leave it with you.' Annie was indeed feeling soothed and calm as she entered the bedroom.

James was already in bed, cat lying up against him, engrossed once more in his oversized library book. He stretched out his arm, welcoming her in. Annie dropped her robe to the floor and joined the two boys in their cosy repose.

'Well, to start with, it was Kirsty I first met – during freshers' week actually. I hadn't really met anyone like her before. She was *so* enthusiastic about everything; just threw herself into things. Come to think of it, the complete opposite of me. She entertained, cooked amazing meals, always had whacky ideas for "excursions" as she called them. There was always some form of physical exertion followed by hot and spicy food and what we used to call her kamikaze cocktails. Kirsty's margaritas were legendary – bucketfuls of tequila topped by a few squeezes of limejuice and heaps of crushed ice. One tequila, two tequila, three tequila, floor!'

James looked startled.

'Oh, come on, James, you were at Glasgow Uni for God's sake and I don't really equate that experience with alcoholic abstinence! Anyway, it never really seemed to get out of hand. I'm sure you did the same.'

'Sorry. Just finding it hard to picture you downing buckets of tequila!'

'Okay, well, moving on… Duncan was also in our year but I couldn't say I'd really noticed him. He was one of the rugby lads and they pretty much kept themselves to themselves. Anyway, one night I was meeting Kirsty in the Café Royal. We ordered a couple of pints and then she told me she'd started going out with someone and that he would be turning up shortly to meet us. She looked almost sheepish, I remember. I distinctly remember her saying "He's not very attractive, quite ugly in fact but a nice sort."'

'Typical Kirsty to tell it as it is.'

Annie ignored James and carried on. 'So in walked Duncan and all I could think was I'm glad he didn't catch the "quite ugly" bit. He was really lovely and really sweet with Kirsty. You need to understand, James, he was such a quiet lad back then and just adored her, which was all good as far as I was concerned.'

James smiled but Annie knew he was unconvinced.

'After a few months of hanging around together, we were all invited up to Duncan's parents' pile in Perthshire.

Virginia and Gordon had also hooked up and we'd become quite a tight little group.'

Annie recalled how Duncan and Kirsty had travelled on ahead and she had endured Gordon's bad driving, all the while feeling less than enthused at the prospect of a weekend away with someone else's parents. Hers were bad enough. She had been dozing off in the back when Gordon suddenly braked. He'd stopped the car at the entrance to the drive leading up to the modestly named 'Drummond House'.

'I have to say, James, Drummond House was anything but modest. It was a *huge* mansion, all towers and turrets. I don't know if you know the area but it sat in splendid isolation near the foot of Ben Lawers. Honestly, it looked like it belonged on the set of a Hammer House of Horror film – remember *The Fall of the House of Usher*?'

James laughed. 'Yes, I know where you are.' Ludovic moved away to a quieter corner of the bed.

'I wouldn't have been surprised to see Vincent Price emerge, creaking open the big wooden door. Anyway, to all our reliefs, the door was opened, not by Vincent Price but by a very ruddy-faced, jolly kind of woman. "Real country stock" my father would have said – and that was Duncan's mother Marjorie. Turned out to be an absolute gem – very much like Kirsty actually, just thirty years older.'

James raised his eyebrows but said nothing. Annie gently put a finger to his lips and carried on.

'Marjorie chatted away, showing us all to our rooms and then shot off, shouting something about drinks in the library and no need to dress up.'

'Sounds less like *The House of Usher* and more Agatha Christie!'

Annie smiled at the thought of a murder mystery playing out at Drummond House. 'Well, that's when we met Strachan.'

'*Strachan*?'

'Yes, I kid you not. Strachan Drummond, Duncan's father. Oh, James, he was awful. His eldest son was off sheep farming or something in New Zealand and that just left the twins, Duncan and Lachlan.'

'Oh my god. There are *two* of them?'

'Right, that's enough.' Annie gently slapped his shoulder. 'Anyway, Kirsty had told us that Lachlan was the blue-eyed boy. Loud and rude like his father, he had joined the family business straight from school – something to do with estates management and property development.'

'Sounds like everything I hate. Not that I'm jumping to conclusions or anything but he's probably turning a quick buck for rich, absent landlords and did you say property development? Well, up there he's probably hell bent on pricing local people out of the property market and keeping them off the land.'

'Well, I don't think you're far wrong, to be honest. Anyway, Kirsty had already told me that Duncan, believe it or not, had been a really studious, quiet youngster and early on had decided he wanted to go to university and become a lawyer. Old Strachan was appalled. He thought both boys would go into the business but Duncan just wanted nothing to do with it. Gosh, when I think about it my parents were thrilled that I was going off to do law.

'That whole weekend Strachan just poked fun at

him, talked down to him or ignored him. It was awful and Duncan seemed to be making such an effort to try and impress his father, particularly on the sporting front. Endless stories about cricket and rugby didn't impress Strachan one bit. He would just follow them up by telling us all about Lachlan's exploits playing for the local rugby team. It was all quite humiliating really.'

'Look, Annie, that sort of family dynamic goes on all the time.'

'Well, I guess you just needed to be there to really appreciate how horrible it was.'

Annie knew he wasn't buying it but carried on. 'Lachlan appeared the morning we were leaving and you could see Strachan was thrilled. He seemed to puff his chest out even more than he had all weekend, slapped the boy on the back and stood grinning from ear to ear as "golden boy" introduced himself to everyone.

'I felt so sorry for Duncan after that weekend, James, and I honestly think you would have too, if you'd been there. There's no doubt, even now, he still tries to be the man his father hoped he'd be. He's just not very good at it, thank goodness, but it does mean he can be really overbearing sometimes. I think it's just because he's struggled to gain his father's acceptance all these years.'

James turned over on to his side to look straight at Annie, inadvertently heaving the cat off the bed. 'Okay, I get that, Annie, but he's a grown man now. He can be his own person instead of this caricature of a drunken old fart.'

'Yes, I know but you haven't seen him at his best and I have. He can be very sweet and he's always been so supportive and, well, just good to me, particularly when all the stuff with Dad was happening – and I don't know if we ever stop trying to do good in our parents' eyes. Anyway, just cut him a little slack, please?' She leant in for a kiss and James pulled her further under the covers.

Ludovic took the hint and retreated to the kitchen.

CHAPTER 4

The next few weeks passed by and Annie and James settled into their new world, creating their own little routines – mundane to most people but new and exciting to them. Annie had mentioned to Kirsty that if Duncan could steer away from cricket and politics then the two men might stand a chance of being able to stay in the same room as one another. As a result, Annie began to involve James in social activities with the rest of the gang and James, in turn, made every effort to be polite and engaging. Annie knew they would never be best friends but James did seem to be more tolerant of him.

'The way I see it, James, it's like establishing certain rules of engagement and if both parties comply then negotiations can be conducted and concluded in a civil manner and to the satisfaction of both parties.'

'Ever the lawyer.' They were walking out on a chill December day to Annie's mother's for Sunday lunch; another little routine that seemed to be gaining some traction.

'Strangely enough, Duncan and I are finding common cause in objecting to the new retail park.'

'Good God, James. How could you? And all the while

Yugoslavia is crumbling. To think I thought you were a man of principle.' They laughed and clung on to each other's winter coats.

*

She had decided to tell her mother about James a few weeks earlier. At the time she wondered if her delivery had been a bit too harsh but then she couldn't see any other way to break the news. It was time. Time to start letting someone into her life. There was to be no discussion, it was what it was and Annie didn't want to explain or justify anything anymore.

'It's your life, Annie. Nothing to do with me.' The response had been sharp and laced with a hint of spite. 'It's just, you know – just be careful.'

No discussion, no justification, that's what she'd promised herself. They were in her mother's kitchen putting away some shopping. All conversation had stopped. The rustling sound of plastic bags being emptied and cupboard doors being opened then slammed shut filled the quiet space until Annie could bear it no longer.

'Look, Mum, I don't know how this is going to turn out but I can't worry myself silly about it. Everyone thinks I'm fine as I am – busy job, busy life. But I can see with James that there's more – that I can have more, I mean.'

'Well, as I said, just be careful.' Her mother carried on with her chores and never once looked round at her daughter.

Annie finally felt the painfully tight ties loosen – the

ties that had bound mother and daughter together since her father had left so many years ago. She couldn't really know how Helen had gone about assimilating this new information but much to Annie's surprise she turned into charm itself when it came to James. She wasn't sure how he'd managed it but James eased into Helen's life as much as he'd eased into Annie's.

'Annie, darling, lovely to see you. My, you look worn out. Have you been working too hard?' Helen gave Annie a perfunctory kiss on the cheek and then turned away, leading them both off into the lounge. 'I'm always telling her, James, they work her far too hard in that office.'

They both ignored Helen's remarks. It was merely a slight variation on the same theme that greeted Annie every time she came to visit.

James followed behind the two Anderson ladies. 'Hello, Mrs Anderson, lovely to see you. You're looking well.'

Annie sensed he was being facetious and turned to give him a warning stare.

'Would you be a dear, James, and pour the sherries?' Helen asked him, nodding towards the highly polished sideboard, upon which various decanted spirits and wines sat.

'Happy to.'

'Now, I've been meaning to ask you two what the plans are for Christmas. I'm assuming you want to be alone so that's absolutely fine. Don't worry about me, I'll make do here or I can pop round to the McHargs.'

'James and I have been talking about exactly that, funnily enough, and we thought it would be lovely to spend our first Christmas together – at home.'

Helen's face fell. *That wasn't how she'd rehearsed this little scene*, thought Annie. It was cruel, she knew, but for some reason, Annie waited just long enough to allow Helen to process the response and what it would mean for her.

'And of course we would want you with us.'

Helen relaxed. 'Well, if you're sure. I wouldn't want to be a burden.' Both women sat, mirror images of each other, hands clasped in front of them.

'Of course you wouldn't be. We were always going to ask you, weren't we, James?'

'Absolutely.' James handed out the sherries and Annie sensed his discomfort as the awkward mini drama played out between mother and daughter.

Sunday lunch passed off without further incident and as they walked home early evening, James suggested a quick drink in the Dean Hotel. Annie enjoyed hotel lounges like the Dean. The hotel facade blended perfectly into the tall, elegant houses situated the length of Clarendon Crescent. She always felt as though she was just nipping into a very wealthy old aunt's drawing room for a quick reviver. Annie settled down onto the plush red velvet sofa in front of a roaring fire and, as it was a bitterly cold evening, James ordered two Whisky Macs.

'Do you mind me asking what that was all about?'

'Sorry?' Annie was savouring the warmth of the whisky and ginger wine as it began to reheat her body.

'What was all that with your mother? I thought you were just going to ask her along for Christmas Day and then you seemed to act out some weird little game with her.'

'Oh yes, sorry. It's what we do. Think it's what we've always done. Everything's played out as a little scene.' Annie laughed unconvincingly. 'Don't worry it's never enough to cause any lasting damage.'

James just stared.

'I know it's not normal but that's what it's been like between the two of us for as long as I can remember. Well, certainly since Dad left. Occasionally there's a burst of spontaneous normality but not *that* often.' She smiled up at him, suddenly realising how peculiarly warped that had all sounded.

Annie had never tried to describe these exchanges before. She wanted him to know exactly how it was, how it had always been, but at the same time she was desperate for him not to think badly of her.

'It must be exhausting. What I don't understand is, if it's so painful, why do you subject yourself to it. Why do you see so much of each other?'

Annie looked up at him, perplexed. 'She's my mother, James, and I love her – dearly. It's just that none of it has ever quite gone away. I mean all the stuff that happened with Dad. We just never seem to be able to quite forgive each other.'

'No, maybe not but all the same – there's no need to go on hurting each other.'

*

James's words stayed with her but everyday life carried on and Christmas and Helen were soon put to the back of her mind. Annie had a couple of tribunal cases running in tandem, a criminal prosecution at the Sheriff Court to prepare for and all needed her undivided attention. Luckily James's work also appeared to be full-on to the extent that he was often at the office until late in the evening and occasionally at weekends. Late one afternoon he called Annie to tell her he was going to stay over at his own flat, perhaps for a couple of days. He had a lot of reading to do and really needed to get his head round some key policy issues that were coming up. Annie understood, of course. Her own workload was starting to get out of hand – but something niggled.

She wondered about surprising him, by turning up and making dinner, so allowing him to get on with his work or perhaps going round early and cooking breakfast so he would be ready for whatever the Scottish Office had to throw at him. *Who am I kidding?* she thought. *Turning up unannounced is all about my insecurity and absolutely nothing at all to do with his welfare.*

So Annie did nothing. She let James be and focused on preparing her client's case for prosecution. By the end of the week she'd heard nothing. Trudging back down to the flat after a gruelling Friday spent mostly at the Sheriff Court and with little to eat, a wave of nausea overcame her. She stopped and held onto the railings that curled round into the Terrace. Passers-by glanced at her but marched hurriedly on. *People don't really want to take on anyone else's problems unless there is a real physical emergency*, Annie thought, knowing she would have scurried past in similar circumstances. Her legs felt like jelly but she managed to compose herself. *Stop thinking the absolute worst*, she thought, and found her way to the front door. Once inside she made a cup of tea, chucked in a spoonful of sugar just in case that was the problem and sat at the kitchen table, head in hands, trying to piece together the events of the last week or so. Could he have been so disenchanted with the mother and daughter mini drama? Was the prospect of Christmas so overwhelming or had she pushed the whole Duncan thing too far and too quickly? Ludovic leapt up on the table and tried to nuzzle into her face. Normally he would have been told in no uncertain terms to get down but she had neither the energy nor desire to push him away.

'You still love me, don't you, boy?' Woman and cat looked straight into each other's eyes.

Sometime later, Annie had changed into tracksuit bottoms and sweatshirt and lay curled up on the sofa, glass of wine in hand, Ludovic lying up against her.

The phone rang.

'Annie, it's me. Look, sorry I haven't been in touch.'

Annie's sense of relief was almost overwhelming.

'It's fine, you're busy.' She felt as though that sounded just a bit too perky and decided to take it down a notch or two. 'I'm pretty snowed under myself. That theft case we're prosecuting has been an absolute pain. Taking up much more time than I had scheduled with the client. So what have you been up to? Come round and tell me about it. It's just me and the boy here, lounging on the sofa. By boy, I mean Ludo of course!' No, that hadn't worked. Still perky.

'Yes, of course. That would be lovely but I'm heading up north for the weekend. All a bit last minute really but I'll be in touch when I get back – promise. Sorry about all this, darling. I'm just not sure whether this thing's going to get off the ground or not and I'll know a lot more after this weekend. I know I'm being really vague here but this could be something really important – I just need to understand things a bit better and I can't really do that from down here.'

'What things?' Annie could feel her relief turn into frustration. 'Surely you can tell me something, James. It's ridiculous just shutting yourself off like this – particularly if it's something so important to you.'

'Sorry, Annie – look that's Graham here with the car. I really must rush. Just bear with me and I'll call when I get back.'

'Bear with you? That's all I ever seem to do, James.' And with that Annie hung up. 'And who the hell is Graham?' she shouted at the inanimate phone.

*

The next day Annie met the girls for teatime wine at the St Vincent. Duncan was on a weekend tour of the Borders with the cricket club and Gordon had gone along too.

'Did Gordon really want to go on this tour thingy?' Kirsty asked as she brought back the bottle of Sauvignon Blanc and glasses from the bar.

'I'm not so sure that he did actually.' Virginia appeared bemused by the whole thing. 'Duncan said something about needing a twelfth man but Gordon knows nothing about cricket so I don't really understand myself. I think Duncan persuaded him by saying this twelfth man job doesn't really amount to much other than bringing on water for the players.'

'Bringing on water? More like the beers,' shrieked Kirsty.

'Oh well, I hope he'll be okay.' Virginia sounded slightly concerned.

'I thought cricket was a summer sport. Can they play in this weather?' Annie regretted questioning the premise of the 'cricket tour' almost as soon as the words were out.

Kirsty carried on regardless. 'As soon as I hear the words cricket or rugby tour, honestly, I just block the whole thing from my mind, Annie. Really don't want to know. You're best doing the same thing, Gin.'

The colour drained from Virginia's face.

'So what's James up to this weekend?' Kirsty appeared impervious to Virginia's feelings of angst. 'Duncan asked him to go too but there was some story about work taking him away for the weekend. Don't think Duncan believed him but when I think what these boys get up to I really wouldn't blame him.'

Annie thought Virginia might pass out.

'I haven't seen much of James this week. Don't really know what's going on with work just that he's got some important project or something on the go.' Annie knew she sounded a bit downcast.

'Oh dear. Don't get upset, Annie. It's no bad thing if he's really involved in his work. Means he doesn't have time for silly things like made-up cricket tours.' Virginia stared at Kirsty.

'That's fine, Gin, but I thought we were getting somewhere. I really thought we could talk to each other about what was going on in our lives. I've told him so much recently and now he's just gone back into himself.

73

He's spending much more time at his own place.'

'Yes, thought I'd seen the lights on. Don't worry, Annie, at least it's work – not like he's gone off with anyone.'

'No, he's not gone off with anyone, anywhere. Not yet anyway.'

*

Annie spent all day Monday trapped in the tribunal offices on Melville Street. She was pitted against a buffoon of a solicitor, probably engaged at vast expense by his client, who could barely remember the poor woman's name and had great difficulty constructing any kind of plausible defence. Annie felt sorry for the woman as she sat, shoulders hunched, looking perplexed as the rotund figure of Malcolm Chalmers of Farquhar and Sutherland once more took to his feet. Annie could see he was starting to sweat, his small head constrained by a too-tight collar, which seemed responsible for popping the purple thread veins on his cheeks and whisky nose.

He's all over the place, thought Annie. She was glad. Not that she had any great desire to thwart Mrs Cuthbert's appeal against dismissal but she had a job to do and knew that up against anyone else, today of all days, she might have faltered. Forensic questioning, however, wasn't really required in this case as Mr Chalmers was losing the argument all by himself.

After closing submissions the Tribunal Chair advised that the panel would issue its decision in writing in the next day or two. Annie wondered why on earth they couldn't just make a decision there and then but after a quick word with her client, who was keen to get away, she gathered up her papers and prepared to leave. Normally she would have returned to the office but Annie just wanted to get home. She left the tribunal room and went to sign out at reception.

As she approached the desk Annie thought she caught sight of the familiar cross-ankled pose of her man lounging in the leather chair by the door. *Could be any tall, greying man*, she quickly rationalised. Suddenly, people were milling about everywhere and her pulse quickened as she tried to direct her gaze past the small groups of lawyers and clients crowding the reception area – just to make sure. One post-mortem finished abruptly and as the earnest little group dispersed there he was, out of his seat, waving and smiling. She walked quickly towards him and in moments she was in his arms.

'Miss me?'

The warm sense of wellbeing left Annie as soon as it had arrived.

'Miss you? Really? I've been wracking my brain trying to think why you would just shut yourself off from me; disappear for the weekend without me knowing *where* you were going, *why* you were going and most importantly *who* you were going with!'

'I know. Sorry, I just needed to get up there and find out for myself what's happening and really try to work out if I've got something to offer that could really help.' He looked completely unfazed by her rant.

'Help *who*?'

People were starting to look. Annie made James promise he wouldn't move as she returned to reception to sign out. When she returned he suggested going for a drink but Annie didn't want any more public displays, of affection *or* anger. They left the office and walked down the road in near silence to Dean Terrace.

Annie hung her coat up in the hall, and then walked through to the kitchen to deposit her briefcase. James had gone straight into the lounge and as she moved to join him she was aghast to see Ludovic rubbing himself against James's legs and positively swooning to the touch of the man who was now scratching him vigorously behind the ears. Traitor.

'Come and sit down,' he said gently.

He took both her hands in his and looked straight into her eyes. Annie felt like she was in some kind of lockdown, unable to divert her gaze away.

'Okay, so you know something about my job at St Andrew's House – rural affairs, land management?'

Annie nodded.

'You also know that I am really interested in how things can be improved for people who live on the land, cultivate it, take care of it, particularly in crofting communities.'

Annie nodded again.

'Land reform was part of my university degree and it was a real awakening for me. I just haven't really known how best to use what I've learned. I seem to have spent so much of my working life trying to get people to take it seriously but the truth is the Scottish Office isn't exactly the place to be concerned with huge amounts of innovation and reform – nothing that's really going to make a difference.'

She continued staring at him.

'Okay, well, there is an area of land, almost entirely crofting land in the south west of Sutherland called Assynt. In short, there's been a myriad of landowners over the past 200-odd years, members of the aristocracy mostly up until the current owner – a Swedish land speculator. *None* of these owners have ever considered how selling and buying the land might affect the people that actually live and work on it. Crofters' lives and livelihoods count for nothing in these deals.'

The intensity with which he spoke slightly unnerved Annie. She hadn't heard him sound so earnest about anything before.

'Now this Swedish company looks like it might go into liquidation and the land will be resold in lots. Different lots, by the way, from the last time it was sold; but the Scottish Crofters Union has been in touch with Government and there might be a chance, just a chance, that the crofters themselves could organise themselves, drum up the necessary finances to secure the land. They would finally be in control of their own future, rather than having to put up with daft ideas imposed from outside or have their own ideas blocked by people who just don't understand the land. Look, I don't want you to think this is just some fanciful notion of a better life. It is beautiful up there but it's bloody hard to scratch out a living on such barren land. Crofting is about working difficult land in the harshest of environments but it's the best way to use that land and it's part of what makes Scotland what it is – I just want to see it properly supported that's all.'

His grip on her hands was tightening as he became more animated.

'Okay, well, I guess it's important to you. I mean it *sounds* important to you.'

'It's important for all of us, Annie. Scotland really is a bit of a basket case when it comes to land ownership. No country has so much of its land in the hands of private landowners and how they got hold of the land in the first place – well, that's another story. It just isn't tolerated in any other modern European country.'

She knew her brow was beginning to furrow.

'Okay, I can see you're looking sceptical. What I mean is that other countries have known for centuries now that land ownership is vital for people to feel invested, connected. It allows communities to grow and care for the place they live. If you are surviving year to year, month to month, unsure if everything you have built and grown is going to be taken from you it pulls at the very fabric of your life, your community and it rips the soul out of your country – our country.'

Annie had never heard any of this before. Why hadn't she heard any of this before? There were questions, plenty of them, but they would need to be for another day. She didn't know enough to be able to share his passion but she could feel it and whether crofters' buy-outs were the answer or not almost didn't matter. She began to understand why it mattered to him and she began to understand why it mattered full stop.

She pulled her hand away from his strong grip and gently stroked his face.

'Okay, well, in practical terms tell me what it means for you, your job – for us.'

'Well, it doesn't really mean anything for my job, as things stand. I'll probably go along to meetings, supporting a minister who may or may not have encouraging words to say, bombard them with bureaucratic niceties, point out all the truly insurmountable hurdles while all the time praising their pluck, their entrepreneurial spirit! The reality, of course, is that I can do absolutely nothing of any practical worth to help them.'

James looked down at his hands.

'They need people like me, Annie. Not just me – they need lawyers, accountants, other professionals. The thing I can do is help them to get their business plan together. I know how to get an "in" to Government. I know what will sway civil servants and ministers so we can get some political clout behind their bid.'

He stopped and drew a deep breath.

'I would have to give up my job. I've asked about a secondment, about some sort of sabbatical, even, but the stuffed shirts aren't interested.'

'And what about your career, your pension…?' Annie tailed off knowing that none of that really mattered to James.

'Yes, but I'm in the fortunate position of not having any dependants, no mortgage. Nothing that stops me grasping this opportunity with both hands.'

'No, of course.' It was Annie's turn to look away.

'I know I'm asking an awful lot but it just seems like after all these years of being weighed down by civil service protocols and red tape I could finally do something I feel passionately about. It wouldn't be for too long and of course I'll be back and you can come up and stay – it's just that it'll probably be quite intense the first few weeks.'

'So, you've made up your mind then.' Annie couldn't help feeling deflated. She understood his words and she wanted to share his enthusiasm but she just couldn't. Finally, after all these years she thought she might just be allowing herself to get close, really close. To have what her friends had: a partner who was there, who would share her life so they could just be – together; but the first sign of something more exciting, something new and different and he was off. She really should never have expected anything different.

'Don't say it like that, Annie. You're making it sound as though I've made a choice between you and going to Assynt. That's not it at all; but it is really important to me. I need to do something with my life that is meaningful; work with good people; do stuff that is going to make a difference, however small in the scheme of things.'

'How long will you be gone?'

'Developing the plan will be a six-month thing and then we can sit down together and take stock from there. It could lead on to other things, not necessarily here; I just don't know.'

'Okay but how am I supposed to plan my life around that? You might be here, you might be there.'

'We'll work something out, Annie.' Suddenly his tone changed. 'It's just I could be doing something real for a change.'

'Well, are we not real? Is my life not real? What I do is real and it's important to me but that's really of no consequence to you. Okay, I'm not saving the country – I'm a boring old employment lawyer. And no, none of that is earth shattering but I'm bloody good at my job.'

She really didn't know where she was going with any of it but it was important to her that he knew it wasn't all okay. She wasn't going to let meek acceptance win the day this time.

'Just go – go to Assynt.'

And with that, Annie broke free from his grasp and marched into the bedroom. She sat on the edge of the bed, head in hands.

James stood in the doorway. 'Oh, Annie, come on. Look, I love you. Please don't make this something it isn't.'

That's right, Annie. Don't make a mountain out of a molehill. It's only work after all. But she couldn't help herself – she started sobbing into her hands.

'Look, we can make this work. Nobody knows what's round the corner but I thought we were in this for the long haul. Chances are I'll be back in six months and then I'll just figure out what I'm going to do to earn a living.'

He squatted down in front of her enclosing her hands in his. Her head fell forward into his chest. 'Oh nice. Tears and snot all over my shirt.'

Annie half-heartedly pushed him in the chest. 'Serves you right. Aren't they going to pay you then?' She looked around at the box of tissues sitting on her nightstand but couldn't summon the energy to go and get them. She knew her face was a mess. James followed her gaze and quickly retrieved the pretty floral box. Annie ripped out more tissues than she needed.

'There'll be a small fee but if we're successful with grant assistance then there is the potential for a salaried position – although I'm guessing it would pay a pittance.'

'If I come and see you I'm not staying in some communal bunkhouse with a bunch of hairy-arsed men – or women for that matter.' Annie made her remonstrations while blowing unceremoniously into the bundle of tissues.

'Don't worry. I'll be in a little place of my own and I'll make sure it's just perfect for you.'

'I hate this, James, I really do. Things just started to settle and it was all beginning to feel so comfortable. I know we're not actually living together or anything but I felt we were a "couple". I'm sorry but no matter how you dress it up it feels like you're leaving me. Do you understand what I mean?'

'No I don't, darling. We still *are* a couple and no I'm not leaving you. I'm going to do something that I feel is important but that doesn't reflect on us. Doing something like this, well, that's just part of who I am and I can't really be any less than that. You're the best thing that's happened to me in a long time but I just feel so stifled at work. I could end up turning out like Duncan!'

Annie couldn't help but smile at the prospect. She had exhausted all her arguments and couldn't face prolonging the agony anymore.

'Let's not do this anymore, tonight. Look, I've got a day off tomorrow. Why don't you just stay here tonight?'

James looked relieved. They were both past eating and like two evenly matched fighters who had lasted the full bout, they collapsed exhausted into their respective corners. They lay in silence for a long time until their hands clasped under the covers. Slowly and tenderly, they made love and then slept soundly through to the next morning.

Annie woke to find James gone. *Surely not already*, she thought to herself until she heard the key turn in the door. His tuneless whistling filled the flat as he clattered about the kitchen. Annie knew he had again bought far too much from the Home Bakery. As she turned over, enjoying the moments before full wakefulness, the warmth of his body was still there on the pillow and the sheets. The sense of him, here in bed and throughout the rest of the flat overwhelmed her. This was what she wanted; this was what she thought was her future. Why did he need to destroy that? The bedroom door opened and in he came with a mug of tea. He set the tea down and swept the hair away from her eyes.

'You are lovely.'

'Yes, well, not that lovely, obviously.'

'Oh, Annie, please. Things will work out for us – they will; and look, when I get the chance I'm going to take you away, just the two of us, to Italy. You know the book I've been reading – well, there's a lovely little spot, high up above the Lakes where an amazing man has created these lovely gardens and I just know you would love it. Just us, enjoying each other and the beautiful things that the world has to offer. We've so many adventures ahead of us, you and I.' James paused. 'I know this is hard for you. I know it is but please you have to give me a chance. You have to believe in us a bit more.'

CHAPTER 5

'Are you sure you still want to go?' Annie was stretched out on the couch watching a 1930s black and white weepie.

'I'm happy to. Get us in the Christmas spirit?' James turned round from the desk, peering over his reading glasses. Every last inch of the antique writing table was piled high with papers.

'Okay, I'll phone Kirsty now and let her know. Are you going to tell them all about Assynt?'

'Don't see why not.' James had turned back and was once more immersed in the world of grant applications and business plans.

It was all so uncomplicated to him, she thought.

'Unless you don't want me to.'

Okay, not completely self-absorbed then. 'No, it's fine.' Annie walked through to the hall and called the Drummonds. 'Duncan. Hi, it's Annie. Yes, we'll both be round tomorrow night. Do you need us to bring anything?'

'Just yourselves, Annie. Kirsty has taken over the kitchen for a change and I must say she's cooking up a storm. It's all finger food but it's looking bloody good. I've got enough champagne, wine and whisky to sink a boat, oh and of course gin, but if there's anything else you want, just let me know and I'll get it tomorrow.'

'No, that's great, Duncan, see you tomorrow.'

Annie returned to the couch to find Ludovic in her place. *Just try moving me, Miss Annie.*

She sidled up next to him, hoping a gentle shove in the ribs might be more than he could stand. He looked at her and then jumped down in disgust. 'I had no idea cats could actually look disdainful but that was it right there.'

James laughed. 'What are you watching, Miss Annie?'

Don't call me that, she thought, *that's what the cat calls me.*

'*Random Harvest.* Ronald Coleman and Greer Garson. It's about a man with amnesia. Falls in love with Paula, becomes a writer, gets knocked down and then remembers his life before Paula. He's some kind of big industrialist and he goes back to that life. All the time he's spent with her has just gone – he doesn't know her at all even when she goes to work for him. She spends the rest of the film waiting for him to come back to her.'

James joined her on the couch and put her head on his lap. 'Bet he does go back to her.'

'Yes, well, they always do in 1930s Hollywood.'

*

'My, you scrub up well, Mr Kerr. Really liking the tweed jacket although it's a bit more landed gentry than man of the people.' Annie was giving her man the once over before they set off for the Drummonds'.

James gently shook his head. 'Well, thank you, my

dear. Not sure what to say to that. A tweed jacket is a tweed jacket as far as I'm concerned. Right, where's that wine? Are you sure that's all we need to take?'

'Oh God, yes. Our little offering will be completely surplus to requirements, believe me.'

'Do you know anyone else who's going?'

'Well, there's Gordon and Virginia of course and I think some of the other neighbours, none of whom you'll have met, I'm guessing?'

'Correct!'

'And I think there might be a few folk from Duncan's office.'

The icy air from the dense fog tumbling down the Terrace hit their lungs as soon as they left the flat. Annie grabbed James's arm and they hurried round into Royal Circus where the dimly lit globes, set high on their black cast iron supports, peered through the mist. She was sure she could hear the swishing of a Victorian gentleman's cloak as he scurried by the railings. Edinburgh was at its best at this time of year. She thought of Leerie the Lamplighter and her father, tucking in the sheets and blankets tightly at each side of the bed and then sitting by her to read from *A Child's Garden of Verses*. She remembered feeling like a tightly swaddled baby; that sense of being completely safe and secure as he told his stories. The memory warmed her all the way to No. 92 Great King Street.

James hit the heavy brass knocker with a flourish. All for effect, thought Annie, as there was a perfectly functional doorbell right in front of him.

As soon as Kirsty opened the door, it was obvious all was not well.

'Strachan and Marjorie are here. They just "popped" in on their way to friends'. God, why tonight of all nights?' Kirsty looked beside herself.

'Great, Strachan. I'm going to meet Strachan!' James grinned from ear to ear.

'Right, that's enough, you. I don't want you causing any bother.' *God, he's like a naughty little boy sometimes*, Annie thought.

Kirsty ushered them inside, grabbing hurriedly at their coats.

'You've heard about Duncan's father then, James?'

'Well, just some basic facts. Annie told me about her trip up to meet Duncan's folks a few years ago. Sounds like a fascinating man. Can't wait to meet him.'

Kirsty looked quizzically at Annie.

No, I'm not sure what that means either, Annie thought.

The first thing Annie noticed as they walked through to the lounge was Duncan sitting quietly slumped in the armchair, beer in hand. He looked so much smaller, she thought, in contrast to Strachan who seemed to fill the room with his presence. He was telling Gordon and some of the other men all about Duncan's brother, Lachlan, and an unfortunate rugby injury.

'Yes, it's a bloody shame. Torn all the ligaments in his thigh. Season's over for him really but still insists on coming into work every day – even on crutches. Don't know what I'd do without him, mind you; he's practically running the business on his own these days.'

Duncan's face suddenly brightened and he jumped up from his detached position in the corner of the room. 'James, old man. Annie, wonderful. What would you like to drink? Was waiting for you to arrive before I cracked open the bubbly!'

'Bubbly, Duncan? Really? Hardly a man's drink, that. I'm sure James would rather have a beer or a quick snifter.' Strachan slapped James on the back with a force that made him stumble forward slightly.

James quickly recovered his composure. 'Bubbly's great, Duncan, thanks. I'll come and help you.'

The two men escaped to the kitchen, emerging a short while later to pass round glasses of ice-cold fizz.

'Perfect!' Annie exclaimed, perhaps just a bit too keenly. She was standing by the fireplace with Kirsty and Marjorie when the two men joined the little group. Strachan was still holding sway in the middle of the room with a group of Duncan's colleagues that included the hapless Virginia and Gordon. Virginia looked wistfully over at the little gathering standing by the roaring log fire. Annie thought she looked like a young, wounded antelope cornered by a pride of lions and felt a sudden urge to rescue her friend and bring her back to the friendly herd. She resisted the temptation in case the alpha male broke away with her.

The friendly little group's tactical positioning could only last for so long and Strachan began to look about for some fresh meat. Annie could see him heading towards James and before she could send any kind of warning signal Strachan was there, once again slapping him on the back.

'Okay, James, time for proper introductions. I know you're Annie's new man! Strachan Drummond, Duncan's father.'

James turned, smiled politely and shook Strachan's outstretched hand.

'Are you an Edinburgh man, James?'

'Glasgow, actually.'

'*Really?* How interesting. What brings you to the metropolis then?'

Annie knew James really wanted to say something about the relative merits of Scotland's two big cities but he was restraining himself.

'I'm a civil servant. Work in St Andrew's House.'

'Well now, this is the first time I've met one of you chaps in the flesh. Thought you always hid yourselves away in these monstrous grey office blocks.'

James smiled but Annie could see in his eyes that this was not an encounter he was enjoying. 'They let me out to meet the masses now and again.'

'So what is it you actually do then, James?'

'Well, I'm rural affairs really. I'm leaving shortly to work with a crofters' organisation up in Assynt.'

Annie stared at him. *Okay, that's it out now.*

'It's not that lot that are thinking about trying to buy the land up there is it?'

'Well, yes it is actually.'

'I've had a few run-ins with the crofters' union myself. Let them sink or swim, I say. If they can't drum up the necessary funds themselves then they shouldn't be getting any help from the state, or the likes of you, James. I'm sure you could put your talents to better use. All good and well managing a few sheep on a smallholding but this is bloody business we're talking about, James.'

'Oh, I don't know. I like the idea of helping them

to purchase the land. You know, ensure the income it generates stays in the local community and doesn't just line the pockets of absentee landlord or speculators. Help them improve the management of the estate. I really think it's the way forward, encouraging new developments, new employment opportunities… that kind of thing.' And with a wry smile, James slapped Strachan on the back.

He didn't break stride. 'Improve the management of the estate, my arse, James. There's a lot of bloody good people invested their hard-earned money in these estates. Crofters shouldn't be getting any preferential treatment. I tell you, it's nationalisation of land through the back door – mad communist ideology, that's what it is!'

Annie noticed Strachan was getting more agitated but James was completely calm. *He's starting to enjoy this*, she thought. Everyone else in the room had fallen silent, engrossed in the sparring match.

Duncan suddenly turned away from his father. There was a slight tremble in his voice as he fixed his gaze on James. 'I agree with James actually. After all, they're the people who really know the land; might encourage families to stay, increase the population and all that.'

Only that tight little group of friends knew what it took for Duncan to oppose his father's position on anything. Kirsty quietly slipped her hand into Duncan's as Strachan, face like thunder, moved away to top up his drink. Gordon and Virginia nervously tried to strike up a conversation about the paucity of lights on the Stockbridge Christmas tree just as James gave Duncan a reassuring nod. Annie didn't know if Duncan truly believed what he had said but it didn't matter. He had stood up to his father, looked ten feet taller and found common cause with James. She slipped her arm round her man's waist and clung on tightly.

Shortly after, Strachan and Marjorie made their excuses and left. Marjorie gave her son a reassuring hug but Strachan was keen to make a point of ignoring him. Point made, Duncan looked relieved to see the back of him.

'So, old man, tell us more about this trip to Assynt. When are you off?'

It was too much for Annie to hope that they could ever be best friends but they were sitting down having a meaningful conversation about crofting! There was nothing superficial, nothing said or done for effect; just two men sharing their thoughts and ideas.

Annie went off to find Kirsty. She was in the kitchen bent over the sink, scrubbing away at a large roasting tray trying to lift the sticky residue of barbecued ribs.

'Leave that, Kirsty, and come back through. Everyone's having such a nice time.'

The roasting tray dropped from her grasp and her shoulders started to shake.

'Hey, Kirsty darling. What's wrong?' Annie turned her round to see tears streaming down her cheeks. She had never seen Kirsty cry before.

'Oh, Annie. I've never seen Duncan talk like that to his father. I mean, I'm glad that he did, I just hope there won't be any repercussions, that's all.'

'Oh, Kirsty, no. It's a good thing he can hold his ground with Strachan. Could be the making of him, you know.'

The two women embraced. Annie wiped Kirsty's face with a tea towel.

'Come on, the night is young!' Annie grabbed another couple of bottles of champagne from the fridge and the two chums rejoined the party.

*

In the days that followed, Annie thought carefully about how the drama had unfolded at the Drummonds' soirée. She happily recalled Duncan's emergence from his father's oppressive shadow but the more significant development, for her at any rate, had been her friends' unquestioning acceptance of James's imminent departure north. They had listened intently to his explanation of what he was about to do, asked intelligent questions and admired his resolve for getting stuck into something he felt passionate about. At no point did anyone express any concern for Annie or for the future of their relationship. She began to wonder if she had really overthought this. If no one else could see what the problem was then maybe she just needed to be a bit more supportive.

Thoughts turned to planning and logistics; working out weekends here and there; calculating how little time they would actually be apart. After all, once she factored in the time spent at work now, it shouldn't really have such a big impact. After careful reflection the negatives began to turn to positives. He was going to do something worthwhile, something that meant a lot to him and something her friends clearly admired him for. She could legitimately feel proud of him.

It was something akin to an epiphany. The dark clouds started to lift and Annie determined to see only good things ahead. Time to start planning for Christmas and looking forward to all that 1991 would bring.

*

James had negotiated his leaving date with the Scottish Office, which gave Annie until the end of February to enjoy what remained of Phase One and to plan for a different but altogether perfectly manageable Phase Two of their relationship. Christmas was going to be wonderful, she decided, and threw herself, with some gusto, into present buying and decorating. Shabby decorations and battered baubles were swiftly discarded in favour of an overall red, gold and green colour scheme. Everything matched and she had even acquired a craft skills magazine from Virginia, which was directly responsible for the gold pinecones sitting in a hand-painted bowl on the hearth. James made the right kind of approving noises as each new element was added, including her beautifully arranged nativity tableau. As she sat one night admiring her handiwork, Annie realised that James was labouring under the misapprehension that quality festive interior design was the norm for her little basement flat. It made her chuckle.

The first fly in the ointment came a week before Christmas. Helen was of course joining them for the big day itself but Annie had been planning an intimate Christmas Eve dinner, just her and James. She hadn't said as much but menus and handmade centrepieces were starting to take shape in her head.

As she was leafing through *Delia Smith's Christmas*,

Annie heard the door, then some rustling of bags followed by opening and closing of the chest of drawers in the bedroom.

James emerged into the lounge beaming. 'Now you mustn't go rummaging about in there, dear.' He collapsed onto the couch and threw his arms around her. 'Bumped into Gordon in St Stephen Street – looked like a man on the edge. No idea what to get Virginia so I dragged him into the Antiquary, we had a couple of pints and I shared with him everything I know about the perfect gift for the woman you love, which by the way is not very much, just in case you were getting your hopes up there!'

He planted a very cold and slightly beery kiss on her cheek.

'Anyway, as I was walking back I thought, why don't we ask them round on Christmas Eve for a few drinks? I think they're having a quiet one and of course Duncan and Kirsty are off to her folks' down the Mull of Galloway so there won't be any socialising with the Drummonds over the piece. What do you think?'

He was beaming, clearly pleased with himself that he was doing right by Annie's friends.

Annie stared at him. 'Good God, James, you've gone from living the life of a hermit to "hail fellow, well met" in a remarkably short space of time!'

He looked suddenly crestfallen. 'Oh dear, I thought you'd be pleased with my suggestion. Show you that I can be sociable, particularly at this time of year.'

She couldn't bear the downcast look. 'No, it's a good idea – I guess I'd just been thinking we might have had Christmas Eve to ourselves – but it's fine. We can have drinks and nibbles.' Annie quietly relegated Delia to the magazine rack at the side of the sofa and squeezed his hand.

As it turned out, Christmas Eve was a relaxed, fun evening and Annie was, in the end, grateful that she didn't have the added pressure of cooking up a sumptuous dinner before the main event with her mother.

Christmas Day dawned and Annie and James spent most of the morning in bed sharing gifts and enjoying each other before the formality of the day encroached upon their private happiness. James scrunched up pieces of wrapping paper and threw them across the room for Ludovic to play with. The cat obliged for all of five minutes before deciding to opt for a more peaceful existence in the lounge. As James headed for a shower, Annie looked around her and reckoned that he had done pretty well on the gift front. He had clearly taken note of her preferred toiletries, including her favourite perfume, although she was less enthusiastic about the cast iron casserole dish. It was obviously very expensive and very heavy but a Christmas present, really? As she had unwrapped the box to reveal the dish in all its functional splendour she couldn't help but smile at him – he had looked so pleased with himself. Just as she thought she'd come to the end of her festive stash, he'd presented her with a final gift. Annie tore off the paper to find a first edition of *Scottish Love Poems*. It was perfect; the best present of all.

James left to pick Helen up at one o'clock and while he was away, Annie added the final touches to her dining table. She wasn't sure if any of it would find favour or not but really couldn't spend too much time worrying.

She heard the car draw up outside and then suddenly

Helen burst through the door, arms brimming with presents. The faux fur coat was topped off this time by a pillbox fur hat. *All very Dr Zhivago*, thought Annie.

'James is bringing in the rest, dear. Where shall I put these?'

Annie showed her into the cosy lounge and pointed to the handsome six-foot Nordmann fir standing to attention in the corner decorated with just the right number of gold, red and green baubles.

'My, this looks lovely, dear. You've certainly pulled out all the stops this year. Must be trying to impress you, James.'

Annie turned to look at him as he struggled with more presents, bottles and what looked like an M&S food parcel.

Then, just as she was going in to kiss her mother and offer some festive glad tidings, Helen suddenly exclaimed, 'What have you done with that luminous white thing you got from Argos last year?'

James almost dropped the whole stash as he tried to stifle a laugh.

'No, seriously, James, it was hideous. I don't know what she was thinking. This is much better.' She walked up to James and squeezed his arm. 'I think you're a very good influence on my girl, you know.'

All her own good work, her own ideas – none of these would have been remotely possible in Helen's eyes without someone else's input. Why did she even bother trying to impress anyone – James or her mother?

At least James picked up on her mood change and after spreading everything out rather unceremoniously on the floor, hurried off to find the sherry. Drinks poured, the unwrapping of presents began. After what seemed like an age, the ritualistic exchange finally appeared to be over when Annie noticed a present cast adrift from the main pile, something that looked like a hefty hardback.

'Oh, James, that's for you!' exclaimed Helen as she turned to look for the cat. There had never been any pets in the Anderson household but in her later years Helen seemed to have developed a strange affinity for other people's animals and small children.

He smiled, relaxed after a couple of sherries now, and ripped the paper off in keen anticipation. It was a copy of the *King James Bible*. James shot Annie a look of utter perplexity.

Helen had her back to them, her attention diverted by her attempts to lavish unwanted affection on poor Ludovic. 'Hope you like it, James. It's all about terrorists in Palestine.'

Annie and James could only stare at each other. Clearly there had been some misunderstanding but it was fun trying to suppress laughter while contemplating Helen's take on the Son of God's good works.

'I think they try to launch a nuclear attack at that American football thingy – the Superbowl I think it's called – well, something like that.'

She was down on all fours now with her ample backside protruding into the air. Ludovic, by this time, had wrestled free and headed for the bedroom.

Helen turned just as James was trying to stifle a laugh while holding the Bible in his outstretched hand. Despite the humour of the situation, Annie thought he looked just a little bit scared, as though holding the word of God too close might result in an unintended conversion.

'Oh my. That was for Jean McHarg. Oh dear, James, I think the poor woman's got the latest Tom Clancy thriller – probably not recommended reading for the Chair of the Women's Guild!'

Any last vestiges of tension disappeared and the three of them sat round laughing as they envisaged present opening at the McHargs.

After a sumptuous meal, they sat fit to bursting and sipping at their orange Muscat. Annie couldn't help but feel very satisfied with her first Christmas dinner. Helen had complimented her all the way through the meal and James grunted approvingly after every course. He did make some half-hearted offer to clear away and do the washing up but Helen was having none of it.

'No, no, James. You sit through there. Annie and I will sort all this out.' Exactly the sort of intervention she had made whenever Annie's father had attempted to help with washing up.

Annie stared at James with a look that clearly demanded some form of resistance but he merely smiled.

'Oh, well, if you insist. Can't say I didn't offer, darling.' And off he sloped.

Mother and daughter assumed their customary roles of washer and dryer.

'I think it's sitting behind a desk all day, dear. You never seem to apply quite enough elbow grease.' Helen rolled up the sleeves of her paisley-patterned Christmas frock and got stuck in.

'Well, you two seem to be settling nicely into cosy domesticity.'

'Yes, it's going quite well.'

Helen stopped scrubbing and turned to look at her daughter. 'I really didn't think you'd want to get all involved with someone, Annie – thought you were quite happy as you were. But then I do quite like him. I know it doesn't really matter in the scheme of things, but I like that he wants to come round to your old mother's with you. Not all men would want to do that – most would run a mile, in fact, unless marital duty forced them.'

'Yes, well, he won't be coming round quite as often, Mum… well, not in the short term, anyway.'

Helen looked quizzically at her daughter. 'Why, what's happened?'

'Nothing's happened. It's just that he's going away with work for a while, six months actually – up north.'

'Oh, I see.' Helen turned back to her roasting tray.

'It's fine, it's just that we'll need to plan things. He'll come back when he can and I'll probably go up there occasionally. It's a really important project he's involved in, something he feels really passionately about.' The lack of any response from her mother made Annie press the case for his leaving. 'So of course I want him to go. In fact, it's really important he goes – and it's not like it's forever.'

Helen's scrubbing tempo increased dramatically. 'Yes, well. I suppose it shouldn't have come as a surprise. Men just like to do their own thing at the end of the day – and just when I thought things were panning out nicely for you.'

Annie knew where her thoughts were going. She slapped the tea towel down next to the sink.

'James and I are not you and Dad. It isn't the same

thing at all. He's coming back to me.' She picked up the towel again. 'I'm not pushing him away.'

She regretted those final words as soon as they had left her lips.

Helen suddenly stopped what she was doing. At the same time, Annie felt herself go towards her mother but in reality it was an emotional shift rather than a physical one. She barely moved. After an uncomfortable pause the two women carried on with their kitchen duties, this time in silence. Annie finished off the drying but her mother had now taken to scrubbing the cooker hob as vigorously as she had attacked the washing up.

Annie made her way back through to the lounge alone to find James assuming his customary position. He was fast asleep, head cocked to one side and snoring. Annie watched from the doorway as he inhaled loudly then puffed out his cheeks and quietly exhaled. The cat seemed determined to match the pose of the replete man and lay stretched out across the top of the sofa, full belly warming James's head and purring in harmony with his adopted master.

Annie joined them, head on her man's shoulder and nestling under the cat's head. James suddenly woke and Ludovic was once more upended from his chosen sleeping platform.

'Oh, there you are!' He drew her in and then looked round, still sleepy. 'Where's your mother? Have you done everything? Sorry, Annie, I should have come through and helped; really not acceptable in this day and age.'

There was a loud meow from behind the sofa.

'Oh God, what have I done to the cat?' James lifted his

arms and stretched, looking round for Ludovic.

'Oh, he's fine. Mother's cleaned every surface in the kitchen and then some. I think she's shut herself away in the bathroom now.'

'Oh no, what's happened?'

'There's just a bit of an atmosphere now that I've told her about you heading off at the end of February.'

'Really, why?'

Annie wasn't sure if he was being deliberately obtuse or just lacking emotional awareness.

'It's Geneva all over again.'

'Oh, good grief.'

Just at that, the door swung open and there stood Helen, the pillbox hat planted firmly on her head now. Warm festive feelings were receding fast. 'James, what time did you say the taxi was booked for?'

'Well, I didn't actually but it's seven o'clock.' He glanced at the vintage clock on the mantelpiece. A present from Annie's father. From Switzerland. 'Look, it's only six now. Why don't you come and sit down and I'll make everyone some tea.'

Helen didn't move. 'I think I'd rather just go now. Can't you ring the taxi firm?'

'Come on, Mum, I'm sorry, I didn't mean to suggest… look, please just sit down. We've had such a nice day.' This time Annie did make the physical gesture and stepped forward to take her mother's hand.

'Well, what exactly were you trying to say then?'

Annie could see James sit forward as though ready to ask precisely what had been said but then suddenly without any prompting, he sat back to let mother and daughter resolve matters. Levels of awareness had clearly returned.

'I don't know. I can't ever really know what went on with you and Dad. I'm sure there were issues on both sides.' Annie guided her mother to sit down next to James. He was looking uncomfortable but Annie wanted her mother in between them; she wanted her to feel that they were united in this. 'James isn't leaving me. It's a short-term work thing, that's all. Actually I'm very proud of him for having the gumption to go and do something like this.'

James took his cue. 'Look, Helen, this isn't going to be for long and you have to believe me that I love your daughter very much and I'm not going to do anything that puts what we have at any kind of risk.'

Annie smiled. She needed to hear that as much as her mother did.

Helen turned to look at him. 'Okay, James, well maybe sometime you can tell me a bit about what you're going to do – although I'm sure it won't mean very much to me.' She was rubbing her fingers, anxiously. 'You might not know very much about the Andersons and their strange lives, I don't know.'

She looked at her daughter but Annie really didn't want to speak anymore.

'I suppose Annie's told you something about her dad and me. I can hardly remember how it all started, I mean Switzerland and all that, but before I knew it everything seemed to just fall apart.' She looked down into her lap. 'All I will say is that I know work and career and everything that brings can seem terribly important – just don't let it all get in the way of what really matters. A lesson, I think, we learned too late, I'm afraid.'

Helen grasped each of their hands. As she turned again to look round at her daughter, Annie could see the tears in her mother's eyes.

'And that goes for both of you.'

CHAPTER 6

In the weeks that followed it occurred to Annie that James had really taken Helen's words to heart. He was forever trying to arrange nice things for them to do, creating special moments. It irked her. She felt he was trying to build up a nice bank of memories that would sustain them during this period of enforced separation but Annie really didn't want the extraordinary. She just needed them to *be* – to enjoy the mundane, the everyday. Then she thought about him in the bunkhouse he was going to occupy for the first couple of weeks. All she could think of was the rank smell of men's undergarments, sweaty and damp, strewn over bunk beds and radiators. She smiled to herself. Maybe he was the one that was going to be in need of nice thoughts to warm him.

They kept up their routine of Sunday dinner with Helen and the three of them seemed to relax more into each other's company. Helen offered no opinion on the desirability of James's 'project' as she called it but rather focused all her energies on his preparedness for an extended trip to the Highlands. Her concern for his welfare extended to the presents she gave for his birthday at the end of January. Annie looked on in disbelief as James unwrapped each item – Helen appeared to have divested Tiso's outdoor specialist shop of its entire January sale stock.

Back at the flat James surveyed his haul. 'Maybe she thinks I'm actually setting out on one of those unsupported Arctic expeditions. Good God, I've even got some of these bloody awful dried meals – beef stroganoff, chicken tikka with rice!'

As Annie picked up a pair of thermal gloves she knew his indignation wasn't all real. He was warming to the thought that Helen actually might care about him.

*

The day before James was due to set off they decided to go for a walk through the Botanics. It was a bitingly cold day but the sun shone high and for the first time that year Annie could feel some warmth in its rays. They walked past a little flurry of lilac and white crocuses, some already trampled underfoot while the remainder were wavering on their flimsy stems up the steep grassy bank. Daffodil stalks had pushed through between the delicate flowers but, unlike their pushy little neighbours, weren't quite ready to share their bright hue with the world.

'Fancy a coffee?' James asked.

Annie thought for a moment. 'No, not really, thanks. It's too noisy up there, I don't want any noise.' She knew that a gaggle of mothers and toddlers always congregated up at the Terrace Café about this time.

James let go of her hand and placed his arm around her, gripping the thick shoulder of her camel coat.

'Fine, let's go and sit at the hothouses and soak up some of these rays.'

They sat just in front of the glass and metal structures that housed, among other things, fragments of the Amazonian rainforest. All hot and humid inside, while they sat outside clad in winter coats, woolly hats and thick gloves. The air was cold but, in their sheltered spot, the sun peered over the trees and warmed their faces.

Annie was feeling irksome, unsettled.

'I still don't really understand why grant applications and business plans mean you need to be hundreds of miles away. I'm sure you could do just as good a job down here.' She was looking down at her feet, stumbling over a final and slightly pathetic attempt to put a halt to proceedings.

'I just need to go, Annie. I want to go.'

'You know, I don't really understand why you moved into Great King Street actually. You're just not very New Town are you? And the Scottish Office – how have you managed to work *there* all these years when clearly all you wanted was to be out communing with nature?'

He didn't rise to the bait. 'I love Great King Street. Wouldn't have met you if I hadn't moved there.'

He turned to smile at her and she held the gaze of his soft blue eyes. Strange how, even now, just a look made her feel as though she might just be able to face anything. It still unnerved her slightly but when it happened and it was just the two of them she almost felt as though she didn't need to be scared again. Did love do that to you? Did it stop you being scared? She said nothing else but leaned into the warmth of his neck and breathed in deeply, hoping that the sense of him might just linger about her for the next six months.

As they made their way through to Inverleith Row it

struck Annie that, apart from the little flurry of colour at the entrance, most of the gardens, even in the late February sunshine, looked grey and brown. The rhododendron bushes sat looking forlorn and hunched over, giving no hint of the riot of colour to come. Then, just as they were approaching the gates, a blaze of purple primulas came into view. Beautiful flowers, standing tall and erect, drinking in the sun. The sight of them warmed her. She never wanted to be scared again.

In the end, James's departure was quiet and unfussy. Everything had been said that needed to be said and so they stuck to the practical tasks of emptying the flat and filling the car. The Drummonds, together with Kirsty's brother Donald, all appeared on the landing offering assistance, refreshments and words of encouragement; Donald was renting the flat for a few months before he headed off trekking in the Himalayas. When they had discussed the rental arrangements some weeks before, Kirsty observed that 'things had panned out quite nicely after all'. They certainly had panned out, thought Annie, as she observed James's little farewell committee, but not nicely. Definitely not nicely.

'Well, we'll miss you, old man, but I'm sure you'll be back with us before we know it.' Duncan stood clutching a slightly tearful Kirsty.

'Yes, be no time at all. Keep an eye on this one, won't you.' James nodded at Annie. 'Might need to give you a call at some point, Duncan, regarding some of the legal issues – if that's okay.'

Duncan beamed. 'Absolutely no problem at all, old man – on both counts!'

The Drummonds retreated quietly, allowing Annie and James to bid their farewells.

'I really don't know the position with phones, darling, but even if there isn't one at the bunkhouse the pub along the road is bound to have one, and of course I'll write – every other day.' He was packing the last of his things into the overcrowded boot. Suddenly he turned, looking distressed. 'Didn't think about stamps and post and all that. There must be a post box close by – mustn't there?'

Suddenly it was Annie's turn to do the reassuring.

'I'm sure there will be.' She put a hand up to the side of his face and he leant against it. 'Stop worrying. Once you get the lay of the land everything will be fine. Don't worry about getting in touch straight away, just get yourself settled in.'

He pressed her hand to his face and kissed it. 'I do love you.'

'And I love you.' A quick, tender embrace followed and before she knew it he had left Edinburgh behind him and headed off to his new life.

The first phone calls were stuttering affairs relayed via a dodgy line from the local pub close to the bunkhouse. There was only time for basic information to be shared: state of the accommodation, working hours, food and drink stocks and a quick round-up of everyone's state of health. There would be much more information forthcoming in James's letters – apparently.

The first of these arrived well into the second week and Annie's heart leapt at the sight of it lying on the hall carpet as she returned home from a less than riveting 'update' session on the Transfer of Undertakings regulations. She determined to have a bath, slip into cosy clothes and make a nice cup of tea before immersing herself in his words.

It wasn't all she'd hoped for. There was a quick run through of his colleagues' biographies followed by a description of current land management issues, including ideas for new farming practices, opportunities for better conservation, potential for improving tourist attractions, possible generation of new employment opportunities – and so it went on.

Annie was bored and ever so slightly disappointed by the time she'd got to the bottom of page three. Not even two weeks, granted, but she had liked to think that he might be lying in his lonely bunk pining just a little bit and thinking of beautiful things to say to her. Finally, towards the end of the dissertation on crofting in Assynt, a ray of hope. He began to wax lyrical about his surroundings; the abundance of wildlife he had already seen, including deer, seals and otters, and was sure Annie would love the area. He described loch-side and woodland walks and how much lovelier they would be if she was with him and then, just to round things off nicely, he had spotted a cottage to rent with lovely gardens leading down to the beach on the shore of a small loch. Would Annie be able to travel up and take a look at it with him anytime soon?

She smiled and reached out to cuddle Ludovic. One squeeze and he was off. *Right, let's think about this.* Annie mulled over the practicalities of heading up that weekend. She would need to rearrange drinks with the Drummonds and postpone Sunday lunch with Helen. Would she drive or get the train to Inverness? Would James be able to pick her up? Where would she stay? Lots of things to think about but they were lovely things to think about.

James rang that night. The train took forever and on a Friday wasn't far removed from the dirt and chaos of a slow-moving sleeper from Calcutta. He suggested driving and a relatively early start to make the most of the daylight. He would of course send very detailed directions so all would be well and, yes, they would book into the hotel along from the bunkhouse. Annie slept well for the first time since James had left. She was setting off on a bit of an adventure and James would be waiting for her at the end of her travels.

The first slight dampener was Helen's concern that she was driving such a distance on her own. 'I do hope you'll stop a lot, not in the middle of nowhere of course. Try to phone me whenever you do stop and do you have enough warm weather gear? I could go back to Tiso's and see what they have. Remember to keep a check on your petrol and you are a member of the AA, aren't you? Will I ask the McHargs' boy to come and check your car for roadworthiness?'

Annie attempted to placate her mother on each of her worry points, all the while knowing nothing would, and so continued making her plans for the weekend.

The drive was much more pleasurable than Annie had anticipated. She loved the quiet roads and breathtaking scenery, certainly once she had left the madness of a Friday on the A9 behind her, and meandered her way across to the northwest coast. What beautiful contrasts Scotland offered, she thought. Lush forests suddenly giving way to heather and boulder-clad hills. Grey clouds dusting the tops of conical mountains scarred by swathes of shale and scree. Edinburgh was her home and she loved it but all of Scotland was her home too. She was suddenly feeling very content with her lot. As she drew closer to Assynt, the feeling grew, knowing that what she loved most of all was just a few short miles away.

'Well, I have to say you made excellent time in your little Fiesta.' She was in his arms outside the old coaching inn that was to be their little haven for the weekend. Annie just wanted to stay like that but James was keen to move things along. He quickly broke free from her embrace and went to get her bags from the boot.

'We'll get you settled in and then I want to take you down to the rocks just there and we can watch the seals for a while.' He pointed to the rocky outcrop that sat alongside the slipway down to the loch. 'You should see all the amazing shellfish they land here, Annie, and of course the crofts supply so much of the meat and vegetables. It could be really self-sustaining if we could just get enough money in.'

He was gazing down at the stillness of the loch now and although Annie desperately wanted to pull him away into the seclusion of their hotel room, she couldn't break the spell. This was the happiest she had seen him.

It was a glorious weekend. The weather was kind to them and they spent much of their time outdoors. Most of their walking was coastal, around wild headlands, but they also trekked high up steep paths and on to heather-clad moorland. It all had an unexpectedly exhilarating effect on Annie. The air was crisp and clean, untainted by city pollutants, and she could feel the benefit on her skin and in her lungs. They were exhausted each day after their exertions but were quickly revived by sumptuous meals and seriously good whisky.

The cottage James had spoken of was walking distance from the hotel and was everything he described. Annie had no hesitation in encouraging the move, particularly when she saw the state of the bunkhouse. (She'd managed a quick look in from the entrance but felt no inclination to explore any further.) In stark contrast, she could picture herself pottering around the cottage, sitting in the garden drinking in the views and cosying up with James in the warm, snug lounge. *My, what a turn up for the books*, she thought to herself. This could just turn out to be the best thing that would ever happen to them.

And with that thought still percolating, Annie prepared for her departure on a clear, bright Monday morning. It was not a repetition of the sad farewell at Great King Street but it was a new chapter gently unfolding in front of them. In Annie's mind Assynt was no longer an alien world that could destroy her relationship before it had truly begun but instead held out the prospect of an alternative existence; something welcoming and vibrant that could only help to nurture them both.

Annie arrived home late Monday afternoon. She was tired from the driving but also felt strangely energised. Bags were unpacked, washing put in the machine and she also managed a cursory round of cleaning. She thought about quickly calling her mother but decided to stay in her bubble until Tuesday and call after work. As she walked into the offices of Saunders and MacKay the following morning, Annie felt glad she had no tribunal or court appearances at all that week. This new air of serenity could so easily have been disturbed by a day of endless legal wrangling; and so her morning was spent reading up on case notes and depositions. Simon had done a wonderful job of ordering what she referred to as her 'purposeful piles of paper' into some kind of chronological order and she felt pleased that she had managed to get through most things by lunchtime. Just as she was about to head out for a sandwich, Bryce popped his head round the door.

'Have you got a minute, Annie? Just need a quick summary on the LRC case.'

'Absolutely.' Annie was more than a little pleased that Bryce had seen her lay hands on the papers at once. Normally she was rummaging about trying to pull everything together in a panic. As she was leaving, the phone on her desk rang.

'Simon, could you get that, please.'

Just as she approached Bryce's door, Simon called out, 'It's your mum, Annie.'

'That's fine, thanks Simon. Tell her I'll call her later. Busy just now.'

*

It was just before five when Annie decided she really needed to turn her attention to properly sorting out her billable time. She hated the chore as much as she hated sorting out her expenses but needs must and she was days behind.

The phone rang and suddenly she remembered she hadn't returned Helen's call. Probably a client though. She'd call her mother right after.

'Good afternoon, Annie Anderson speaking.'

'Oh, Annie, thank goodness, Jean McHarg here.'

A sudden feeling of panic swept over Annie. 'Jean? Why, what's wrong?'

'Oh, my dear, it's your mother. She's quite alright I think but she wasn't feeling at all well over the weekend, in fact didn't come to church. Anyway, she thought she had a touch of the flu but today she had a terrible pain in her chest and so she rang me – I think she'd tried to ring you, dear. Anyway, Alasdair called an ambulance straight away. "You don't mess about with chest pain", he said, and of course he's quite right. So anyway, the upshot is we're all here at the Western General, dear.'

'And you're sure Mum's okay?'

'Well, she's hooked up to lots of wires and things but she's sitting up and talking. Although I have to say she does look quite ghastly.'

'I'll be right there.' Annie thought she was going to be physically sick. As she put the phone down and grabbed her coat and bag all she could hear was the sound of her heart thumping.

'Simon, I'm off. It's Mum, she's in hospital. I don't know...'

She walked quickly past everyone and straight out the door. Simon was calling after her but all the sounds around her seemed strangely muffled. As she started to run towards Queensferry Street, a taxi trundled slowly round the corner and she wildly flagged it down. As she jumped in, the driver turned to exchange some pleasantries but as soon as he saw Annie and heard the words 'Western General, emergency admissions', he automatically switched to caped crusader mode and sped off towards the hospital.

Feelings of panic and fear ebbed away as Annie entered the admissions area. Helen was indeed sitting up, hospital gown falling off her shoulder. She smiled broadly at the sight of her daughter.

'Oh, Mum, what on earth has happened to you?'

'Oh, just a silly little thing with my heart, nothing for you to worry about. Oh dear, I am causing such a fuss.'

As Annie sat by the bed, Helen weakly placed her hand over hers. Annie thought how suddenly very old and tired she looked.

'Let me just speak to the doctors, Mum.' Annie got up and saw the McHargs standing at the edge of the curtained bay. She must have walked straight past them. 'Oh, Jean, Alasdair, I'm so grateful. Thank goodness you were around.'

'Oh, it's nothing, Annie. We just marshalled the forces really. She'll kick on now you're here.' Captain McHarg always spoke as though he was still brigading his troops.

'What did the doctors say?'

'Well… oh look, here's Doctor Gilchrist now.'

'Hi, you must be Annie. Doctor Gilchrist. I'm the A&E Registrar. Let's just have a quick chat round here.'

She followed the impossibly young medic down the corridor, his white coat billowing out behind him before they stopped at the nurses' station.

He spoke slowly and quietly. 'Mum's had a mild heart attack. Nothing too serious and doesn't look like there should be any lasting damage but we're going to keep her in for a few days to keep an eye on her, do more tests and sort out the medication she's going to need.'

Annie appreciated his reassuring manner.

'Okay, gosh, I can't remember Mum ever being very ill – well, not seriously ill. Should I stay here tonight?'

'Look, we're going to move her up to the cardiac ward now so why don't you sit with her for a while there and then just come back in the morning? You'll need to get some sleep.'

She did as instructed and after sending the McHargs home with a promise to phone in the morning, Annie sat with her mother until she appeared to drift off to sleep. Before she knew it, it was time for lights out and so she gently kissed her mother, trying not to wake her and went to put on her coat and scarf.

'Don't leave your neck open,' said Helen weakly.

Annie smiled and stroked her mother's greying hair, making sure it was nice and tidy, just as she liked it.

'I'll bring all your hair things, toiletries, oh and of course your nightie – in the morning.'

'Thank you, dear. I'm sorry to be such a nuisance.'

'Nonsense. You'll be right as rain in no time.'

'Annie.'

'Yes.'

'I know it's not always been easy – and there are things. Things I needed to tell you.'

'Mum, don't. It's all fine. You don't need to say anything. Just get a good night's sleep and I'll see you in the morning.'

Annie was just about to leave the ward and turn into the corridor when she felt inexplicably scared. She suddenly wanted to be a little girl again, when her parents seemed happy and she felt safe and protected. But she realised there could be no going back. That warm and comforting memory would need to be left behind for now. None of it really mattered – what had gone before – none of it. Annie knew that she would be giving her mother the best care and attention. She wanted her mother to feel safe, not scared.

She turned to look back. Helen smiled and did her best to summon up an enthusiastic wave. Annie smiled and returned the gesture, trying hard to appear nonchalant and unworried.

When she returned to the flat she sat in the cold darkness for what seemed like an age, still wrapped in her coat and scarf – Mother would definitely not approve – but eventually managed to stir herself to make a cup of tea; eating was beyond her. At some ungodly hour she changed into her nightie, lurched into bed with Ludovic at her feet and began a night of fitful sleep.

*

The alarm went off at six thirty and Annie woke tired but cosy. She was about to shut off the incessant arguing that had already started on the *Today* programme and turn over for a few more precious minutes, when a strange sense of all not being well hit her. Then she remembered the events of last night. She lay for a while, letting things settle in her mind. *Better get a shift on*, she thought. She dragged herself from her slumber and trudged towards the bathroom. As she did so, she saw, out the corner of her eye, the red light flashing on her answerphone, demanding her attention. How could she not have noticed last night? She stood shivering in her nightie, arms wrapped round herself and played back the message.

It was James. Was she out enjoying herself? He hoped so but not too much and then there was a number for her to ring back on. Just hearing him was a comfort but she would need to get to the hospital, call the office; speaking to him would need to wait till later.

Just at that moment, the phone rang, suddenly and shrilly, interrupting her train of thought.

'Miss Anderson? Miss Anne Anderson?'

'Yes, that's me. Who – who's this?' Annie stumbled over her words, unsure of the strange voice.

'So sorry, Miss Anderson, it's the hospital. I'm afraid it's your mother. Can you come straight away?'

Annie was aware that there were other words but she found herself disengaging from the conversation and suddenly all she could see in her mind's eye was her mother waving to her as she left the ward. She tried to return to the moment but something was choking her, something heavy and aching that had moved up from the pit of her stomach and into her throat.

'I'm afraid it all happened so quickly.' Finally that's what she heard and then nothing. A blank space had opened up between the nurse at one end and Annie at the other. It was bad news, the worst kind of news.

'Miss Anderson? Are you there? Is someone with you?'

'Yes, no. I'm fine.' She knew there were questions but she also knew they were useless in the circumstances. She didn't want to hear anymore. 'Yes, I'll be there as soon as I can.'

Annie walked into the bathroom in a daze. She washed

her face, brushed her teeth, tied her hair back and then went back to the bedroom to dress. She looked at herself in the mirror. *Come on, you can do better than this. Your mother would never step out the door without putting a bit of makeup on.* She sank down on the old piano stool that functioned as her dresser chair, and assembled her Estée Lauder makeup carefully across the dressing table; the same makeup her mother wore. She felt sick as the feeling of utter sadness overwhelmed her and the tears fell. Annie cried until she was empty.

When she got to the hospital, Annie thought how strange it was that nurses were still scurrying around, doctors were making their rounds and sullen-faced porters were still transporting patients. Clearly not everyone had got the news. As she approached the nurses' station, the staff nurse walked towards her. Annie noticed that her name was Florence. She could never really have been anything else, Annie thought. Odd that the woman who had saved so many sick soldiers could do nothing to save her mother.

As Florence walked up and took Annie's arm, she was struck by how kindly she looked, as though the pain of this moment was as much hers as it was Annie's.

'Would you like to see her?'

'Yes, if that's okay.'

Florence took her by the arm and led her into a bright and airy side room. It was like stepping out of the hospital. There were no clinical smells, no intrusive whirring noises or high-pitched sounds of monitoring equipment. The room smelt fresh, the curtains a pale marigold, the walls a cool magnolia.

Annie noticed a small vase of flowers placed at the window. Nothing too intrusive, just a simple mark of respect. The bed was made perfectly, not a crease in the blankets, neatly turned down and tucked in firmly either side. And there lay her mother, face slightly sunken and grey in pallor but peaceful, completely peaceful.

'Is there anyone you would like us to call? Any other family perhaps, who could be with you?'

'No. There *is* no one.' As she said the words she felt her legs start to give way. Florence took her arm and sat her down at the side of the bed.

'I'm going to get you a cup of tea.'

'But she seemed fine. She waved to me, last night, I mean. She was smiling.'

'I'm so sorry. It was a massive heart attack, in her sleep. She just died in her sleep. It couldn't have been more peaceful.'

Florence put her hand on Annie's shoulder.

'I'm fine, thank you. I just didn't expect… I might just have been different with her, that's all. If I'd known.'

Florence drew up a seat next to her. 'Everyone does that. You don't need to, you know. She wasn't here very long but she didn't speak to us about anyone other than her daughter. Just you, how proud – and lucky she was. Now let me get that cup of tea.'

She would think back to this time and remember these little kindnesses but not now. Now she could barely hear the words.

CHAPTER 7

Annie left the hospital with the nurse's words vaguely ringing in her ear and holding a death certificate in her hand, knowing she had to speak to people but not really feeling like she wanted to. This was the final time Annie would be running errands for her mother. Not that she'd done much of that recently but it was important she carried out the last rites of registering the death, calling the lawyer and arranging the funeral on her own. The expressions of sympathy and offers of help would need to wait; this was between her and her mother.

It was a strange out-of-body experience but Annie did what she had to, all in one day, with nothing but adrenaline to sustain her. In the evening after forcing down a slice of toast she entered into the rigmarole of calling her friends and the McHargs. It was so hard to say the words and to hear the cries of anguish on the other end. Virginia, bless her, wanted to come round straightaway just to sit with her but Annie declined; Kirsty, characteristically, was all about the practicalities but again Annie turned down well-meant offers of help. In truth there was only one person she wanted with her at that moment and he was 200 miles away. She had left her call to James to the last.

'Oh, darling, no. I'm so sorry, *so* sorry.'

The genuine distress in his voice overwhelmed Annie and she began to cry, more at the relief of sharing the terrible news with him than anything.

'I'm leaving now. I'll be with you in just a few hours.'

'No, don't be silly, James. Wait till the morning, I don't like you driving through the night.'

'I'll take my time, don't worry, but I can't be up here thinking about you like this. I wouldn't sleep anyway.'

Annie put up no further resistance. She put the fire on, pulled down the throw from the back of the couch and settled down to wait for him. She knew it would be hours. She must have slept, for before she knew it, he was through the front door and like the warm security blanket she desperately craved, wrapped her up in his arms.

*

The funeral service was a simple affair: traditional hymns and little fuss – all very Church of Scotland. Annie even managed a smile at the high-pitched warbling that came from the army of fur-clad women filling the pews behind her. All the while, she felt like she was playing a part in a very dark play. All eyes seemed to be trained on her, the dutiful daughter. She acted out her role and spoke her lines as convention dictated. James was by her side throughout.

Only after the funeral tea and when she was back in the flat with James did Annie feel like she'd returned to something resembling real life.

'She really liked you, you know.'

122

'I liked her. She made me laugh, even when she didn't mean to – all her strange little quirks.'

'When do you need to go back?' She was lying in bed with her head on his chest, steeling herself for his answer.

'I'll stay as long as you need me.'

'Well, I'm not sure how I'm supposed to react to that. The honest answer would be I *need* you here – all the time.'

'You know what I mean. I want to make sure you're okay before I go back.'

'Funny how men always want things to just be okay as quickly as possible. If I say I'm alright, you'll be happy and off you'll trot.' She looked up at him but he just looked perplexed. 'Tell you what, why don't you stay for a few days. I think that would really help and then you can head back up the road.'

Her words had suddenly changed into something he could readily understand. She smiled as the worried look left him and he closed his eyes to sleep.

*

Annie hadn't expected to feel quite so empty, quite so bereft, but then how could she have expected anything. There was no warning, nothing to prepare for. In complete contrast to her father, her mother's passing had been so sudden and shocking that it had prompted an almost visceral response. Aside from the sadness, a pain had started deep down; somewhere in her stomach, a pain that just wouldn't shift. It scratched and gnawed at her, never letting her forget for a second. She hadn't shared any of this with James and let him head off believing that, although still clearly grieving, she was absolutely on top of things and coping admirably with the aftermath of her mother's untimely death. She was sure that's what he told himself and his colleagues back in Assynt. As she thought about going back to Helen's penthouse apartment to sort things out, the pain started to grow in intensity. Once again offers of help flooded in; James wanted her to wait until he was down at the weekend, but once again this was something she wanted to do alone.

As she entered the flat, it struck Annie how amazingly pristine everything was, almost as though Helen had been preparing for this day. Nothing out of place and everything in a highly polished state. The rich deep hues of mahogany furniture; the various decorative fine antiques including her much loved collection of Meissen porcelain all stood immaculately dust free as though waiting to be photographed for the next Lyon and Turnbull auction catalogue.

How could it be, that there wasn't a thing out of place? *People don't live like this*, Annie thought to herself. There should at least be the odd newspaper lying about or an unplumped cushion not quite at the right angle, but no, everything was in order, standing to attention, awaiting inspection. She made her way through to the dining room and opened up the first drawer in the large Victorian sideboard. Annie knew this was where various important documents were kept; Helen always pulled them out for Annie to see just before she set off on one of her bridge cruises. True to form, insurance documents, bank and building society information was all neatly filed away in separate coloured folders and clearly marked. Annie couldn't help but smile.

She took everything she needed back into the lounge and then wandered through to the bedroom. Oh goodness, all her clothes. Annie's heart sank as she opened one of the wardrobes. What was she going to do with all the furs, the dresses, the best Jenners could offer in twin sets? What on earth? Then she remembered reading something in the *Evening News* about the charity shops in Davidson's Mains that seemed to inherit all the fox furs and silks from the large mansion houses up at Old Barnton, a place where all the old moneyed families of Edinburgh had settled at the turn of the century. Barnton was to the north of Edinburgh what Morningside was to the south and, as she started to lay some crisply ironed blouses on top of the bedspread, Annie couldn't think of a better home for Helen's wardrobe. She would be more than a little pleased to be in such grand company, Annie reasoned.

As she wandered round the side of the bed her foot brushed against something solid, nudging it further under the frame. She bent down to pull the object from its dark hiding place and discovered a Gabor shoebox. Annie sat on the edge of the bed and pulled off the lid. Amongst some early family photographs were her father's wallet, passport and a number of letters with the familiar Helvetia postmark. Annie had corresponded regularly with her father when he went off to Switzerland but these were addressed to her mother – in her father's hand. She'd had no idea. Looking closely at the postmarks she noticed that they extended to the time when her father was living with Céline; then at the bottom of the pile there were letters addressed to her father, clearly in her mother's handwriting. *This is bizarre*, she thought. All the time he was away, she had been forbidden to speak his name in the house and yet all throughout this period, her mother and father had remained in contact.

She held the letters in her hand, unsure what to do. She couldn't bear the thought of reading anything hurtful and cruel between them, not now, not after everything. She studied the front of each letter carefully and noticed that none were addressed to the apartment her father moved into after he became ill and no further letters had been sent to Helen after he had made the move. Well, that made sense, thought Annie. When she had broken the news of his illness, Helen had clearly been shocked.

Then, right at the bottom of the hidden stash she noticed that a photograph, slightly gnarled at the edges, had been carefully placed in a small cellophane packet. She pulled it out from its protective covering and peered at the image in front of her.

A baby, in a plain white romper suit was sitting up on a rug, smiling and holding its hands out towards the camera. The rug, pale blue and white checked, was spread on a pristine green lawn. In the background some steps led up to a stone terrace in front of a dazzling white *art moderne* building.

'Hugh and Céline's house,' Annie whispered.

*

Annie left her mother's flat with the letters filed away into the coloured folders and the photograph carefully tucked away in the zipped pocket of her handbag. Her mind was racing all the way across to Great King Street. Could be

126

endless reasons why a small child was photographed in front of the house her father had shared with his mistress. Céline, of course, had stayed in the house after he'd left so it might be a friend's child or niece – or nephew for that matter. *Come on, Annie, think – was it a boy or a girl?* She pictured the image in her mind's eye as she sat in the queue of traffic snaking its way through Stockbridge. No, she decided, the photograph gave no clue as to the sex of the child.

'Tea, coffee – wine?'

Annie was sitting at the end of the large oak table in Kirsty's kitchen. Coat still on and clutching the bag that was perched on her lap.

'Annie? Are you going to at least take your coat off?' Kirsty was holding the kettle aloft with one hand and a bottle of Sauvignon with the other.

'Yes, in a minute. I think I'll have the wine if that's okay.'

'Of course. Duncan's at the cricket club – committee meeting I think he said. Anyway he's not going to be back till around eight. He's bringing in Chinese if you fancy?' Kirsty set down two large glasses and proceeded to fill them.

'No, no. Just the wine thanks.'

'Well, it's six o'clock on a Tuesday. I've had a shitty day at the office so that's why I'm straight into the vino. You're sitting there with your coat on, looking like you've seen a ghost. Spill the beans, sweetie, what on earth is going on?'

'I've been at Mum's. Starting to clear things, sort stuff out.'

'Oh, Annie. How many times? You really shouldn't be

doing that sort of thing on your own. All far too raw just now. You need someone with you who can just focus on the practical bits.' Kirsty sat, hands cradling her glass and looking straight into Annie's eyes, searching for some clear acknowledgment of the point she was trying to make.

Annie dropped her eyes. 'Yes, Kirst, I know but it really is something I feel I want to do alone – just the first bit. Just being surrounded by her things, looking at what's left behind of our family. I promise when it comes to the "practical bits" I'll call on everyone to help. That's not it really.' She paused and then reached into her bag and pulled out the photograph. 'That's not what I wanted to talk to you about.' She handed the photo over to her friend. 'I found a shoebox under Helen's bed and this was in it with other things belonging to Dad.'

'Gosh, he's a chunky little thing. Is it a "he"? Who is it? Where is this?' Kirsty examined the photo from all angles turning the little cellophane packet over and over in her hands.

'I don't know who it is but the house is the one Hugh and Céline lived in. The baby might be a relative of Céline's or perhaps belong to a friend, I don't really know.' Annie looked at Kirsty to see if her mind was turning up any other possibilities.

'Yes, but why would Helen have it?' Kirsty looked quizzical.

'Unless, it didn't belong to Helen. Maybe it belonged to my dad.'

'Oh, I see. Just in with the stuff he brought back home.'

No, Annie thought, *she isn't going anywhere near the place my mind has travelled to*. She watched Kirsty continue to study the image and then finally, after what seemed like an age:

'But what on earth would your dad be doing with a picture of a baby?'

Yes, her thoughts were now preparing themselves for the final approach. Cabin crew take your seats for landing.

'Unless… surely not at his age. It might be his?'

A couple of bumps on the way in but destination safely reached. Cabin crew – doors to manual.

'Bloody hell, bit of a dark horse old Hugh! How the hell do you process that, Annie?' Kirsty sat back, looking shocked and proceeded to polish off the Sauvignon.

'I don't know, Kirsty, I really don't know.'

*

At home that night, Annie desperately tried to make sense of it all. And so what if this child was her father's? Why had he needed a new family? What was wrong with the one he had? She'd tried her best to be his daughter – to *still* be his daughter even after he'd made a new life for himself. She'd gone to him and his new woman after all – plenty of people in her situation wouldn't have bothered. Kirsty wouldn't have bothered, that's for sure. But no, that wasn't enough – he needed another child, a different child. Annie quickly checked herself before her thoughts spiralled out of control. She needed to construct a case, establish the facts, piece together timelines. It was the only way she could manage what was in front of her.

She found an A1 sheet of paper and a black marker pen in amongst some of James's paraphernalia and proceeded to spread everything out on the living room floor. How long was Hugh with Céline? How long had they stayed together in that house? How long was he in the apartment after falling ill before coming home?

Sitting cross-legged with the cat alongside, who was clearly anxious to see what new game was afoot, she plotted out what she knew of her father's time in Geneva.

He had left for Switzerland in 1973. She couldn't be sure when he started the affair with Céline but it was a good five years before he announced the news. Okay, so that was 1978. Ludovic decided this really was something he needed to be a part of and proceeded to walk across the paper every time Annie added another date or significant event. Bloody cat.

It couldn't have been terribly long after the announcement that he moved into the house with Céline. The relationship might have been going on for ages, Annie reasoned, but it looked like they made it public just as they'd decided to set up house together.

Right, that's enough. The cat had casually stuck out a paw and deftly ripped a tear through 1978. She picked him up and dumped him unceremoniously onto the sofa.

She tried to recall her trips over to Switzerland. Did Céline ever talk about having children, wanting them? Did Hugh? No, that would have been just too crass to talk about wanting children in front of the one child Hugh had, to all intents and purposes, abandoned.

So when was the cancer diagnosis? When did he come home?

Annie's head was starting to throb. A stressful day had culminated in quickly knocking back two large glasses of wine. Seemed like the best thing to do at the time but the soothing effects had now given way to tension and tiredness. She stretched out on the floor looking up at the heavily corniced ceiling.

Well, he was back late in 1981 but he didn't see the end of 1982. But how long had he lived on his own? Couldn't have been that long, probably the beginning of 1982. So they were together less than four years? Yes, but who's to say she didn't visit him in the apartment? They seemed to part on fairly amicable terms, after all.

So many questions.

Later in bed her mind kept turning over all the possible next steps. James had called earlier but she had been distracted. His voice was gentle and soothing but words weren't really registering. He would see her as early as possible on Friday so she decided it would be better to tell all then. A bit more thinking time was required.

As she lay, brain gently whirring, she knew the sense of detachment wasn't just about this unexpected turn of events. In all honesty she hadn't anticipated the feeling of suddenly being cast adrift. The anchor had broken free and there was a sense from some of her friends and colleagues that, without having to face the possible burden of caring for a parent sometime in the future, a new life awaited; so much for her to explore and enjoy. She could chart her way, unfettered by any familial responsibilities. *Perhaps that was how orphaned adults were supposed to behave*, she thought, but for Annie the sadness was rooted in knowing that the only people who had truly known her from birth to womanhood were gone. All memories, unique to Hugh and Helen, were quickly dissolving. She would never again look for their company, ask for an opinion or seek their guidance. Neither would she hear their views on anything from clothes choices to politics, desired or otherwise. Yes, she had good friends, a man she truly loved, but just at *that* point, right at *that* moment Annie felt completely alone. And now, just as she felt like she might sink to the bottom of that particular pit of emotion, here was something new. Something borne out of betrayal perhaps but it offered up the possibility of a connection – back to her father, back to family. She could drag herself up and out. She could see that a new destination might emerge from the thick haze that was obscuring her horizon. Well, at the very least, it was something to steer towards.

She told James about the photograph on Friday night. Not straight away. They had missed each other and Annie just needed to enjoy him again. After cooking dinner together, they settled down and she asked about Assynt, the cottage in particular. Just for a while Annie wanted to escape the maelstrom of her mind and bask in the tranquillity of the Scottish Highlands.

'Of course, I'm telling you all the good bits and I think to be honest, you've only seen the good bits. Yes, it's beautiful, Annie, but so much of the land is barren, a lot of it overgrazed and so isolated. I've only been up a few weeks and my God it can be lonely. I just know I couldn't stay up there long term.'

Well, that's reassuring, thought Annie. 'But you still think the buy-out can happen?'

'I do. Small-scale farming like crofting is the only way to manage that kind of land. Just needs proper support, business ideas. Anyway, let's not talk crofting tonight.'

They were in each other's arms on the couch. The fire was roaring and there was barely audible classical music coming from the radio in the kitchen. Annie strained to hear and then suddenly a soaring violin melody pierced their bubble.

'*Lark Ascending*?' she asked.

'I think so.'

A piece of music evoking vivid images of green and rolling English countryside. The complete antithesis of James's beautiful, sprawling wilderness. She lifted her head from his chest and told him all about her week.

*

'And have you read the letters?'

'Yes. Bizarre really. It's all so everyday, so mundane. They exchange information on money matters, the purchase and upkeep of the Edinburgh house. Mum tells Dad about what I'm up to, even though I'm writing my own letters to him. She even tells him what's going on at the Women's Guild! He talks about the weather, his work, things he misses, what it's like to live in Geneva. It's almost like they're pen friends.'

'What, the whole time he was with Céline?'

'Yes. They stop abruptly when he moves out into the flat. I presume he stopped writing but I don't know if she tried to keep in contact or not.'

'How on earth do you fathom that lot out? Your mother could barely speak to him when he came to visit and then understandably wanted to hear nothing about Céline – and yet they still had that connection. Just so strange...'

'I know. Shall we have some tea? I think I'd like some tea.' Annie slowly lifted her head from his chest feeling the indentation of his thick cotton shirt on her cheek, warm and rough. She looked at him but he was staring into the distance, brow heavily furrowed.

'And there's nothing about a baby in any of these letters?'

Annie stretched her mouth letting her skin relax and start to fill in the little dents in her cheek. 'No, nothing. But then he's hardly going to surprise her with that little bombshell, is he? "Hi Helen, guess what's been happening in my life?"'

'And there was nothing else in the shoebox?'

'No. Just everything you've seen. Tea? Did you say yes to tea?'

'And so you're assuming the baby is Hugh and Céline's?'

Annie stared at James in anticipation of a plausible alternative explanation.

'Well, why else would the photo be there?'

She knew she was sounding slightly exasperated but a sensible alternative was the least he could offer up after all the detailed questioning.

'Well, maybe we should go back to your mother's flat and have a good root around. Just in case you've missed anything.'

He sounds like a detective returning to the scene of the crime, Annie thought to herself.

'And have you thought about what you might want to do? If you think the baby really is your father's?'

Looked like the question portion of the discussion still had some way to go.

'I don't really know how I feel about it to be honest. I had thought about writing to Céline but I don't know if she'd still be living at the house. It's the only address I have for her, other than the pharmaceutical company where they both worked. But then it's *nine* years ago, James. Surely life would have moved on for her by now. And what if she doesn't want any contact? I'm sure she could have found me by now if she'd wanted to.'

'I'm guessing she wasn't at your dad's funeral?'

'Oh, good God, no. I did write to let her know when he died and she wrote a lovely letter back. I know it all seems very strange but I never felt bitter about Céline. She saw my father's good qualities and she happened to fall in love with him – and I guess he fell in love too. I really didn't regret that she made him very happy for a while. But having said all that, I was glad he was with my mother at the end. And now this new thing needs to get thrown into the mix. It never occurred to me they'd want to have a child. God, it must just all sound so complicated to you.'

James put his arm round Annie and drew her back in. 'Well, life's complicated. *Love's* complicated. So many kinds of love, so many facets to how we feel about people that come in and out of our lives. It's the hurt that love can cause – that's the killer.'

He paused, shutting his eyes. Annie wondered if this might be the time to go and make the tea but just as she started the extrication process all over again…

'But you can't blame love for that. It's the way people are, human beings and all their weaknesses. I think sometimes you just have to stop for a minute. Appreciate the love you do have in your life, live in the moment, that kind of thing.'

She lifted her head and kissed him. 'Well, there we are. That doesn't sound too complicated.' Finally, she stood up and walked through to the kitchen.

'What are you doing?'

'Going to make tea,' she shouted as she switched on the kettle.

'Great. Can I have coffee?'

*

They headed back over to the penthouse apartment on Sunday morning. James immediately opened up the sliding doors in the lounge and stepped onto the balcony looking out over Edinburgh's roofscape. He proceeded to reel off the name of every important landmark he could see. Annie thought he sounded as though he'd discovered something new and startling at every turn.

'There's the Forth Rail Bridge over there and then over there, the Castle and is that the spire of St Giles?'

'James. We're not here to look at the view. Come back in, it's cold with these doors open.'

He did as he was told and slammed the doors shut. 'Right, where should we start? Are you sure you're okay doing this? Maybe you should look around in your mother's bedroom. I'll just stick to the lounge and dining room.'

'Yes, I'm fine. First time was the worst. I know what I'm facing now – well, maybe I don't.'

Annie was back in amongst the fox furs and hatboxes. There wasn't quite an old person's smell but there *was* a mustiness coming from the mahogany wardrobe that housed all Helen's outer garments. She reached up to the top shelf and pulled the hats down. Nothing else there. She went over to the nightstand feeling slightly awkward about rummaging around in her mother's more personal items and then smiled to herself thinking it unlikely she would find any packets of contraceptive pills or tubes of lubricant. She searched both drawers but found nothing of any import. Lavender drops for her pillow was about as risqué as it got. There was a nightstand at the other side of the bed but that wasn't used as her father hadn't slept there when he returned home. The guest bedroom had been converted into a makeshift palliative care ward and that was where he had spent his last months. As she moved towards the doorway she could hear James clattering about, pushing and pulling at drawers and cupboards. *He would make a pretty hapless burglar*, she thought.

'Is that you finished in the bedroom?' he called.

'Yes. Just going into the guest bedroom.' She paused at the door. 'Well, no, not quite finished.'

Annie turned and went back to the identical little bedside table at what would have been her father's side of the bed. The top drawer was completely empty but in the bottom drawer, hidden right at the back, was a Bible in a zipped black leather casing. Annie hadn't seen this Bible in years. She remembered it from when she was a little girl; the feeling of it in her hands, closing and opening until her mother told her to put it down in case she broke the zip. She opened it up for the first time in almost twenty years. The smell of cold church pews filled the air.

At the front was a small prayer card decorated with

forget-me-nots. Printed across the top were the words 'For Those Who Live Alone'. She read through until the last line: 'I live alone, dear Lord, yet have no fear, because I feel your presence ever near.' Annie's eyes welled up as she read. She kissed the card and placed it carefully back into the front of the little hymnary. She was about to send the Lord's word back to the dark sanctuary of its protective cover when she noticed something protruding from the back of the Bible. It was white and of a firm texture in stark contrast to the delicate yellowing pages of testament and hymns.

Annie sat on the edge of the bed. It was an envelope addressed to her father. She opened it up, pulled out a piece of paper, clearly not written in her mother's hand, and read:

> *'Dear Hugh. Annie told me how ill you were and so I hope you don't mind me writing. I did wonder when I hadn't heard from you these last weeks. She told me that you know you haven't very much time and so I decided I had to contact you. I am so grateful for what you have done, for both of us. I wish things had been different but, now that I know there isn't much time left, I wanted you to have a photograph of our son and to let you know...'*

The letter stopped abruptly. It had been folded in half and the bottom part was missing. What did she want him to know? She heard James come into the bedroom.

'It's all gone very quiet in here. Thought I'd see what was going on.'

138

Annie held up the torn sheet of paper.

'What's this?' he asked.

'It's a letter, well, a piece of a letter from Céline to my father.' She paused.

'I have a brother, James, a little brother.'

James sat beside her on the bed and put his arm round her.

'Well, now we know for sure.' He reached for the letter. 'Why do you think it's torn like that?' he asked.

'I don't know, James, but I have a brother.' This was no longer some hypothetical scenario she was facing. Fine to let her thoughts run riot when none of it was real. But this was real. There was a boy and he was her brother.

'Yes, yes. Sorry, I know that's a lot to take in. Where did you find the letter?'

'It was tucked away at the back of Helen's Bible. I only opened it up because I used to play with the thing when I was young. I loved touching these delicate little pages, hidden away inside their zipped cover – but putting a letter like that in *here*, well, she obviously didn't want anyone to find it. Anyone except me, that is.'

'It certainly is an odd place to hide such a thing. Surely she didn't carry it into church every Sunday?'

'Oh no. It wasn't her everyday Bible. I wonder if she knew I would find it some day. She must have known that I would open it up as soon as I found it.'

'But there was never any hint? Absolutely no suggestion from either of them? How could they keep such a thing secret?'

James was looking and sounding incredulous.

'No, nothing, and I can't even be sure that my father

read this letter or saw the photograph. What if Helen opened it? Maybe she didn't want him to see anything from Switzerland or if it arrived when he was really very ill then maybe he just wouldn't have been able to read the letter or understand what the photograph meant. But then at the hospital – I don't know, but I think she wanted to tell me. Oh, I don't know – maybe not.'

'Well, is there a postmark? Would that help?'

Annie's head was beginning to hurt; a dull throb signalling brain overload. She looked down at the envelope. Postmark Geneva 20th October 1982.

'When did he die?'

'15th December 1982.'

CHAPTER 8

James left later that night. She didn't want him to go but at the same time needed the space to think and decide what she was going to do next. His thoughts and suggestions were well intentioned but it was all just too oppressive. She had to consciously stop herself from sounding dismissive and eventually closed down the discussion, explaining she was tired and wanted to just relax for the next few hours. They took a familiar walk back to the flat along by the Water of Leith and spoke about their respective weeks ahead. On returning, James cooked an early supper and they collapsed in front of the television. They weren't particularly focusing on the programme in front of them but neither were they bothering with any kind of chat. He seemed to know, finally, that she just needed peace and quiet. Before they knew it, it was time for James to go.

'You're having to deal with so much alone, Annie. I feel terrible leaving you.'

'Don't, darling, don't. It'll be fine. You know me; once I've got a plan of action sorted everything will be absolutely fine. And then hopefully I'll get up to Assynt, maybe not next weekend, perhaps the following...'

She knew he was leaving unconvinced by her

assurances but that was hardly surprising; she sounded less than convincing in her own mind.

By the following morning Annie had resolved to write to Céline at the only address she had. If nothing came back in the next few weeks then she could always contact the Stolz pharmaceutical company. At least they might be able to help with a forwarding address. If Céline was still in the same house and chose not to respond then Annie would know she wanted to sever all connections. Having made the decision, her head cleared a little and she felt able to give some attention to her appointments for the week.

At home that night, Annie worked on a presentation she was giving to law students on the cut and thrust of employment law demonstrating why it was the single most exhilarating specialism the legal profession had to offer. Not exactly the title of her talk but that was the tone she was striving for. It wasn't an easy task but at least it was a welcome diversion from the tumble of words, the sense of something that she needed to formulate into a coherent and sensitive letter.

The phone rang; it was Kirsty.

'Annie, darling. Could I pop round to see you sometime this week? Something I'd like to chat through with you. I feel terrible knowing you've got all this stuff to deal with – Hugh, Helen, the extraneous child, all that. Unearthed anything else on that front at all?' She didn't pause for a reply. 'It's just you're really the only person I can speak to about this, I think.'

'Of course, Kirst, how about tomorrow?'

'Great, Duncan's meeting his brother tomorrow night,

would you believe. I'll be round about seven? Don't cook anything; I'll grab a bite before I leave the house.'

The following evening, Annie had set out olives and crisps and chilled a bottle of Sancerre. Bit more expensive than her normal wine choice but she felt she deserved it. She'd lunched with Bryce and a couple of the firm's more extravagant clients at Cosmo on North Castle Street so wasn't at all hungry. The upmarket Italian was reputedly a favourite haunt of Sean Connery's although Annie had been going for years and never managed to cross paths with the great man. She dreamed of standing at the bar and ordering a vodka martini while listening to 007's deep Edinburgh burr behind her.

The doorbell rang and Annie snapped herself out of her Bond fantasy to go and answer the door. Kirsty stood looking slightly bedraggled. Her unusually pale pallor and disorganised demeanour prompted Annie to ask if she felt okay.

'I think so, oh I don't really know.' She walked into the lounge, coat still on and collapsed onto the sofa. 'I could really do with a large glass of something, I know that.'

Now it was Kirsty's turn to spill the beans and for Annie to offer whatever comfort and kind words might help in the circumstances. She poured out two glasses of wine and sat alongside her friend on the sofa.

'Okay, what's the problem? You look a bit out of sorts.'

'I feel terrible coming round here like this with my *news* when you've just got so much to think about.'

'Honestly, Kirsty, it would be lovely to hear about what's going on in someone else's life for a change, believe me.'

Kirsty looked down at the glass in her hands.

'Thing is, I'm pregnant. Unbelievable really.'

No advance warning; no lead up. She placed the untouched wine back on to the coffee table.

It was such an abrupt announcement, Annie struggled to mask her shock. She didn't really know why but she had just never imagined the Drummonds having children. After a moment's hesitation, she replied, 'Oh, that's wonderful, Kirsty.' She regained her composure, quickly put her glass of wine down and embraced her friend. Kirsty sat completely still, almost rigid. Annie realised that 'wonderful' perhaps didn't accurately match her friend's take on the situation.

'I mean, it's a bloody miracle, to be honest.' Kirsty forthright as ever. 'Duncan's usually far too tired or far too pissed to get an erection that lasts more than two minutes never mind go the whole hog and actually impregnate me.'

Annie had to stifle a laugh. 'But did you *mean* to get pregnant?'

'Well, we had talked about it. I mean, you know me, Annie. I've never really liked the whole sex thing. I don't really like the way I look with no clothes on so never thought anyone else would. Suited me down to the ground that Duncan never seemed terribly interested and whenever he did have a go he very rarely finished what he'd started. Honestly, if he'd been one of Dad's bulls he'd have been turned into burgers years ago. But there we go – pump, pump, squirt and that was it, which, when you think about it, is all you really need from one of your prize specimens.'

She took her friend's hand. 'Oh, Kirsty, I'm sorry for laughing.'

Annie felt strangely happy at the thought of a new baby Drummond but the description of poor Duncan's performance in creating the little thing had left her struggling.

She quickly collected herself. 'It really is lovely news. Aren't you both thrilled?'

'Oh, I don't know, Annie. I don't feel as though I have any maternal instincts at all. I just thought if we really wanted to go down the reproduction road then we'd need to start sooner rather than later. Duncan was awfully keen, which is ironic given what I've just told you. But decision made and here we are – I just hope I like the thing when it comes out.'

'Oh, Kirsty, you will. Of course you will.' Annie wasn't entirely sure herself. Kirsty had never given any hint that she wanted to be a mother and was often quite rude about other people's children, complaining to restaurants about unruly youngsters and asking neighbours if they could stop their babies crying in the night. She could only hope for the best.

'I am a bit worried about telling Virginia.'

Annie smiled sympathetically. Virginia and Gordon had been trying for children for years. Annie had always seen Virginia as the perfect embodiment of Mother Earth and it had come as no surprise that she talked about having babies almost as soon as the forest-themed wedding invitations had hit the doormats. A few years had passed, there was some talk of IVF but then nothing. There was no happy announcement and no further discussion about which room would be turned into the nursery. Virginia had stopped talking about babies.

'Look, I'm sure she'll be really happy for you. It's just how you present it to her, I suppose.' Not the usual Kirsty in a china shop routine.

'Well, maybe we could go round together?'

'Yes, that's fine; we'll do that sometime soon. Maybe you should have a cup of tea, Kirst? It'll be a while before you can start back up on the vino.'

'Oh, God. Yes, tea would be best. And actually I'm not sure I really fancy the wine. Just so used to having a large one when I feel a bit stressed about anything. That's when I knew really. After our little session last week, I realised I just wasn't enjoying the taste. Started to feel a bit off colour and then counted back to see when I'd last had Matilda in. Realised I was late by about three weeks so picked up a pregnancy test and there it was – "in foal" as my mother used to say!'

'Matilda?'

'Oh sorry. That's what Mum used to call her period.'

Oh dear, how on earth was that conversation with Virginia going to go. Annie was feeling anxious already.

'Well, if it's that early maybe we should just wait a bit to tell Gin.'

'Yes, of course, whenever you think. It'll be you next, Annie, I'll bet.'

Annie wasn't sure how to react to that. Children had never featured in her plans. It struck her just then that she was completely ambivalent about the whole thing. She would be supportive to any friends that might find themselves having kids, whether it was finding the right way to respond to Kirsty's incessant use of animal husbandry terminology when describing the creation of life or, on a completely different level, trying to understand Virginia's more spiritual take on bringing a new life into the world. But for Annie it seemed that just getting on with life, navigating her way through all its twists and turns, was hard enough. If she could do that with someone to help take the tiller from time to time and with a few fair winds of love and friendship at her back, then she might just stay afloat.

'I don't think so, Kirsty. There's enough going on in my life at the moment. Let's not overcomplicate matters.'

They spent the rest of the evening catching up and discussing what Annie might say in her letter to Céline. Kirsty's suggestions, such as asking Céline why she couldn't have just picked up the phone and called Annie to tell her she had a brother, were none too subtle but Annie listened and feigned gratitude. Finally, Kirsty made for home.

'I do hope it's going to be the making of Duncan,' she said putting her coat on. 'I hope this might be the thing that finally makes him happy.'

'He's happy, Kirsty, he's happy with *you*. Okay, sometimes he gets a bit *too* happy but…'

'No, he's not, Annie. He's really quite *un*happy. Almost as if he doesn't quite understand his place in the world, what he's here for. Hopefully baby Drummond will give him that.' She smiled as she patted her tummy. 'As long as Strachan doesn't get his claws into him.'

'Him? So you think it's going to be a boy?'

'Oh, I don't know. I think I'd like it to be and then we can bring him up to be absolutely nothing like Strachan or Lachlan! And by the way, I'm done with the whole surnames for first names thing. If it is a boy I think we'll call him Bob.'

'Oh, Kirsty, I think you're going to be a great mother.' They gave each other a hug and agreed to meet up again in a couple of weeks.

Annie had intended writing the letter that night but Kirsty had exhausted her. Her mind was full of baby Drummond and Kirsty's conflicting emotions. There really was no room for anything else. James rang just as she was getting ready for bed and she told him the news.

'Well, I didn't see that one coming, did you? Bet the first thing they do is get the wee thing's name down for Fettes. Strachan will make sure of that.'

'Actually I think Kirsty is going to make sure Strachan has very little to do with any decisions about baby.'

'Easier said than done.'

'And darling...'

'Yes?'

'I had no idea children were on the cards and it's early days yet so no spilling the beans, particularly to Virginia or Gordon.'

She went to bed and tried to switch her thoughts back to the letter she planned to write. After an age spent tossing and turning she decided on a slightly different course of action. There would still be a letter but not the one she had initially intended. It was a gamble, a bit of a risk, but somehow it felt gentler, kinder. She resolved to talk over her thoughts with James and decided a trip up to see him would be best, for all sorts of reasons. It would do her good to get away from Edinburgh for the weekend just to escape the noise of the city as well as her own thoughts.

She turned her nightlight off but was still restless. Annie had spent her life steering away from turmoil and upset; always trying to find the path of least resistance; holding things together. Ever since her father had left the family home she found change, any kind of change difficult. She had stuck resolutely with the same small group of friends; stayed at the same law firm despite numerous attempts to tempt her away to more lucrative positions. Now everything seemed to be shifting. The loss of Helen, her sense of what family was and what it meant to her; everything was churning around endlessly. Knowing that the Drummonds' life would change forever also seemed to unnerve her slightly. Of course it was good news but what did it mean for their friendship? Would they all start to drift apart as priorities changed? Was this unsuspecting boy in Switzerland supposed to restore some equilibrium to all these disturbed thoughts and emotions? Did she expect him to fill some void? Was there a void to fill? Was that not all a bit much to lay at the door of a ten year old who was presumably completely oblivious to her very existence?

If only she could just empty her mind completely, just for one night.

*

When she arrived in Assynt the following Friday evening, a surprise awaited her. James had signed a lease for the cottage earlier in the week and had just picked up the keys. She followed his car along the narrow road around the loch until they reached the house. It was exactly as she'd remembered it. As she got out the car Annie breathed in deeply. She felt, once again, the crisp, fresh air slide down into her lungs as she looked out at the tranquil gardens and woodland stretching down from the front of the house to the shores of the loch. This was the ideal place to stop asking questions and chart the way ahead.

'I can't believe how much has happened in the short space of time I've been up here,' James remarked as he took Annie's bag from the boot of her trusty Fiesta. 'And you're having to deal with it all on your own.' With his free arm he pulled her close in to the lapel of his musty tweed jacket.

'I'm not on my own. I've got the gang down there and I've got you up here. Whether you're with me, physically, or not.' She quickly looked up at him. Just for a second she felt vulnerable, lost again. 'I have got you. Haven't I?'

'Of course you've got me.'

He held her in tightly, so tightly she struggled to breathe.

As they turned to walk towards the cottage, hand in hand, Annie felt the tension leave her body.

'It is strange, though, that I can meander through life for years with very little happening of any great significance and then everything just seems to get completely turned on its head, all at once.'

He said nothing but squeezed her hand. She didn't know how it was all going to work out but just then, at that moment, she felt safe and reassured and really that was all that mattered.

James had made a massive pot of chilli with enough heat to make her eyes sting accompanied by enough rice to feed all the neighbouring crofts. He poured large glasses of warm Merlot to slosh it all down with and they ate as the sun went down over the loch. As Annie savoured each mouthful she could feel the heat rise through her body; it was a simple but hearty meal.

'Well, you've got a rosy glow.' James smiled at her across the table as he refilled their glasses.

Annie relaxed back into her chair. 'I'm just feeling so chilled, finally. This place is like some sort of magnificent de-stress zone. It's lovely, James. It should be on prescription.'

They sat enjoying the food, talked about the cottage and little else of any note. It was bliss.

'Let's finish our wine outside.' James stretched his hand across the table.

'But I'm so cosy and warm. It'll be cold out there.'

'We'll wrap up. It won't be for long.' James stood up, breaking the spell, and went to the small cupboard at the entrance to the cottage from where he produced two huge padded jackets.

'I'm going to look ridiculous,' Annie protested as she disappeared inside the thick mass of fabric.

'Well, you're not going out clubbing. The odd deer or otter might have something to say about your state of dress but apart from that, I really don't think you've got anything to worry about.'

She smiled sarcastically at him.

They walked gingerly down to the small picnic bench at the bottom of the garden. There was little light from the night sky and James took her hand as they negotiated the narrow stony path. Annie held on tightly to her wine glass with her other hand, making sure not to spill a drop.

The absolute stillness and enveloping darkness slightly unnerved her; she just wasn't used to it. She almost stumbled into the bench before sliding in, relieved to be setting her glass down.

'I can't see a thing,' Annie said peering into the night.

'Wait a minute. Just let your eyes get adjusted and then look up.'

As she lifted her eyes Annie felt overwhelmed by the sheer vastness of the sparkling canopy above her. 'Good grief, how can there be so many stars? I didn't know there were so many. I usually feel so proud of myself when I can spot "Orion" or the "Plough".'

'What a townie you are. It's just because you don't have all that light pollution up here. There's nothing to obscure the beauty of the night sky.' He took her hand again and they sat in silence for a few moments.

In Edinburgh everything had seemed so closed in that she thought her brain was going to explode but here there was space and time, endless amounts of it. All the thoughts and worries that had been churning round didn't disappear – they just seemed less significant.

James broke the silence. 'It probably won't feel like it just now, Annie, but I think this place does give you some perspective. Everything you're going through, well, it's just a moment in time, probably not even that when you consider how old some of these stars are. It'll all become clear and settled soon enough and you'll move on with the next phase.'

She knew he just wanted it all to be better and not for entirely selfless reasons.

'Well, I don't know about that, James. I can't just neatly

package up all these thoughts and feelings and put them behind me but I have been thinking about what to do next. I'll tell you when we go back in and get comfy – see what you think about my plans for travelling through *this* little piece of space time!'

He looked slightly crestfallen that she hadn't wholly bought into his theory for moving on with life but he smiled at her regardless. They clinked their glasses together and drained the last of the wine.

Once back inside James threw a few more logs onto the fire and they settled down into the sunken old sofa.

'Okay, so what are you thinking?' he asked, pulling her closer.

'Well, you know how you said you'd like us to travel once you'd finished your stint up here?'

'Yes, think I bored you slightly talking about the botanical gardens at Lake Maggiore. Look, here's the book.'

Annie looked on in disbelief as, from the side of the sofa, out came the massive book he'd been studying so fervently back at home.

'James, it's a *library* book. You'll be racking up late payment charges.' With everything else he'd had to cram into his car why on earth lug a weighty tome like that all the way up here?

'No, I booked it out again just before I came up – but yes, you're right, forgot about the whole charges thing.'

'Okay, well, moving on. I wondered if we might travel to Geneva en route?'

James said nothing but sat, brow slightly furrowed, tapping his fingers on the arm of the sofa.

Eventually Annie had to break the silence. 'Well?'

'Yes, sorry. I think we could do that. I was just thinking how we would do it. We could maybe fly to Geneva, rent a car from there and head down to the Lakes. I think that would be a really lovely drive.' He smiled to himself. Annie knew he was mapping out a route in his head.

Annie stared at him. 'Okay.' Nothing about why they might be stopping off at Geneva then. 'And what do you think about my idea? I mean, going to Geneva?'

'Yes, that sounds grand. But you're not just going to turn up on the doorstep, are you?'

'Don't look so worried. No, of course not. I'll write to Céline and hopefully we can take things from there.'

'I just mean you might have to be prepared for things not working out exactly as you want them to.' He looked concerned.

'Well, I guess the thought had crossed my mind but we always got on fairly well and who knows? She might have been waiting to tell me all about my brother but just didn't know how to. I might actually meet him.'

The first part of the plan was starting to take shape and she didn't really want to think about any possible negative outcomes. 'So do you think we could do it? When do you think you'll be finished up here?'

She could feel James tense slightly as he shifted uneasily in his seat.

'Well, the crofters have formed a co-operative now and there's a lot of high-profile backing. A sale might well go through by the end of the year if everything works in their favour – but I think my job here will probably be done by the end of the summer.'

'I thought there might have been the chance of

something more long term?' She knew this wasn't quite how James had expected things to pan out.

'Well, now there's the real possibility of finance from outside agencies to help the crofters meet the purchase price – which is obviously great. But there's not going to be any financial help for admin costs and that includes supporting a job like mine. Anything would need to continue on a volunteer basis, so I guess I'm just going to have to turn my mind to what I could do after the summer.'

For the first time since she'd met him, Annie thought James sounded really quite unsure of himself.

'It does seem a shame after what you've given up. Are you managing okay now if they aren't paying you?' With all that was going on Annie hadn't thought too deeply about what he was doing and how he was doing it.

'Well, I don't feel like I've particularly given anything up by leaving the civil service. Anyway, before I came up, I said we'd take stock after six months so that's what we'll do.'

He got up and started to tidy things away, close the curtains and generally shut things down for the night.

'We'll talk about what I'm going to do later; let's just concentrate on Geneva for now.'

He smiled at her but Annie sensed that she had stumbled into an area where James felt less than comfortable. He clearly wasn't going to discuss how he was supporting himself so she decided to take the hint – for now.

Annie woke the following morning from a deep and restful sleep, snug under the thick duvet and patchwork eiderdown that covered the bed, almost reaching down to the floor on either side. The bed filled the little wood-panelled room with barely enough room for any other furniture. She could hear James outside filling the wicker basket with logs from the wood store ready to take up its position again on the slate hearth. She lay for a while enjoying the solitude until she could smell the irresistible twin aromas of almost burnt toast and sizzling bacon. With one mighty heave she threw back the bedclothes and walked to the window.

On pulling back the makeshift curtain that covered the single glass pane she could see the clouds had rolled in overnight and spread themselves out over the rocks that pierced through the thick grass and heather-clad hills. It was a dramatic but sombre sight. In the distance, tumble-down ruins of stone buildings, long since abandoned, seemed to crumble under the weight of a harsh environment. The weather had torn through the very structures that held these communities together but as she'd learned from James so too had the brutality of market forces. It was hard to think about such things in the middle of this beautiful wilderness but it looked like James was going to be at their mercy too.

Later in the day they walked round to a small bay, a few miles' walk from the house. As they turned round the headland, the dark brooding rocks suddenly gave way to a strip of near-white sand. They sat on a grassy bank looking down onto the green-blue waters sweeping gently into the shore. James pulled a thermos of coffee from his backpack.

'Are you sure you can wait till the end of summer before we get to Geneva? Don't you want to go sooner?' He handed her a steaming hot cup of milky coffee.

'Actually it gives me time to sort an awful lot of stuff out. I can organise the flat, decide what I want to do with it, get all of Helen's affairs sorted and then I think I can deal with all of this with a clear head.'

'And how are the Drummonds? I forgot to ask about them and their news? It's strange imagining Duncan as a father.'

'Well, Kirsty hopes it will be the making of him and I think it will. I'm sure it will.'

James put his arm round her. 'Even when things are kind of thrown at you out the blue you always end up seeing the positive, don't you?'

'No, not always. But what's the alternative, really?'

'And children? Have you thought you might like to have children one day?'

She looked up at him, so quickly she hurt her neck, taken aback by the directness of his question. She paused before answering.

'Just because Kirsty is "with child" doesn't mean I've started to get broody. In fact I can't say I've ever had the desire to have any. Quite unusual, I suppose. And I've always felt so bad about that because Virginia has been desperate to have kids. I guess if I found I was pregnant I'd be okay with it but managing my own life seems to be tricky enough.'

She paused, unsure if he would be disappointed in her answer. He said nothing but carried on drinking his coffee and looking out to sea. It suddenly struck her that James may well want to have children. After all, why wouldn't he? They had never talked about it, in fact the thought had never crossed her mind and she wasn't entirely sure why.

But he said nothing and carried on looking out to sea.

Annie chose not to engage in any further discussions around shared futures, children included or not. Something niggled about James's life choices; the decisions he was making appeared to be very spur of the moment and yet he had doggedly carved out a twenty-year career in the civil service right up until this year. Was it some form of midlife crisis that had sent him up here on a whim? With hopes dashed of anything more permanent on the job horizon he seemed reluctant to discuss options with her. As she drove back home on the Sunday it struck her that she knew very little of James Kerr. She thought she knew the kind of man he was, the qualities that she found so attractive, but there were whole swathes of his life that he just hadn't shared with her. If she were working in human resources she would seriously question the glaring gaps in his personal profile. What was it called? She wracked her brain while *Gardeners' Question Time* droned in the background. Hinterland, that was it. She knew absolutely nothing of James Kerr's hinterland.

CHAPTER 9

When she got back there were a couple of messages from Kirsty on her answerphone. It was Duncan's birthday at the weekend and they were having a few people round. Could she come and of course bring James? She felt happy at the prospect of being with her friends again. Virginia and Gordon were going to be there, so the whole pregnancy thing might be tricky, but there was a comfort in knowing she was going to just hang out with her chums on Saturday night. She had discussed the next couple of weekends with James and they had agreed that there was no need for either of them to hare up and down the length of Scotland for a while. She was fine with that; they would sort something out in the next couple of weeks.

She had ascertained that the birthday boy's invitees were for the most part people she had already met. Once again that comforted Annie. Familiar surroundings, familiar folk, usual chat. The only unknown quantity was going to be the appearance of a few guys from the cricket club. You never really knew with these kinds of men. They could be boringly dull, stand in a corner and talk sport all night or be gregarious loudmouths hanging on to the last vestiges of their sporting youth and encouraging everyone to get involved in tediously sexist drinking games. To her great relief the three unknown men didn't appear to fall into either category. They were all new to the area and had only recently joined the club. It was typical of Duncan, thought Annie, that he would be such a welcoming host to people he barely knew. Baby Drummond could do worse than inherit some of his father's genes – just some of them.

Two of the men had recently joined Duncan's law firm and had just moved into the Stockbridge area and the third was a nervy young man from Cheltenham who fidgeted so much that he inadvertently stepped back into one of Kirsty's monstrous ferns and knocked it off its wooden pedestal. He was so effusive in his apologies Annie thought he might crash into something else so she carefully led him by the hand away from potted plants and other loose impediments.

The biggest surprise of the evening, however, was the appearance of Lachlan. No sign of Strachan or Marjorie, thank goodness, but it was the first time, to Annie's knowledge, that Duncan's brother had been invited to any kind of social gathering at No. 92. Something was afoot, she decided.

Aside from the usual greeting at the front door, Kirsty had been absent for much of the first part of the evening. Duncan had been telling everyone that she was putting the finishing touches to his famous rogan josh – given it was his birthday she had insisted that he could start the thing off but she would take over for the final flourish. However, the commotion from the lounge would normally have signalled a rush to the scene by the lady of the house, probably with dustpan and brush in hand; she was nowhere to be seen. The heady aroma coming from the kitchen was making Annie salivate and she decided this was an opportune time to go and investigate.

Virginia spotted her movement towards the kitchen and came to plead with her friend.

'Please, I can't take any more tales of the Borders rugby tour. Even Gordon's joining in with all the laddish banter. Where's James when you need him to talk about normal stuff?'

'Sorry to disappoint, Gin, but it's just me tonight. James and I have been doing enough travelling back and forth so we thought we'd both just stay put for a while. By the way, I was getting a quick rundown of the highlights of the cricket club annual prize giving. Just the highlights mind you – lucky me – before poor Nigel knocked that triffid over. Have you seen Kirsty?'

'Just assumed she was in the kitchen. Anyway, how are you? I just got that mad phone call before you headed north: letters, photographs, your father and Céline – and a brother, really?'

'I'll tell you all about that later, let's see if we can find Kirsty.'

Annie opened the kitchen door to find the two large pots of spicy heaven bubbling away madly. She quickly turned the heat right down but the pot of rice that was at the back of the hob had been left to its own devices for far too long. Annie could tell from the slightly acrid smell that, although white and fluffy on top, it was beginning to suffer from a seriously burnt bottom.

She left Virginia to salvage supper and went in search of the hostess. She found Kirsty in the bedroom sitting in a little wicker chair in the corner, sobbing.

'What's wrong, Kirst?' Annie knelt down in front of her friend.

'All day, bloody morning sickness for one thing and now Lachlan.'

'What about Lachlan?'

'He's decided he wants a bit of adventure in his life and fancy's joining Ranald, you know the eldest, in the back of beyond – well, New Zealand.'

'So, why the tears? I thought you might be glad to see the back of him.'

'Yes, although he's a much nicer person when he's away from Strachan's influence. No, I don't really care whether he goes or not it's just that he's asked Duncan if he might want to move up to Perthshire and take over running the business with his dad. Quite frankly, Annie, I would rather die than move anywhere near the Drummonds.'

'But what has Duncan got to say about it?'

'He's actually started talking about all the positive things that might come with a move to Drummond House. "Lovely environment for baby to grow up in, parents on hand for babysitting, escaping the pressures of city life for us" – that sort of thing.'

Annie noticed her friend quietly tearing a paper hankie to shreds as she spoke.

'You couldn't possibly live in the same house?' Annie asked incredulously.

'Oh no. The parents are going to downsize in any case. I don't think I told you but Strachan had one of those mini-strokes – I think it's called a TIA. Hardly a surprise. The way he goes on something was bound to burst eventually. Anyway, the idea is that we would have the house but they would be living pretty close by – absolute horrors.' Kirsty looked distraught.

'But I thought Duncan didn't want to have anything to do with the business. I thought he wouldn't be able to stand working with his dad.'

'I know, I know, Annie. He just keeps talking about "the bigger picture" whatever that means and he thinks his parents will really be taking a back seat. He has all these ideas about what he could do with the business, which seem like complete madness to me. And then he sounds so excited that I think maybe this is what he needs, maybe what we both need. I just can't get my head round it – maybe it's just my hormones, could it be my hormones?'

The hankie was now a little shredded mound at Kirsty's feet.

'And so you'd leave Edinburgh? And what about what you need? What about your career? Why does everyone want to leave Edinburgh all of a sudden?' Annie knew she was starting to sound a bit shrill and a bit self-interested.

'Oh no. We'd have a bolthole here. We just couldn't afford to keep this place on, that's all.' She reached out and grabbed Annie's hands. 'If it does happen and I'm not saying it will, you mustn't think we're leaving you, sweetie. We're the absolute best of friends and always will be.' And with that she started crying again.

At that point the door opened and Virginia burst in. 'What's going on? I think I've salvaged the curry but we'd better get down there and eat it. Everyone's asking for you.' Then she saw Kirsty's tear-stained face. 'Is everything alright?'

'I think you should tell Gin everything. I'll go and

let everyone know you were just feeling a bit queasy but everything's fine now and you'll be through shortly.' Annie squeezed her friend's hand and then left them to it.

A little while later, Kirsty and Virginia came into the lounge hand in hand.

'You alright, darling? Annie said you weren't feeling too great.' Duncan came bounding over and put his arm round his wife. Virginia quietly peeled away.

'Yes, I'm fine. Nothing for you to worry about.' Annie watched as she put her arm round Duncan's solid girth and kissed him on the cheek.

Virginia walked over to join Annie who was telling Gordon all about the cottage in Assynt. 'It's lovely up there, Gordon, you'd love it. It's just so peaceful and, of course, the scenery is stunning.'

'Yes, it must be. Brilliant hill walking up there too. Must try and pay James a visit before he finishes, maybe drag Duncan up and see if we can have what I would call a proper boys' weekend. Out in the hills all day, hearty meal when we come home and a few drams to finish off. Better than all that cricket and rugby nonsense.'

'Okay, Gin?' Annie looked sympathetically across to her friend.

'Yes. All good, Annie. It's all good.' Virginia smiled as she took Gordon's arm.

Annie knew there was nothing disingenuous about Virginia's response to Kirsty's news. There may well be pangs of envy about Kirsty's pregnancy or sadness that she couldn't conceive, but Annie could see she was trying hard to make sure any negative feelings stayed below the surface. Virginia would comfort Kirsty through her mood swings, counsel her on healthy organic eating and start to turn her hand to knitting and crocheting in preparation for the arrival of baby Drummond. She really was the best of friends.

Over the next few weeks, Annie focused on getting Helen's affairs in order and clearing out the flat. Her friends and James all chipped in and there was an endless convoy of car trips to charity shops or charity vans arriving to pick up larger items of furniture that no one wanted. There were some laughs as they stopped to look at photographs of Annie and her parents in identical knitted Arran jumpers held together by oversized brown leather buttons. It was the only time she remembered Helen ever knitting. The fad had lasted a couple of years and the thick woollens were a necessary prerequisite to spending summer holidays along the East Neuk of Fife, where battling an icy cold wind was just part of the fun.

Eventually the flat was all but cleared and Annie arranged with the solicitors to put it on the market. One Sunday evening after a day spent wiping down, cleaning and dusting, it was just Annie and James who were left, standing looking out at the panoramic views of Edinburgh.

'I still find it hard to believe she's really gone. I still go to phone her or think I'm still going to turn up for lunch on a Sunday and then I remember. It's like being kicked in the stomach every time.'

James stood behind her with his arms round her waist.

'It's going to take a while, Annie. That pain, it'll never go completely but it will lessen and then maybe it'll be easier to think about the good times. Strange, it's hit me a bit harder than I thought it would. She was nothing like my own mother but I was very fond of her; she was so direct, straight to the point. Bit brutal sometimes but she did have a good heart.'

This is it, Annie thought. *This is the time*. She turned round to face him.

'So tell me about your mother.' She held him round the waist and looked up into his pale blue eyes.

'Really? Now?' His brow furrowed.

'Yes, I'd like to hear about her.'

'Well, they're mostly all good – my memories of her.'

He took a moment to gather his thoughts and as he began to talk about his mother, Annie could feel his body relax.

'She was very elegant – tall, slim. I was only little but I thought she was beautiful. Never saw her without any makeup on. Always dressed immaculately. I remember her coming up to say goodnight to me before she went out for dinner with my father. She had this long emerald green dress that she wore with a wonderful black jacket that looked as though it was covered in diamonds. She shimmered, sparkled even, and I just thought she looked like a princess but then when I think about it, she really didn't have to bother with any domestic drudgery. We always had "help" – a cook *and* a housemaid.'

'Bloody hell, James.'

'Yes, I know.' He looked mildly embarrassed. 'Anyway, we were together all the time till I went to school. We did lovely things, always going on outings, picnics. At that age she was my world. Perfect really.'

He took Annie's hand and led her to sit on the one

remaining piece of furniture, a small sofa due to be picked up by the British Heart Foundation.

'The thing I remember most about her is her voice. People say that goes after a while and you really struggle to remember what someone close to you sounded like. I never have. I can close my eyes and still hear that voice – like velvet with a soft Highland burr.'

'Where was she from?'

'Grantown on Spey. Descended from the famous Grants of Rothiemurchus.' He spoke those last words with an exaggerated flourish.

'Oh my, that sounds terribly grand. What were they all about?'

'Owned land essentially.'

It occurred to Annie that James's passion for land reform might have some perverse connection to his landowning ancestors but she didn't want to explore that just now. She needed to keep him focused. It was the first time he had opened up to her about anything family related.

'And how old were you when she died?'

'Nine, I was just nine.' His eyes dropped, the weight of loss and memory too much. 'Everything changed after that and I was sent off to boarding school. Gordonstoun.'

'I've heard of it. It's a pretty brutal regime, isn't it?'

'It wasn't all that bad. It just wasn't really for me, that's all.'

Annie swept back a bit of hair behind his ear.

'Did you lose her suddenly?'

'She had cancer. She seemed to be in and out of hospital but I didn't really know what was going on. I think it happened quickly at the end; I'm not sure. I think it did.' He held her hand, pressing it against his cheek.

'Must have been awful for you. Losing her when you were so young.'

'Yes. Yes, it was.' He took her hand from his face and stood up. 'Right, come on. This is getting altogether too morose.'

Pressing him when he wanted to shut the conversation down might not help but she carried on in any case.

'Okay, and what about your father? How did he cope?'

Maybe she'd gone too far. She wasn't sure.

'Well, he didn't really. Kind of withdrew. I guess that's why I was sent away.'

'But did you get on with him?'

Suddenly his eyes widened. 'Why do you need to know all this? One minute we're talking about Helen and then… look, let's just say we got on better when I was older. He didn't really have much time for me during school holidays or anything like that. Come on, let's go, I'll need to start heading up the road.'

He held out his hand and pulled her up from the sofa.

'It's just you've never spoken about your parents. I'd just like to know a bit about them, that's all.'

His expression softened and he kissed the top of her head.

'Okay, when we get back to yours. Promise.'

They closed the front door behind them and Annie slowly turned the key in the lock. Suddenly she had left James's world and was back with her own mother.

'I don't know if I'm going to be back here again. The neighbours are going to let the charity people in and then the solicitors are handling all the viewings. I just didn't think I wanted to be involved.'

She placed her hand on the frosted glass panel in front of her. The now familiar feeling of sadness surged briefly but like a flash flood it receded almost as quickly.

James put his arm round her. 'Come on. Let's go home.'

When they got back to the flat James started packing his bag in the bedroom and Annie went to make a pot of coffee to help him stay alert for the long drive north.

Once in the lounge, Annie opened up the parent conversation again. 'I thought about your dad the other day when I passed Hendersons. Remember when we had our first rather awkward lunch date? You said he was a good friend of that actor. The one with my favourite name.'

'Moultrie Kelsall.'

'Yes. What a name. Still makes me smile.' She hoped her expression might make him relax into full disclosure. It seemed to work.

'Have you heard of Kerr and Boyd?'

'Kerr and Boyd? They're publishers, aren't they?' Annie put her coffee down on the small side table and then just as she assimilated that tiny snippet of information, 'What, he was the Kerr?'

James kept his hands resolutely wrapped round his cup. 'Yes, he was the Kerr. For a long time they were *the* publishing house in Scotland. My father and my grandfather that is, before they were bought out by one of the big London names.'

'Wow, that's impressive. Wish I'd asked sooner.'

'Really?' His reaction was devoid of any emotion.

'Well, *I* think it's impressive. Were you involved at all? If it was a family business, I mean.'

'No, I wasn't. Father made no secret that he wanted me there but it just didn't interest me – that whole world. I wouldn't know what makes a good author or a good book. He seemed to have a nose for what would sell – I wouldn't have had a clue. I know if I'd shown any kind of interest he would have tried to hang onto the business but in the end I think he kind of gave in.' He looked down at the floor. 'I didn't care then but as I've got older I wish I'd done something. Made the effort to work with him even if at the end of the day it hadn't worked out and we were bought over anyway. Instead I did my own thing, which is fine I guess, but I've lived off his wealth; reaped the rewards. I've taken the money and done absolutely nothing for it. When he died it all just fell into my lap and I couldn't even be bothered to raise a finger to help him when he wanted me to.'

Finally, he was bearing his soul to her and for the first time she put her arm round his shoulder.

'Oh, James, it's only natural that he would have wanted you to join him – I guess that's what happens in family businesses. In the end everyone has to carve out their own path in life and that's what you've done. I'm sure he would have wanted you to do what made you happy. I'm sure he would have been proud of what you're doing right now.'

It suddenly struck her how alike James and Duncan were. Perceived dereliction of duty weighed heavily on them both – just in different ways.

'Don't you see, Annie, it's almost worse. He never forced me to do anything. He supported my choices but all the time I knew he was disappointed. I've begun to understand a bit of what Duncan's been going through, you know. Don't get me wrong, my father was the polar opposite of Strachan but still, the expectations and not meeting them...'

So he saw it too. She rested her head on his shoulder. They were both good men, striving to make their mark, needing to do something meaningful and although they might not recognise it, still struggling to be good enough in their fathers' eyes.

It was a slow, arduous process but she was starting to better understand his character. The events, the places and the people that shaped him. It was important to her. He was opening up his heart and when she looked she saw a little bit deeper into his psyche. Some things she wouldn't understand, actions or reactions she couldn't fathom but her feelings for him only grew. Every new thing she discovered confirmed that, despite his flaws, she had found in James a man who helped her see things – often new things or just the same things differently. Everything felt brighter, sharper when she was with him. There were rough edges, plenty of them, but he was the right man; the right man for her.

CHAPTER 10

Over spring and the early part of summer they worked their way to a settled routine of reciprocal visits. The weather had been good and longer days made travelling easier. The contrast in pace of life between her two homes could not have been starker. Her time in Assynt was unhurried and tranquil; in Edinburgh it was timetabled and carefully costed. Her city life also meant living every moment, along with Virginia, of Kirsty's pregnancy.

'I find I can't walk past a jar of Marmite', was a favourite behavioural oddity that baby Drummond seemed to induce and which made Annie wonder precisely how many jars of Marmite Kirsty encountered in everyday life. There were daily progress reports once she had emerged from all day morning sickness into blossoming pregnancy but it was, in Virginia's words, 'all good'. After a shaky start, Kirsty faced pregnancy with the same vigorous enthusiasm she had once reserved for equestrian point to point or a competitive game of hockey.

As for leaving the city, Kirsty had resolutely told Duncan that she couldn't possibly consider a move to Drummond House before baby was born and that seemed to suit everyone concerned. Lachlan was going to postpone any move to New Zealand until after the birth and Duncan was going to test the water with his father on taking up the reins of the business. He had persuaded Kirsty that he would drop any plans if he thought Strachan would interfere in any significant way, but given his father's health he was convinced that wouldn't be an issue. Annie knew Kirsty wasn't so sure.

*

It was a hard letter to write.

Annie sat at the writing desk, now cleared of James's forms and plans, looking out at the terrace and across to her neighbours' back garden. A cherry tree stood heavily in bloom; small clumps of blossom, the hue of sticky marshmallow, covered every bough. Sometime in the next few days, perhaps even sooner, should there be anything approaching a strong gust of wind, the petals would fall like pale pink snowflakes.

Spring planting. She hadn't even thought about spring planting. Some marigolds, pansies perhaps, although they could be a bit hit and miss. Her eyes swept round to the back of the garden. The privet hedge at the back needed a trim. Gordon normally did that for her and advised her on composting. Same thing every year and not once had she listened to anything he said.

Annie pushed her chair back and pulled out the narrow little drawer at the front of the desk. She lifted out the photograph of her baby brother and placed it by her writing pad. Taking a deep breath she clicked the end of her pen and began.

It was a hard letter to write.

*

Weeks passed and Annie heard nothing. She played over and over in her head the phrases, the words, the tone used. Reaching out and showing empathy. That's what she had striven for but perhaps Céline just didn't want to reciprocate. Perhaps she had created a new world for her son; perhaps with a new father; perhaps there could be no turning back the clock. No intrusion from one life into another. As Annie mulled over all the possibilities, her anxiety grew. However much she'd tried not to want this, she knew she was clinging to the hope that she could connect to someone, someone with a sense of shared heritage. Someone who could help keep her father's memory alive and with her. How could she have let this build up to the point where she was distraught at the prospect of not meeting him; not being able to plan a life with him in it? James was right. It obviously wasn't going to pan out as she'd expected.

Spring gently sidled up to summer and as the trees burst forth into full leaf, the sun began to exert some real warmth and the last vestiges of early morning frost soon receded. Blankets were discarded from beds, central heating was turned off and Kirsty was starting to blossom, not that she necessarily saw it that way.

'I'm going to have to start buying some of these bloody awful maternity sacks soon.' Kirsty was lounging back, legs splayed and with an oversized sun hat covering most of her face. They were sitting outside Café Florentine on a beautiful Saturday morning. The sun was already splitting the sky at ten o'clock and everyone was sporting short sleeves and summer shorts or skirts. It always tickled Annie to see bemused tourists staring at all the freckled, milk-bottled limbs on display as they steadfastly stuck to wearing woolly jumpers and jackets. After all, hot in Edinburgh might be bordering on mild in Madrid.

'When does James come back? For good, I mean.' Virginia's floral skirt was pulled up to her knees and her blouse was unbuttoned as far as the top of her bra. She was determined to absorb as much vitamin D as possible and didn't much mind what the local residents thought of her state of dress. She leaned across the table, lifting her sunglasses on to the top of her head giving her friends an unrestricted view of ample cleavage.

'Good God, Gin, put the puppies away. Poor Annie is going to feel awfully inadequate what with my paps swelling up to a ridiculous size now too.'

Annie laughed. What an altogether dishevelled little group they were. The weekday facade of smart professional women had disappeared overnight.

'Yes, well, I'm certainly in the lower divisions compared to your premier league assets, girls. As for James, well he should be back by the end of next month.'

'What's he going to do?' Virginia asked while munching down a warm croissant, flakes of which had now stuck to her exposed chest.

'Well, he's going to join an environmental agency as a consultant.' Annie shifted slightly in her seat. 'So he's quite excited about that.'

'What does that mean?' Kirsty screwed up her face and Annie wasn't sure if it was because of the sun or James's career choice.

'Why don't you ask him when he's next back? He'll be able to give you a far more sensible answer than I can.' Annie shut her eyes to take in the sun's rays and to signal an end to questioning about James.

Virginia missed the signal. 'Well, I think that's great. He's such a clever chap you know, Annie. So knowledgeable and he's really done so much to help with that land buy-out up north. There must be loads more he can do.'

'Thanks, Gin.' Annie kept her eyes shut. 'I worry he's a bit of a lost soul at the moment but if he can get his teeth into something with this agency then hopefully it'll all be good.'

'What about Switzerland, any news on that front?' Kirsty being characteristically direct.

'I've just written to Céline actually, just the other day.' *Well, that was an out and out lie*, she thought to herself. It had been weeks and no word back. 'So, we'll just leave that and see where we get to. She may have moved on of course.' Annie was thinking emotionally as well as physically.

'And you're okay? If you don't hear anything, I mean.' Virginia sounded concerned.

'Yes, I think so.' It was another lie but she wanted to seem detached. 'We'll see. No point worrying until I hear back, or not as the case may be.'

Annie trundled back to the flat carrying bits and bobs for a nice summer salad later that evening. She turned the key in the door and heard Ludovic's familiar welcoming meow before he suddenly appeared looking for the tasty morsel his mistress had surely brought back for him. He raced back to the kitchen to sit in nonchalant anticipation. Annie picked up the pile of takeaway menus from the doormat and an exhibition brochure from the local art gallery before walking through to the lounge. Dropping the pile of papers onto the sofa, she passed through to the kitchen. Ludovic watched as shopping was emptied from bag into fridge. Nothing. Disappointed yet again, he slunk back to the lounge to resume his lookout position at the French windows.

Annie poured a large glass of cool water before returning to the lounge.

A white envelope. There on the floor. Slipped out from the little heap of junk mail. Probably a bill. Electricity was due but then so was the credit card. Charity begging letter perhaps. Money urgently needed to save donkeys in Spain or dogs in Italy.

Her heart beat faster and thoughts raced as she bent to pick it up. Just a plain white envelope, nothing extraordinary, nothing to differentiate it from any other piece of everyday mail. She quickly turned it over to reveal the Helvetia postmark. Nothing extraordinary – only the stamp that connected her to a past life and now perhaps to a new future.

*

'Hi Gin, it's me, Annie. What are you up to tonight?'

'Nothing special. Such a gorgeous night we were just going to go for a stroll before dinner. Why? Do you fancy joining us? Just down to St Bernard's Well; we're practically passing your door in any case.'

Annie was tempted. The old well was an ornate construct that sat by the Water of Leith. The supposed health-giving waters were encased within a beautiful circular temple with a marble statue of a healing Greek god at its centre. Could be just what she needed but Annie decided to decline Virginia's offer. She just wanted to sit and gather her thoughts for a while.

'Actually, I just wondered if you'd like to come round here. I've just got salad stuff but I thought maybe we could have dinner, a few drinks and Gordon could give me the annual compost lecture.'

'Okay, lovely. Does the hedge need trimming? He always loves to get his hedge clippers out. Oh, and I've just baked a brown rice asparagus quiche so I'll bring that round, shall I?'

'Oh well, if you're sure. You don't need to bring anything – honest.' Annie was sure she sounded less than convinced at the prospect of brown rice anything.

'No, no. It'll just go to mush if we don't eat it tonight. We'll nip out now for our walk and then come round later – around six okay?'

Lovely, Annie thought. *Saturday night supper is going to be something that readily turns to mush.* 'Yes, yes that all sounds great.' Annie paused. 'Gin?'

'Yes.'

'I got a letter from Geneva today. Céline. She's written back to me.'

'Oh, Annie, that's wonderful news. Just wonderful.'

Virginia at her enthusiastic best. Positive thoughts were what Annie needed right now and who better to encourage and bolster her than Virginia.

Annie set out little bowls of olives and crisps and started to prepare the salad. She pulled out a tray of 'continental cheeses' from the fridge still tightly wrapped in cellophane. It was clearly enough of a marketing strategy to indicate to the British consumer that these cheeses were continental; enough to distinguish this little tray of produce as 'foreign'. No need to identify country of origin. What was the point? It was cheese and it wasn't British and that's all anyone needed to know.

Shortly after six, the doorbell went and Annie opened the door to a beaming Virginia.

'My, this is exciting news.' She flung one arm around Annie and with the other offered up a large canvas bag containing a bottle of wine and some potted cuttings alongside a square plastic box, which Annie guessed held the intriguing proposition of a brown rice quiche.

'Thanks, Gin, that's lovely.' And off they strolled into the kitchen.

'Gordon's just gone back to get the hedge clippers. He'll be here shortly. We'll let him get on and then you can tell all.'

'I know. It's exciting, isn't it? I'm a bit of a mess to be honest. Just all these thoughts going through my head. I really just want to get on a plane now but I can't really and of course I have planned to travel over there with James in any case. Anyway, will Gordon want a beer? I put some bottles in the fridge.'

Gordon appeared shortly afterwards brandishing a set of hedge clippers in one hand and holding a book on composting in the other.

''Thought I'd just leave this with you,' he whispered.

'Thanks, Gordon, that's great.' Annie smiled. After years of failing to make an impact talking about compost he was going to make her read about it.

He made his way to the far end of the garden with his bottle of Grolsch and the girls knew that would be him happily occupied for the next hour or so. They retired to the lounge with glasses of wine and Annie retrieved the letter from the desk drawer.

'Here it is, Gin,' her outstretched hand inviting her friend to share the news.

'No, Annie. I don't think I should. Just you tell me, in your own words, what it says. I think that's better.'

So funny how different her friends were. Kirsty would have practically torn the thing from her grasp before she'd had the chance to say anything but Virginia just wanted to hear her take on what was in the letter and what it meant.

'We've just been at cross-purposes, I think. Dad knew from the very outset that Céline was having his child and had made all the necessary financial arrangements to support her. She hadn't wanted to just assume that he'd be involved in his son's life but she was very careful to ask if he wanted her to keep in contact. He did, for however long he had left, and he'd apparently discussed the situation with my mother. Oh, Gin, I just can't imagine what Helen's reaction would have been. I think there were moments when she tried to tell me but then I suppose she just couldn't open all that up again. I would never in a million years have known that there was anything wrong, anything new or different. I mean the focus was really on Dad and his illness – but then she had perfected the art of evasion.'

Annie thought back over the years when her father was away and how her mother slowly and deliberately built and then gradually shored up her defences. Nothing was allowed to get through until, faced with the man she loved, still loved, faced with his imminent demise, the facade had simply crumbled.

'She could be a really tough cookie, darling. I mean, I don't know all the rights and wrongs of your parents' relationship but she was very good at putting up a front. Well, I thought so, anyway.'

Virginia smiled at her in a way that just made Annie want to lie down with her head in her friend's lap and simply open up about everything she was feeling. Virginia was *the* psychiatrist's couch.

'Yes, you're right. Anyway that final letter from Céline to Dad, you know the one with the photo in it?' Virginia nodded. 'Well, there was a bit missing and I'd said as much when I wrote to Céline. So she replied that she'd told my father...' Annie paused for a second. 'Well, she just wanted to say that she'd always make sure their son knew everything about his father, what a good man he was.'

Annie's voice broke. She had become quite adept at putting feelings into little compartments, something she'd clearly inherited from her mother, but now they were simply pushing at doors and tumbling out from their dark recesses.

'I think Mum must have destroyed that bit of the letter.'

'But why not just destroy the whole lot after your dad died?' Virginia looked confused.

'Honestly, I've gone over and over that in my head. Sometimes I think she wanted me to find it, Gin. Maybe she was going to tell me – eventually. Well, I like to think so or was she just going to leave it for me to find? I don't know, I'll never really know.'

181

It was Annie's turn to feel confused.

'Thing is, Céline seems to have assumed that either he would have shared all of this with me while he was alive or that after his death my mother would have. She's been labouring under the complete misapprehension that I knew everything and that it was just too painful for me to acknowledge. When I wrote to tell her that Hugh had died, well, she just assumed I couldn't even contemplate reaching out to her or her son. Maybe because it would have hurt my mother too much.'

Annie took a large sip of wine. Courage, Dutch or otherwise, was required.

'And now, after all this time. Oh, Gin, she *so* wants me to meet him and to be part of his life. Can you believe it?' She clung on to her friend and they looked at each other, laughing and crying.

'Well, that's a good job done even though I say so myself.' Gordon had just come in through the French windows and stood holding a bag full of hedge clippings. 'What's been going on here then?' He looked quizzically at his wife and her friend as they sat still clinging to each other on the couch.

'Oh, Gordon. Thank you. Thank you *so* much.' Annie had got up and flung her arms round him. He responded by nervously patting her on the back.

'That's alright, Annie. Just the hedge. I do it every year.'

CHAPTER 11

Annie sat with case notes covering the writing desk. She had carefully transferred James's papers onto the coffee table, a move that had proved too much of a temptation for the cat who was now sitting atop one small pile, staring at her. *That cannot possibly be comfortable*, she thought to herself but turned away unwilling to give him the satisfaction of any kind of reaction. She looked at her watch. Six thirty. James was a bit later than normal but she knew he was throwing himself into work and even entertained a vague notion that he might be socialising with some of his new colleagues.

She had been worried that he would be disappointed with an early return from Assynt but she needn't have been. He'd gained a lot of kudos from his work with the crofters. He was enthusiastic about the agency he was now with and about working with a handful of estate managers and landowners who were much more forward thinking than some of the old guard and who were at least keen to try out some of James's new ideas. He couldn't get anywhere near the large shadowy corporations that owned so much land but that was fine. Small steps, he kept saying.

Small steps working in land reform perhaps but pretty

big steps for Annie and James. They were living together. It hadn't been the easiest transition in the world. She'd had to make room for him, not just his clothes but also some of his things. Although they'd decided he would leave all his furniture behind at the Great King Street flat, the one thing he'd desperately wanted to bring with him was an oversized watercolour of a sprawling Highland landscape. It appeared inordinately bleak and harsh to Annie but his mother had painted it and so she had agreed that it would indeed look wonderful above the fireplace. Her shining gilt-edged mirror was removed and replaced by the dark monstrosity. At first it seemed to cast a dark shadow across the whole room but as time wore on the painting mellowed and gradually began to meld into its surroundings. Annie found herself sitting contemplating the brushstrokes, the textures and warmed to the thought that James's mother was now part of their everyday life. The things that had really worried her – different routines, different likes and tastes – only occasionally surfaced but not enough to make any real waves. She found herself compromising in some areas but then so did he. All the worries about being with someone just seemed to fade away. They had of course been spending an awful lot of time together before he'd journeyed north but even so Annie couldn't have imagined that actually living with someone, full time, could be this straightforward. *Something has to give*, she kept thinking. *He's bound to need to get away from me at some point.*

Just then she heard the key in the door.

'Just me.'

'Who else would it be,' she wanted to say but instead

got up from behind the desk to greet him. There was still that slight feeling of giddiness, excitement even, when she moved from one space into another, knowing he was there. She wondered if that would ever leave her. She hoped not.

'I've booked our flights to Geneva, looked at places for us to stay and arranged the car hire to take us down to the Lakes.' He looked very pleased with himself as he handed her details of hotels and guesthouses.

'Great, well done you.' She took his hand as they walked into the lounge.

'And you're sure you don't want to stay with Céline?'

Céline had invited them to stay but it felt like too big a step all at once for Annie.

'No, it's fine. She understands and it's just a couple of days. I just want to tread carefully, for everyone's sake really. So we'll look at hotels tonight and get that organised and then we'll be off.' She squeezed his hand tightly. 'Just four weeks, James. Just four weeks and we'll be there.'

After changing clothes, they made a start on dinner.

'I meant to ask how your day went, you were a little bit later tonight.' She was in the fridge looking for the asparagus.

'I met Duncan, actually.' James had his back to her vigorously scrubbing at a pile of new potatoes. 'He's really anxious to get me working with him on the estates the Drummonds manage. You know, once they move up there. Sounds really promising. There's a new landowner who's really interested in diversifying, doing things in a more sustainable way and he's also interested in sorting out a better relationship with the tenants and local community. Well, that's certainly Duncan's take anyway.'

He turned round to see Annie looking all wide-eyed.

'Well, that does sound good, James, but it also sounds like it's a done deal. The Drummonds, I mean – moving.'

'Isn't it? Have I got that wrong?' He looked anxiously at her, obviously worried that he'd either divulged a state secret or completely misunderstood Duncan.

'No, probably not. It's just Kirsty doesn't seem to have quite got on the Duncan bandwagon yet. She doesn't want to think about any of that stuff until after baby's born.'

'Oh right. Oh dear. Probably shouldn't have said anything.' James turned sheepishly back to his Jersey Royals.

*

The beginning of September arrived and Annie and James sat in the departure lounge at Heathrow waiting for their connecting flight to Geneva.

'I had no idea there was so much history to Geneva. For some reason I've just thought it was some modern, brash place filled with drugs companies and tax avoiders.'

James didn't look up as he spoke. They were surrounded by different nationalities all heading to the same destination and he was immersed in a heavy hardback book charting the development of the city from sixteenth century to present day. Anyone else would have just bought one of those Berlitz travel guides but not her man. Heavy hardbacks were his thing. Annie was imagining the seating arrangements on the flight as he sat elbows out, book propped up on the small foldaway tray, and prayed that the person sitting beside him would not be too inconvenienced. She could of course offer him the window seat but she loved sitting at the window so – no, that wouldn't be happening.

'Birthplace of John Calvin, Annie. Did you know that?' Now he looked at her, peering over his reading glasses. The incessant background noise of tannoy announcements, raucous laughter from the bar and crying children had made no incursion at all into his sensory world.

'Nope, can't say I did.' Annie had a newspaper on her lap but she couldn't concentrate. She was rehearsing her meeting with Céline after all these years and was trying to think about what on earth she could say to a ten-year-old boy she'd never met before. Not just any boy – her brother. *What if he's a little horror? What if he hates me? No, banish such thoughts immediately. Okay, but how do older sisters relate to younger brothers in any case? So much younger.* She had no reference point.

'Yes, well, apparently John Knox lived there for a while, studying at the feet of Calvin. The Scottish Reformation started right there.' He let out a yelp. 'Says here Calvinism made Scotland the moral standard of the world. Bloody hell.'

Annie smirked. So her father, pillar of the Scottish Presbyterian community, left his birthplace to live in the place where it had all started and to all intents and purposes threw their morality right back at them. Well, what exactly would Calvin have made of modern-day Geneva in any case, she thought. Her father's lapse in moral standards was nothing in comparison.

Their flight was on time and after picking up their luggage, they jumped into a taxi and headed for the Old

Town. James had booked them into a small hotel very close to the Place du Bourg de Four, the oldest square in Geneva and where they had arranged to meet Céline the following afternoon. It was nearly dark when they arrived and Annie just wanted something light to eat, a bath and then bed.

'Don't you fancy exploring?' James was perched excitedly on the edge of the bed, surrounded by numerous maps kindly provided by the pretty young receptionist.

'Really, James? I just thought a quick bite to eat in the hotel would do us for tonight. We've been travelling all day.'

'Okay. Compromise. Let's go into the square and grab something to eat, soak up a bit of the atmosphere and then straight back here.' He had moved up behind her as she started to hang things up in the ancient old wooden wardrobe and began kissing her neck.

She stopped for a second. The thought of sitting out in the still warm night, enjoying a romantic meal and a glass of chilled wine suddenly sounded rather appealing.

As she nodded in agreement, James grabbed Annie's hand, picked up the pile of guides and maps and before she knew it she was standing in the middle of the square beside medieval fountains and surrounded by restaurants and cafés teeming with tourists and locals alike.

He picked out a small restaurant with the words 'typical Swiss food' emblazoned across its canopy. 'Let's try here.' Although still reasonably warm, there was a slight chill to the air, so they decided to eat inside at a wooden table surrounded by paintings of old Geneva buildings. Annie plumped for a simple dish of ham and potato rosti while James went all out for steak tartare.

'Are you okay, darling?'

'Yes, fine. Just a bit preoccupied. You know – about tomorrow.'

He looked concerned. Any other time Annie would have lapped up the atmosphere of the place, the different languages, the cuisine. She would have loved to explore again the cobbled streets and hidden courtyards; it had been such a long time since she'd been here. Just not this trip. Maybe next. 'It's okay, I'm fine – honest. It's a lovely meal.'

The following morning, it seemed to Annie that James had decided it was best to keep her busy and so they went on a relentless tour of museums. The Reformation and clock-making seemed to be at the heart of most things and Annie trundled along happy to absorb whatever she could by osmosis – it certainly wasn't by intently listening to James or any of the tour guides. Then, finally, she noticed that they had somehow made their way back to the Place du Bourg de Four. She looked at her watch. It was nearly two. James took her hand and they walked toward the café, their pre-arranged meeting place. She found herself pulling his hand back, trying to slow their pace. She wanted to see them before they saw her.

They seemed to be going against the tide. Tourists in shorts and large sunhats, locals in cool linen and designer shades. Then suddenly they were through the meandering crowd, a few metres from the café.

Céline's hair looked the same. Same style, still very Audrey Hepburn and still jet black. Her head was down, oversized sunglasses perched on top, perusing a menu.

Annie tugged firmly at James's hand, urging him to stop.

'That's her,' she whispered. She quickly looked round the haphazard arrangement of tables with round gold tops and rickety wooden chairs. There was an elderly couple sitting at the table next to Céline. He sat smoking a small cigarette, Gauloise perhaps. It didn't seem to leave his lips even when he exhaled little puffs of smoke through his fingers and up through the thick bristles of a very handsome moustache. His wife sat impassively next to him, long grey tresses piled up and held fast by a dazzling silver pin, delicate pearls caressing a worn, leathered neck. She too smoked but held the little reef aloft, fixed into a long black holder, distancing herself from its effects. Annie glanced back at Céline. There was no one else with her. No child.

James stood looking down at her. He didn't appear to know what was expected of him and then, just as Annie was about to signal a move forward, Céline looked up. Her eyes were squinting in the sun and so she pulled her glasses down.

'Annie. Oh, Annie, it *is* you.' Suddenly she was up out of her seat and crossing the cobbles to greet them, arms outstretched. 'You are not changed. Not changed at all.'

Annie slipped her hand away from James and held her hands out not knowing if she was expected to shake or hold hands or even hug. Céline bypassed any awkwardness and went straight to hug. Annie felt relieved. She would never have to play that moment over in her head ever again.

'And you must be James. How lovely. And how tall!' Céline had stepped back from the embrace to briefly shake James's hand and then returned to slip her arm into

Annie's and to lead them both back to the little black cast iron table with its round gold top.

'Coffee, tea or wine perhaps?' Céline beamed at them both.

'Oh just tea, I think.'

'Yes, tea please.' James quickly concurred.

'*Je voudrais du thé, s'il vous plait,*' Céline asked the waiter who had suddenly appeared at her shoulder.

'I cannot believe you are here. All these years – and misunderstandings, I think.'

'Yes, yes. Misunderstandings.' Annie couldn't believe how little she had changed. They weren't so far apart in years and yet Annie felt slightly crumpled and haggard opposite Céline's clean lines and smooth skin.

'I just don't know, Céline – why I wasn't told. It was all so complicated. Hugh and Helen, well, it was just all very difficult. Sometimes I'm so angry with them. With both of them and I think I have been for a very long time. I suppose I've just managed it well. But now? Now, I just think what's the point?'

She hadn't meant to say things all at once but there it was, the little rubber bung popped out and words flowed. She stopped and looked down at her lap as James reached across to take her hand. 'The main thing is we're here now.'

'Yes, *ma chérie*, we are here now.'

The tea arrived in a large pot with three pretty little china cups and mismatched saucers.

Céline poured the tea. 'I am sorry that Hugo cannot be here to meet you. I am afraid he is in school but I will take you home with me and you will meet him there. Yes? He is very excited.'

191

'I love that you called him Hugo.'

'Of course. Yes. How could I call him anything else? He is my son and he is all I have left of your father.' Céline handed round the little cups. 'I am sorry. Perhaps I should not tell you these things.'

'No, it's fine. It's lovely really.' Annie wasn't sure if it was Céline's directness or slightly stumbling English that had taken her aback but on a positive note it had allayed any fears that mother and son might want to cut ties with all things Anderson.

Annie took a sip of tea. The groundwork that would help re-establish a connection to her father, to her family was about to be laid. It was a delicate thing; the wires were fragile, frayed even, and they would need careful handling.

Céline set off again. 'Sometimes I think I overthink things. I want Hugh to be proud of our son and I try to see him in everything. I look for signs in Hugo. It is too much for one little boy, I think.'

She pulled a hard white napkin from the red plastic dispenser in the centre of the table and held it up to her trademark bright red lips.

'So many times I wish I had never left your father. I was young and I was scared and he was so kind, so generous, even then. Even when I left. But then he was with your mother at the end and maybe that was the right thing after all. I don't know.'

She suddenly looked down to her little tea cup, her eyes filled and the little napkin was held ready to catch any drops of moisture. Annie quickly abandoned her own brief moment of quiet introspection. The years of questioning, the years of feeling pain all had to be laid to one side.

192

'Oh, Céline, there are so many things we don't know. What was for the best, what we could have done differently. I've spent such a long time trying to forget how lost I was when Dad left and then when he set up home with you, well, I've just tried to keep a lid on all of that.' She moved her hand to find James and quietly slid under his strong grip. 'There's been too much pain and I really don't want to go back there. I think in the end all we can do is look forward, make the best of what we've got now.'

*

They arrived at the white *art moderne* house late into the afternoon. The clean, angular lines of the house exterior were reflected in Céline's design of the interior. Nothing much had changed since Annie had last visited although every so often she did notice traces of a young child's presence: small scuffed shoes in the rack in the hall, discarded action figures and then the plethora of framed photographs. The house seemed to stand impervious to the occasional rough handling of its smooth finishes by the absent-minded young occupant. It was clear that he belonged to the house as much as the house belonged to him and minimal disruption was tolerated.

Suddenly the front door opened and Annie and James both jumped as they heard the quick and noisy clatter of school shoes on oak wood flooring and then, with only moments for Annie to settle her thoughts, there he stood – framed by the doorway to the sitting room.

'Hugo, *mon chéri*, stop running all the time.'

'*Pardon, Maman.*' The little boy uttered his apology

193

quickly as though impatient to move on to the far more important business of greeting the two guests.

'That's okay, darling. We are going to speak English now. Okay?'

'*Oui, Maman.*' He smiled at her while shaking the satchel from his back and letting the heavy bag fall to the floor with a thud.

'Hugo!'

'*Pardon, Maman.* Sorry. I mean sorry.' Hugo smiled mischievously at his mother.

He picked up his bag with one hand, wiped his nose on the back of the other and then stood staring at Annie, white polo shirt hanging out at one side of his grey shorts, blue tie slightly askew, one grey sock up and one down. Standard state of attire for schoolboys that seemed to transcend national borders, she thought to herself. His dark colouring was so much the product of Céline. Annie really didn't know where the mop of black curly hair came from but it was his eyes; the shape of his face; his thin lips. These were the shared Anderson features that she fixed upon. She smiled at him and he smiled back, his dark eyes glinting in recognition. They could only be brother and sister.

'Hugo.'

He turned to look at his mother.

'This is Annie. I told you all about Annie. And this is her friend James.' Céline nodded to her son and held her hand outstretched, guiding him towards the two strangers on the sofa.

He looked a little nervous and shuffled towards Annie with his head down. Then suddenly he lifted his head, looked straight at her and with an air of unexpected formality, offered his little hand. The one with the trace of snot on the back.

'How – do – you – do?'

'Very well, thank you, Hugo. And how are you?' Annie smiled again as she shook his hand. 'Your English is *really* good.'

She overdid the shake in an attempt to make a little joke out of this heavily trailed meet and greet and immediately felt the tension leave the little boy's body. He laughed. And then just as she felt they were both relaxing into the encounter, for some inexplicable reason, James shot up out of his seat, all six foot five of him. Towering over the young boy he slapped him on the shoulder. Annie saw Hugo's eyes shudder in his head.

'Hi there, Hugo, great to meet you. How's school?'

The little boy murmured something and then shot off to take refuge in the protective space by his mother's side.

Annie couldn't bring herself to look at James but just sat staring straight ahead and smiling at Hugo, albeit more forced now, hoping to re-establish the sudden, severed connection.

And then to her astonishment Hugo shouted out, 'Do you like cars, James? Do you like Formula One? Would you like to see my race track?'

Before she knew it both of them were off to inspect the replica racetrack at Monza that he had built in his bedroom along with a fine selection of Ferrari and McLaren model cars (James waxed lyrical once they were back at their hotel). Typical, she thought. Boys bond over such superficial nonsense and all the while she was trying to connect meaningfully, emotionally to her little brother. So a few spins round a racetrack, picking out their favourite teams and she was suddenly an irrelevance.

In the years that followed, Annie would often wonder if that was the moment in time when the bond between James and Hugo was so firmly fixed. She was very close to Hugo *now* but that relationship had developed over time and she had grown into the role of big sister – sometime confidante, sometime surrogate mother. The connection with James, by contrast, had been instant. She used to think it was just bonding over boy things but it wasn't just that and neither did it seem to neatly fit the father and son mould. There was something more important at play. Kindred spirits, perhaps.

'That is the boys for you.' Céline smiled and ushered Annie into the kitchen to help her with tea. *Some things just never move on in the world of gender stereotypes*, Annie thought, as she set out sandwiches and arranged cups and saucers on a silver antique serving tray.

*

As they departed Geneva to make their way down to Lake Maggiore, Annie reflected on how well the visit had gone. They drove slowly, snaking behind the trail of cars and camper vans heading for parks scattered around little marinas or to exclusive hotels perched at the edge of the lake. Her window was down and she could feel the baking warmth of the wind caress the side of her face.

'He *is* a nice little boy, isn't he, James?'

'I think he's great. Bundle of energy. A really inquisitive

mind, that's what I like about him.' He took one hand off the steering wheel and placed it on her knee. 'He just seems to want to learn things all the time. I was like that at his age.'

Annie turned to see James smiling contentedly at the road ahead.

Finally they reached Hotel Gardini, the former monastery that was now their twentieth-century hotel, sitting on a promenade by the lake and close to the ferry stop. Two women emerged from the entrance just as they drove up, all dressed in black right down to the thick tights and flat black shoes. Mother and daughter, Annie guessed. They were greeted politely rather than effusively just as a young man in a smart green waistcoat appeared from nowhere and swiftly carried their bags off into the depths of the hotel. They quickly registered and trailed after the women in black along the twisting passageways. Annie thought of solemn monks silently treading through the cloisters in their rough brown habits to evening vespers. And then, finally, just as they'd passed another little vestibule housing some fake religious artefact, they reached their room; small but perfect. Annie walked straight over to the open French windows and stepped out onto the little balcony that looked down the side of the hotel to the bright blue lake beyond. A gentleman in a panama hat was sitting below her in a wicker chair sketching the majestic scene in front of him. *Straight out of Somerset Maugham*, Annie thought to herself.

That evening they dined on the small terrace and tucked into a tasty if ill-defined meal entitled 'Fish of the Lake'. It was served lightly battered with green beans and little duchesse potatoes entirely in keeping with the simple, elegant demeanour of the hotel and its guests. Annie reckoned that the genteel vision was only marginally disturbed by James's insistence on bringing down *Gardens of Northern Italy*. Once again the weighty tome had appeared when Annie least expected it, having made the journey along with its equally oversized partner, *The History of Geneva*.

'Villa Taranto tomorrow, I think, darling.' He lifted up the book from the side of the table.

'No, James. Put it down. You're not doing that here. We're having dinner.' She whispered and smiled at the same time to preserve the image of domestic harmony.

He opened his mouth to say something but in the end seemed to think better of it and repositioned the book.

The following day they made their way to Villa Taranto. Annie couldn't argue with anything he had told her about the gardens. Created by a shipping magnate from Galloway in the early 1930s, Captain Neil McEacharn had invested all his money into creating the spectacular paradise that they were now walking through. Dahlias, lotus flowers, gigantic water lilies and tumbling waterfalls all framed by the Alps in the distance. The man had poured his heart and soul into the place and the profusion of colour, the sheer vibrancy of the place filled Annie with joy.

'Isn't it just incredible?' James was looking out at the snow-capped mountains. 'To create something that you know thousands of people will enjoy for generations to come?'

'Yes, it is.' They were sitting on a bench under a Douglas

fir. *Yet another Scottish botanist spreading his tendrils around the world*, thought Annie. They had climbed steeply to see the breathtaking views and Annie could feel her once cool cotton shirt start to stick. She took off her sun hat and turned to look at James. He was sitting back, hands clasped, gazing down at the lake below.

'When were you last here?'

'Oh, it's a few years ago now. I first came here with my parents when I was a boy. I thought it was magical and then later – well, I was just fascinated with the design of the place and of course the plants: where they'd originated, why he chose what he did, how different aspects of the garden suited different plants. And look, you can see what he did to maximise the views.' He looked towards the distant mountains. 'And then when he died he left it all to the Italian State, for everyone to enjoy. That's something I really admire.'

He turned and took her hand in his.

'To be honest though, I'm not sure I ever got the real beauty of the place before. Before now I mean.'

CHAPTER 12

That August, Céline brought Hugo over to Edinburgh during the school holidays to sample all the Festival Fringe had to offer a lively, inquisitive young boy. Hugo loved it. He would pore over the programme and pick out all the things he wanted to see that day. He loved anything raucous – over-the-top theatrics preferably accompanied by ghostly stories with a bit of blood and gore thrown in. To top it all, the excitement was only heightened if James managed to get away from work to join in the fun.

Annie noticed that Céline occasionally interspersed the moments of festive fun with talk of Annie's father, Hugo's father: where he had worked, where he had played rugby. The little boy looked on in respectful silence as his mother showed him his father's old school. Annie thought Hugo was a little bit overawed at the sight of Fettes College; an imposing building that resembled a cross between a French chateau and an over-engineered baronial castle.

As they walked away Hugo tugged on James's sleeve. 'I think Dracula lives there.'

'Could well be, Hugo, could well be.' The two of them laughed.

On the second Saturday of their stay Hugo had

persuaded his mother that he would be perfectly happy if she wanted to meet up with some old colleagues who were now working in Edinburgh. They were all sitting having lunch on the High Street.

'Please, Mama. I am fine. I will be with Annie and James.'

At least he put my name before James's, Annie thought.

'Honestly, Céline, we would love to and we'll go out for tea – pizza, Hugo?'

'Yes!' Hugo punched the air like one of his football heroes and then grabbed Annie's hand. She felt a little tremor travel up her arm.

'Well, if you are sure it won't be too much bother.'

'No, of course not, absolutely no bother at all.'

And that was that. One Saturday in the late August of 1991, the little band of James, Annie and Hugo was firmly formed.

*

Annie was sitting at her writing desk, preparing for the continuation of a tribunal hearing the next day. Another riveting local authority case. Caretaker dismissed on grounds of capability. Final straw for the council was his decision to stop phoning in to advise of his impending absences. No landline at home and he had decided to stop using public telephones as he could pick up any manner of diseases that might just exacerbate his existing condition. A condition which various medical advisers were unfortunately having some difficulty in nailing down. When asked if a friend or relative could phone in, he calmly let it be known that no one in his circle of family, friends or indeed neighbours possessed a telephone. He hadn't flinched. He was entirely content that this was a perfectly plausible defence. It was cutting-edge stuff.

She sat back in her seat and let her mind drift away from all things legal. It had been over a year since she had met James and so much had happened – good and bad. Summer was transitioning into autumn. Trees, shedding their leaves, were getting ready to shut down for winter. Kirsty Drummond, bucking the trend, was more than ready to burst forth with new life. She was a week overdue and everybody knew it. Another evening listening to a blow-by-blow account of every twinge and ache beckoned.

'Bloody hell, when is this thing going to pop?' She was half-sitting, half-lying on the small comfy chair Duncan had brought into the dining room as the six friends had gathered at No. 92 for another one of his speciality curries. They were all the rage in the Drummond household at that moment but Kirsty could only do sitting on a hard seat to eat hers for short bursts at a time.

'I'm sure it'll be any day now, darling.' Duncan was sitting at the head of the table, back to his wife and rolling his eyes. 'What with all the extra hot curries and quick marches up and down Great King Street, really can't be long now.'

'Well, if you'd just get on and have sex with me like the midwife told you to, then it might be here by now.' Kirsty was sitting looking at her stomach like it had been invaded by some alien life force.

'She didn't *tell* me to have sex with you, dear. It's an

option, but I think we'd probably both have to be in the mood.' Eyes rolled again. James and Annie were trying hard not to laugh while Virginia and Gordon just kept their heads down. Annie wasn't sure if Virginia was red from embarrassment or too much chili.

'Well, *I'm* in the bloody mood, Duncan. I need to get this thing out of me.'

Duncan ever so slightly shook his head. He clearly had no more words.

James got up from his seat to pick up another napkin from the sideboard. Annie noticed him place his hand on Duncan's shoulder, just for a moment, as he walked past.

How his view of the world and his place in it had mellowed over these past twelve months, Annie thought to herself. Tolerance, empathy. Not always the easiest concepts to master but he was getting there. Annie recognised the signs. She was just a little bit further round that particular learning curve, that was all.

'Shall I start clearing up?' Virginia ignored Kirsty in the corner and addressed her question to her fellow diners. Without waiting for an answer she was suddenly up collecting dishes and urging Gordon to do the same. They tidied up and everyone left the Drummonds still talking about sexual desire and the relative merits of positioning during pregnancy.

The following day Duncan rang to say they were heading to the hospital. Kirsty's waters had broken while she was waddling round the New Town for the umpteenth time. Annie had just got in from work.

'Oh, at last, Duncan, you must be relieved.' They would all be relieved.

'Too bloody right. Must go. Can you hear her? She's starting to wail now.'

'Look, just get her there in one piece. No mad driving and let me know when it's all over.'

And before they knew it, in fact a mere five hours later, little John Duncan Drummond was born. Kirsty stayed true to her word and there wasn't a Scottish surname anywhere other than its proper place, as far as she was concerned.

'John. You can't go wrong with John.' That was Gordon's underwhelming take on the naming saga.

'It's a lovely name. Such a clean, strong-sounding name for a little boy.' Virginia piped up.

Annie had nothing to say about the name. It was fine. She just didn't harbour the same visceral hatred of surnames for first names. Virginia and Gordon had called just after midnight to discuss and she was tired. Too tired to give much thought to baby names.

The friends, other than James, who was with a client in Perthshire, had gathered at No. 92 following Kirsty's return home. Duncan had begged everyone to come down to the hospital to see the new arrival but Annie resisted. It was touching that Kirsty and Duncan wanted their friends to be the first to mark such an important milestone but Annie knew they risked breaching hospital protocol. In any case, Kirsty's parents would be driving up, although, so far, there was no sign of Strachan and Marjorie.

Baby John and the impending move of the new little family to Drummond House dominated the following weeks. Kirsty had changed. Grown perhaps more than changed. It wasn't just the whole maternal thing kicking in. Clearly she was knackered but there was this rather odd benign glow around her. The parents had been up to make sure all was well with mother and offspring but they couldn't really leave the farm for too long and were away back down the road to tend to their own brood of sheep and cattle.

The surprise package in all of this was Strachan and Marjorie. They had turned into doting grandparents; doting but not overbearing. They were staying in a little guesthouse nearby and seemed to be always around on the edge of things. Kirsty lay back on the new recliner, breast out and baby clamped. She looked exhilarated and exhausted all at the same time.

'You know, I really don't mind the sleepless nights. I never was one for a full eight hours what with the snoring whale next to me.'

Annie had never seen her like this. People say parents can look besotted with their babies but she'd not been around many to make an informed judgment. Here it was, right in front of her.

'Remind me I've said this to you in a few weeks' time when I'm ready to call social work.' Kirsty smiled weakly as she looked at the soft dark downy head, nuzzling and slurping.

Just then Marjorie appeared from the kitchen with tea and cakes. She laid the tray down then took her apron off.

'Okay, dear, I'm just nipping to the shops. I've got the list. Is there anything else? I told Duncan's dad I'd meet him in Stockbridge and we'd have lunch there but if you need me we can always come straight back.'

'No, all good thanks, Marjorie. I've got Annie for the

next couple of hours and Duncan should be back soon. We'll be fine.'

Annie raised her eyebrows. She didn't mean to, it had been an involuntary reaction. So everything would be fine because *she* was there in the event of a newborn baby emergency.

'So everything going okay with the in-laws then?' Annie poured the tea in readiness for the end of feeding time.

'Yes, I know. Who'd have thought but Marjorie's been an absolute angel and to be honest Strachan's just been hanging about, not saying or doing very much at all. A bit awkward, a bit in awe of baby I think sometimes. Out of everybody he's been the really emotional one. Duncan keeps talking about how much he's softened and John has brought out his good side. I thought maybe the blood clot just zapped the impossibly arrogant Strachan and left us with this slightly overwrought model. But then I look at him, the way he looks at John.'

Baby had momentarily slipped off his feeding station, only to be gently nudged back into place by his mother. It looked to Annie as though she'd been doing this all her life.

'I don't know, but I was thinking about it earlier when he was here. Maybe he just doesn't need to have an agenda with John. With the business, the boys – he must have felt it was all on him. Driving everything forward, trying to make a success of it all. But maybe with John, I don't know.' She looked down at her son and stroked the tiny strands of fine hair behind his ear. 'Maybe he can just be his gramps – maybe that's enough.'

Annie smiled. 'Whatever the reason, it's good that you're happy having him around. It'll make all the difference when you move.' She had decided just to make the assumption that they were all heading north and await the reaction.

'Yes. Yes it will. Not so much walking into the lions' den.' John had fallen asleep, satiated, little lips still pursed. Annie helped her friend out of the recliner so she could put him down in the bedroom next door.

That's that, she thought. Friends were shifting, worlds were changing but somehow it all felt less unsettling than before. Change because of loss could weaken, even diminish, but the last few months had brought new lives into her world, adding new dimensions, strengthening connections that were already there and creating others. The life that she'd deliberately kept small and tight was expanding and she wasn't even going to try and stop it.

Kirsty tiptoed back into the room. 'God, the paps get sore, Annie. And look at the size of them, they're ridiculous.' She clambered back on to the recliner. 'But at least they're finally being used the way nature intended – not just a pair of fun bags, are you?' She was lying back holding each breast up in her hands.

Annie could only laugh. Some things, reassuringly, would never change.

*

In the years that followed, life for Annie and those closest to her settled down. Routines were established and some order restored. Life was different but she had reintroduced some structure and that made her happy.

Hugo came over at set times during the school holidays and was about to make his first trip alone. The friends would gather at Drummond House at least once a month and this summer Hugo was going to join them for the first time. He was sixteen and growing fast. It seemed like no time at all since they first met the mischievous little ten year old in Geneva.

James and Duncan were closer than ever and, according to James, 'making real strides improving estate management in Highland Perthshire'. The whole thing still struggled to pique Annie's interest but then James wasn't that interested in legal practice, so it was all fine. Strachan had another mild stroke some months earlier and had completely stepped back from the business but spent his time happily doting on his grandson who, much to everyone else's surprise, appeared to return the favour by heaping generous amounts of unrestrained affection on his gramps. All of which seemed to soften the blow for Strachan and Marjorie when Lachlan declared he was gay, four years after shacking up with a sheep famer somewhere near Dunedin on the South Island.

Virginia and Gordon remained in the same jobs; same house and joint chairs of the Campaign for a More Sustainable Stockbridge. How it could become any more sustainable was beyond Annie. There were more allotments, compost bins and bicycles in Stockbridge than the rest of Edinburgh and its environs put together.

Annie had been made partner at work. The firm was doing well and she was reaping the rewards. She was focused on building the firm's client base and didn't much miss the tedium of run-of-the-mill tribunal cases.

James, Hugo and her friends remained at the centre of her existence.

A warm Saturday afternoon in the early August of 1997 at Drummond House brought the six friends together with Hugo and baby John. John, or Johnny as he was more commonly known, was quite the little bruiser at the tender age of five. James joked he was like a wee sumo wrestler when he was running around in nothing but shorts, planting his feet firmly down on each side as he pondered his next move, folds of chubbiness ripe for squeezing. He was potentially the most squeezable child she had ever come across and it took great powers of self-control not to leap up and grab the wee mite by his Michelin arms. She contented herself with watching Hugo running after him around the perfectly mowed lawn, which just made Johnny squeal with delight.

Annie lay back in her sun lounger on the patio sipping her gin and tonic watching the boys and glancing over at Kirsty who was giving Virginia a tour of her flowerbeds. Who would have thought? Kirsty Drummond – a gardener. Gordon returned to the shade after erecting a badminton net at the far end of the garden. He was wearing a large Australian sunhat with corks dangling down to ward off midges. Combined with his khaki shorts, sports socks and sandals he looked a riot but Annie had long given up being shocked at Gordon and Virginia's state of attire. It was just who they were.

Duncan came round to top up the gins. He still enjoyed his gin – and wine and beer for that matter, his widening girth stood testament to that – but he possessed a degree of restraint now, across all aspects of his personality, that just hadn't existed before. Kirsty had been right. He seemed to have found his place in the world; he looked happy.

'So, chaps. A new Scottish Parliament – are we for it or against it?'

Annie hated when they strayed into the world of politics and much as James and Duncan were now on the same wavelength across a range of issues, there were still areas of contention. She lay back again and closed her eyes, hoping to shut out the intrusion into this perfect pastiche of an E. M. Forster novel.

'Definitely yes for me, Duncan. Think how much easier it would be to get to politicians in Edinburgh on some of our land reform ideas. No one's interested in Westminster or the Scottish Office for that matter.' Annie could hear James's voice and now waited in suspense to hear what Gordon had to say.

'Gordon? If that is actually you behind the swaying corks.'

Gordon ignored Duncan's last comment. 'Well, on balance, I have given it a lot of thought and, well, Gin and I have been chatting it through quite a lot recently.'

Annie looked at him out the corner of a barely opened eye. He was leaning forward, shrouded in cork.

'And I suppose when you look at the negatives but then weigh them up against the positives, I guess, and of course I'm not speaking for Gin on any of this, but I guess, I *think,* I'll probably end up voting yes.'

'Bloody hell, Gordon, you sounded positively constipated trying to get that out.'

Duncan turned towards Annie who, having breached her self-imposed blackout, quickly shut the guilty eye. Too late – she'd been spotted by incoming enemy fire.

'And finally, Annie, who's pretending to be asleep in the corner there. Thoughts?'

She'd had a few moments to prepare her response. 'Well, actually, I'm going to read up on each side's arguments and then make a decision. I've got loads of stuff – just haven't had the time to look through it all.'

'Very sensible, Annie. That's the best way to approach these things.' She could always count on Gordon to back up a rational position.

Although she had returned to complete blackout status she could hear James moving about in his seat.

'But what does your instinct tell you, Annie? What does your gut say?' James sounded concerned, anxious that she hadn't yet made up her mind.

'My gut doesn't say anything. It's not the sort of thing my gut gets excited about.'

After all, she spent so much of her working life dealing in facts; hard evidence. It wasn't easy getting out the mindset. No judge was going to have much truck with Annie presenting a case based on gut instinct. In any case, on this issue, well, yes, she did have an inkling about how she might vote in the upcoming referendum but like any good lawyer she wanted to be sure of her facts; as sure as she could be. And she wasn't going to disclose her position until she was quite ready to do so. Case closed.

'Hugo, can you take Johnny and wash his hands. Time for his tea. Duncan can you get his tea ready – it just needs heating up. James, Gordon can you get everything set up for the barbecue. Daddy Drummond will want to get stuck in once his boy's been fed but if you can just make sure everything's ready that would be a *huge* help.' Kirsty was barking out her orders and everyone jumped to it. Well, nearly everyone.

'I just set up the badminton net, Kirst, doesn't anyone want a game?' Gordon was brave enough to challenge the Chatelaine's authority.

'Oh, I'll play with you, darling,' piped up Virginia.

'Sure you would, Gin, but no time for that now. Chop chop. Tell you what, once everything's on the go, we'll get some badminton in.' Kirsty slipped her arm into Gordon's, planted a big kiss on his cheek and marched him off, corks swinging vigorously from side to side.

The men had assumed their positions, leaving the three girls to chat on the patio. The sun was still warm. Annie looked over at James and Gordon standing at the shiny new barbecue. They were deep in conversation, Gordon emptying out the bag of coals and James holding a pair of large tongs aloft. And there stood Hugo by his side, hands in the pockets of his shorts and hanging on James's every word. His mop of black curls was less unruly now – he was at an age when such things were starting to matter – and he was tall. He was going to be taller than his father; not as tall as James perhaps, but he wouldn't be far off. She often thought how much like father and son they were. There was no genetic connection, obviously, and Hugo clearly retained physical characteristics from her father but perhaps it all came back to the question of nature or nurture. Did it matter? If the people around you, blood relatives or not, guided you in positive ways, just made life more interesting, more enjoyable when they were with you,

212

were there for you when you needed them – that was all that mattered, wasn't it?

Her moment of peaceful contemplation was shattered by James's laugh. Hugo laughed too, right in there behind him. She pushed her lounger back to observe James, not something she was prone to do. They were normally alongside or directly opposite each other, sitting or lying. Very rarely did she have the opportunity to just watch him. He was getting greyer now but it suited him. His skin was softly tanned and his eyes still a beautiful watery blue. Annie noticed how, from time to time, he would turn to bring Hugo in to the conversation and she loved him just a little bit more for it. James's relationship with Hugo was effortless – always encouraging, always reassuring. She breathed in deeply and surveyed the scene. *Everything I want in life is right here*, she thought. And with that Duncan burst through into the garden with trays of raw meat.

'Right, let's get this show on the road.'

'Do we know where the meat comes from?' Virginia gently enquired.

'Killed a lot of it myself, Gin – killed a lot of it myself.' Duncan thumped the large tray down next to Gordon.

Virginia and Gordon exchanged startled looks and Annie knew they were struggling to decide if that was acceptable in terms of sustainable food production. Kirsty ended their torture by once more replenishing the drinks.

Duncan was throwing venison, fillet steaks and bits of pheasant onto the hot grill. He was a serious marinade man and the tempting aromas of thyme, garlic and homemade barbecue sauce all being brought to life by smoky charcoal was making Annie salivate. The gin and tonics had been discarded in favour of chilled Sancerre or ice-cold beers and those in the group not actively involved in the cooking process had left their relaxing recliners and were now standing round the little party of basters and grillers, ready to jump on the first morsel that might be thrown their way, like hungry lions. All thoughts of badminton had been erased from their collective minds.

'Oh, salad, I forgot the salad,' Virginia shrieked as she broke away and skipped towards the kitchen. 'All done, just need to make the dressing.' Her words were lost to the friends who stayed rooted to the spot. Salad wasn't quite the unwanted guest at the party but it certainly wasn't the main attraction.

Kirsty rejoined the group having put Johnny to bed and the pride was finally sitting around gorging itself on heaped plates of protein. Some were in the sun, some lying out under the shade of a tree, meat juices slowly trailing down their chins. Gordon and Virginia seemed to have abandoned any further questions regarding the provenance of their supper and were ripping into barbecued flesh with uncharacteristic ferocity. The neglected salad was starting to wilt under the sun's still warm rays.

'So, Hugo. How's school?' Duncan barked. Just the thing a sixteen-year-old boy wants to talk about when he's on his holidays.

'Oh, it's good. Yes, good.' He took another bite out of his blackened piece of deer. 'Thank you.'

'Any ideas what you might like to do? Your sister says you're a very bright young lad.'

Oh thanks, Duncan, thought Annie. *He doesn't want*

to know that I speak about his academic progress to all and sundry.

Hugo didn't look up. 'I'm going to come to Edinburgh. I want to go to university in Edinburgh.'

Annie looked at James who merely lifted his eyebrows. Everyone else looked questioningly at Annie. What did they want her to say for goodness' sake? He was perfectly capable of deciding what he wanted to do with his life.

'Well, that would be lovely, Hugo, having you in Edinburgh, wouldn't it, James?'

Annie was staring in a way that demanded a positive response. Now all heads turned toward James.

'Yes, of course, great. You'll have to work hard though, Hugo – to get in.'

'I know.'

He was beyond nonchalant. Annie smiled and reached across to gently squeeze his arm. She liked the thought of her little brother coming to live near her. What Céline would make of it she had no idea but it was a nice thought to end this holiday on. Hugo looked up at her and smiled.

CHAPTER 13

A referendum on whether a Scottish Parliament should be reconvened in Edinburgh after 290 years filled the newspapers and daily news bulletins. James was enthused and had become engaged in the local campaign to vote For. That was good up to a point but she didn't really want the subject dominating every conversation. She was already reaching saturation point from every media outlet.

'Why don't you come along to a meeting?' James was sitting at the writing desk in the lounge, folding campaign letters and stuffing them into envelopes.

Annie was interested and, as she had promised, read every piece of literature that came through the door but that was enough as far as she was concerned.

'No, honestly, James. I'll be glad when the thing's over. I know how I'm going to vote and that's that. Are you out again tonight?'

'Yup. But won't be late – honest.'

He gathered up his bundles of envelopes and stuffed them into a carrier bag before dropping down onto the sofa.

'What are you going to do?' He pulled her back away from the comfort of the sofa cushion to put his arm round her and kiss the side of her cheek.

'Kirsty's bringing round photos of Johnny's first day at school. We'll just have a blether, bit of a catch up.' She turned to look at him. 'How are you going to feel when this is all over?'

'When what's all over?' He used her knee as a lever and pushed himself back up again.

'The campaign. You've got awfully political all of a sudden.' She rubbed her knee. Age-related wear and tear meant her joints didn't cope well with heavy loads.

'Really? I don't think so. I guess most of the stuff I've worked on, been interested in has been political – at some level anyway. Actually, I'm thinking I might join the Green Party. Virginia and Gordon have joined.'

'Well, yes. But they're all knitted cardigans and grow your own bean sprouts. That's not really you, darling.'

'That's a bit rough, Annie.'

'Sorry. No, I love them to bits, you know that. They just don't always inhabit the real world. Well, not the one I seem to have to encounter every day.'

He was putting on his jacket and looking round for his keys, all the while wittering on about a broad church, something else about it takes all sorts, and finally ending on the imminent demise of traditional politics as we knew it.

'Don't close your mind to these things, Annie.'

'I haven't closed my mind to anything.' She suddenly worried that she'd appeared just a bit too flippant. 'I know there's much more to Green politics than bean sprouts.'

He blew her a kiss and then was off – apparently to create a new legislature and save the planet.

For the next hour or so, Annie looked at seemingly

endless photographs of Johnny in his pristine little uniform. He was being privately educated in a Perthshire establishment that placed as much value on a robust regime of outdoor pursuits as it did academic excellence – all very Duncan. The choice of schooling had not met with James's approval but Annie had gently advised him to zip it. Johnny was not their child. It might feel like co-parenting sometimes but he was entirely the Drummonds' responsibility and they had to make the educational choices that they felt were right for him. Such choices were of course beyond the reach of lesser mortals, well, at least those mortals who didn't have the Drummonds' financial wherewithal, but they remained theirs alone to make.

'Isn't he darling?' Kirsty was beaming.

The little sumo was, for the first time, not bulging out of his clothes. He had a blazer on, the length of which completely covered his shorts and was nearly at his knees. The sleeves stopped way beyond his hands and the shiny brown satchel strapped to his back was almost the same size as the sturdy wee chap himself. He wore a cap with a large peak under which glowed a round chubby face. *Pleased as punch with himself*, Annie thought.

'Yes, he is.' Annie remembered the first time she had seen Hugo in his school uniform. He'd been a few years older but there was that same look of impending mischief; an uncanny likeness perhaps or more likely a look of small boys the world over.

Kirsty wasn't down in Edinburgh much these days. The Drummonds had bought a tiny mews flat as their new 'crash pad' (Kirsty's description) and Great King Street was going on the market soon. James pointed out that the money spent on the mere crash pad could have housed two families somewhere on the outskirts of Edinburgh. *Why would anyone want to live on the outskirts*, thought Annie, but then she knew how insensitive that sounded, so kept her New Town thoughts to herself.

'We're going to have a last hurrah at No. 92.' Kirsty gathered up the photographs and put them in her bag. 'You know, just to say goodbye to the old place.'

Annie noticed the tears in her friend's eyes.

'Silly really. I mean it's just an old flat but oh, when I think of it, so much has happened there – good and bad.' She pulled herself together, let out a laugh and put her arm round Annie. 'Anyway, let me know if a week on Saturday suits you both. Couldn't possibly have the final shindig without you, Annie.'

Annie was in bed when James finally got in.

'So how did Johnny get on?' He was undressing slowly, with his eyes almost shut.

'Great. Charging about on his first day, so no surprise there, and knocked some kid into the sandpit. Complete accident but created a bit of a rumpus. Some little Spanish boy in the class called him "Torito" and it seems to have stuck.'

'Torito? What does that mean?'

'"Little Bull", according to Kirsty. She was mortified but Duncan thinks it's great. Thinks he'll gain a lot of respect with a name like that.'

James let out a tired laugh. 'Oh my. The Drummonds. You just couldn't make them up, could you?'

'No, indeed you couldn't. By the way, we're invited to their last party at No. 92. Week on Saturday.' She put down her book and watched him finish undressing. He was tanned and lean after a long hot summer spent mostly outdoors.

'Week on Saturday. Okay. Oh, I can't wait to get into bed. I'm knackered.' James threw back the bedclothes and climbed in. He yawned loudly and reached across for her hand.

'Night, night, Annie.'

She'd hoped her flickering embers of desire might just have been stoked into life by a passionate embrace or kiss but the embers, such as they were, had been quickly doused by those tired little words.

'Night, night, darling.'

The next morning she was up early, showered and dressed quickly. She came back into the bedroom to pick up her bag and found James stretching sleepily, showing no signs of joining the day.

'How's it going? The merger, I mean.' He spoke while yawning. Unfortunately it made him sound as though he was merely feigning interest.

'Buy-out more than merger.' *Where were those packs of tissues?* 'It's going well. Hope it'll all be done and dusted in the next week or so.'

Annie had been asked by Bryce to lead the buy-out of a smaller rival. Law was a competitive business in Edinburgh and too many companies were chasing too little work; Ogilvie's was a good fit. She was really enjoying the process and with a small capable team around her she led the negotiations like an old pro. The trick appeared to be to sound utterly confident in everything you were offering and absolutely resolute when the same offers were thrown back at you. Yes, you needed to give things away but you needed to make them sound far more critical than they actually were. She knew Saunders and MacKay had the potential to be one of the 'Big Three', she knew what it would take and most importantly how the business needed to grow to keep them there.

'How about you? What are you up to today?'

'Oh, just a meeting – with a client – in the office – later today.' He stretched again, his long, lean, muscular arms hitting the headboard before finally dropping onto the duvet. 'Meant to say, I met a really interesting chap last night.'

'Oh really?' She wanted to sound interested but she wanted to get away. Her head was filled with spreadsheets. She wasn't sure it could absorb anything else.

'Yes. He's just been made Branch Secretary.'

Branch Secretary? she asked herself. *Oh there they are, the tissues. Oh yes the Green Party. Branch Secretary of the Green Party.*

'Anyway, he runs a small publishing company.'

Annie's ears pricked up at the word 'publishing'. She stopped what she was doing and turned to him. 'Really?'

'Yup. Little independent focusing on nature and the environment. Anyway he'd heard my name and we ended up having a little chat.'

'And so what do you think to that?'

'Well, two things really.' He'd emerged from his soporific state and was sitting bolt upright now. 'He's interested in my thoughts on Assynt and land management in general. Wonders about me writing something but more than that, Annie – he thinks I might have something to offer on the business. They're really just starting out and keen to grow. Might be because of Dad's name, I don't know, but even if it is, I might just be able to prove my worth.'

She put her bag down and went over to sit on the bed. He had seemed to be dipping into things since he left the Scottish Office, nothing that seemed to hold him for any length of time. This might be different, something that might just work for him on a number of different levels. Is that what he was thinking?

'You don't have to prove anything, darling. But it does sound as though it might be worth looking into.'

He smiled. 'For some reason, the thought of it has really excited me – the thought of being part of a publishing house. I could use what I'd gained from Dad, maybe with a bit of investment but also some of his know-how, contacts. I know it's not the same thing but it would *feel* that maybe I was doing what he wanted me to, finally. But not just for him – it would be on my terms too, in areas that really interest me.'

Yes, that was what he was thinking. His enthusiasm was filling the room. Annie could feel it.

'Well, it looks like you might just be about to take him up on his offer, whoever he is.' She smiled at him.

'Jack. Jack Chalmers. Well, I hadn't thought but just then, talking it out like that, with you, well, I think I just might. I just might.' He'd screwed up his face and she knew the possibilities were all starting to take shape. 'See how good you are for me?' And with that he grabbed her round the waist and pulled her onto the bed.

The party at the Drummonds' was two days after the Scottish people decided that they would indeed like to have their Parliament back. The result was broadcast to the nation with just the right level of gravitas for the occasion; no American-style hoopla save for a few cheering politicians and groups of campaigners who had gathered at the count; all reasonably dignified. Certainly everyone Annie knew declared themselves satisfied with the outcome. Well, everyone that was apart from Duncan who voiced some vague concerns about being 'dangerously overgoverned'. James tried to get him to explain what that might look like but he merely muttered something under his breath and stomped off to the kitchen. The subject was then quickly put to bed and they all started to reminisce about favourite times at No. 92.

'Oh, James, remember that first dinner when you droned on about Yugoslavia crumbling while we tucked into our crab and avocado?' Kirsty laughed. They were sitting round in the big bay-windowed lounge with James taking up his customary position in the old leather armchair in the corner.

'Oh, I don't think he droned on, Kirst. He was quite right – we were all talking nonsense while really terrible things were happening in the world.' Virginia had perched on the arm of James's chair and was right in there supporting him. For a brief moment Annie thought she should perhaps have been filling that role but it was only fleeting. Her attention had been diverted by Johnny who had rushed in and dumped two lumps of Play-Doh in her lap.

'Well, maybe I took life just a bit too seriously back then. Think I'm also slightly better behaved at the dinner table these days.'

'I'll say. And you know, we can't always do much about

all these terrible things that happen in the world.' Kirsty looked serious. 'We just crack on and do our best with what we've got here. Well, at least I think we try to.' She suddenly looked embarrassed and the friends started to look around at each other. Kirsty wasn't prone to being philosophical about anything.

Annie knew James wanted to say something in reply but to her surprise he suddenly stood up.

'Well, this is all very serious. Come on now – I'm only here because the Drummonds usually know how to throw a good party. Come on, Duncan, let's get the drinks topped up.' Duncan had only just reappeared after his minor strop and happily marched back into the kitchen.

Annie felt the awkwardness evaporate. She knew he still didn't always feel comfortable in group situations, even with friends as close as they were. He was always battling something – his notion of snobbery, ignorance even. Whatever it was it hadn't gone but he had found better ways to deal with people; discuss rather than berate; offer up a view rather than lecture on the basis of a predetermined position.

Some point later in the evening, the three girls found themselves in the master bedroom. Kirsty let out a sigh that seemed laden with sadness as she pulled out a small leather book from one of the side tables.

'Look what Duncan made me.' She opened up what Annie then realised was a photo album.

'He's put together photos from our time here. Fourteen years of memories.'

She quickly closed the album and started to stroke the shiny new leather.

'It was lovely of him but it just made me realise how much I'm going to miss the place. Silly really.'

'No, it's not. It's been your home. Your first home together. It's natural.' Annie tried to sound reassuring. Virginia said nothing but just sat down on the big sleigh bed at Kirsty's side and put her arm round her friend.

'It's just, it *is* my home. I know who I am here. Drummond House – well, it's lovely of course and brilliant for Johnny but I have no idea who I am there. How to behave. When to stay in one room and when to move into another. Maybe because there's so bloody many of them.' She let out an unconvincing laugh.

'Sometimes I feel like the house is laughing at me. No. 92 never laughs at me. It knows me, everything about me.' Suddenly she dropped the album onto the bed. 'Oh God, listen to me. I sound like I'm losing my marbles.' She moved gently out of Virginia's embrace, signalling a return to customary stoicism and fortitude.

'I mean, really. Some people have nowhere to live and I'm crying about moving to a house with too many rooms.' She slapped both knees and stood up. 'Get a grip, Kirst. James is right, you know – sometimes we lose sight of the big picture.'

Annie just stared at her. 'No, we're not getting all political again. Anyway, it's important – where you live, I mean. Big or small. In the town. In the country. A home gives you security and then later, when you've been somewhere a long time, well, it's just part of you – I think.'

Kirsty and Virginia smiled at Annie. They knew exactly what she meant. The three friends left the bedroom and went back to join the men in the lounge.

CHAPTER 14

In the course of the next two years James did indeed join the little publishing outfit, aptly named 'Evergreen' and had completed the first draft of his book on land reform. He had absolutely loved the process of writing, engrossed in research that was often historical in nature and which sent him off to spend hours in secondhand bookshops – all on the pretext of work. The fact that their bookshelves were now heaving with political biographies and accounts of epic explorations across the globe gave lie to that assertion. He was also enjoying being involved in managing the business and was prodding them to branch out into other areas. As a result, Jack Chalmers had become a firm friend and was a regular visitor to Dean Terrace.

They were sitting round the dinner table one Friday night, replete after a seafood bonanza cooked up by James. He had raided Armstrong's, the fishmongers, and Annie and Jack had been treated to scallops with creamed leeks, langoustine in a lemon and butter sauce and then John Dory, seasoned with cumin and paprika, fried off and served with a simple salad.

'Michelin star stuff this, darling.' Annie reached out to take James's hand in hers. He smiled back at her.

Jack had finished off the John Dory but returned to the langoustine shell, trying to prise out any last vestiges of sweet meat that might have escaped his first foray. His lips glistened with a sheen of lemon butter and he carefully licked them from time to time to ensure his elegantly shaped beard remained untainted. Annie thought he had the look of an American frontiersman about him. Impressive thick moustache curling up at the ends and a long grey wavy mane that swept back from his face and tumbled down almost to his shoulders. Well, maybe frontiersman crossed with Raffles, for Jack Chalmers was a bit of a dandy. He liked his velvet jackets, patterned waistcoats and brightly coloured trousers did Jack, which of course had him pegged, in Annie's eyes, as a model New Town resident.

When James had described the man as 'really interesting' it had been no exaggeration; if anything it was tending towards understatement. He had travelled the world and met a ton of interesting people – the Dalai Lama and Gracie Fields among them. It was that kind of insight, more than anything, that intrigued Annie. The circles you would have to move in to cross such diverse characters. She had once been introduced to Stanley Baxter at a book event somewhere on the Royal Mile. That was fifteen years ago and that's how rock and roll her life had been.

After their meal, they had retired through to the lounge and were all sitting nursing chunky glasses of Edradour. Jack was swirling his golden liquid round and round as if the heavenly elixir was about to serve up some ancient secret from its hidden depths.

'Been trying to persuade your man to stand for Parliament.' He'd stopped swirling now and held the glass against his yellow brocade waistcoat, nestling it into his heavy stomach.

'Really? To do what?' Annie was shocked. James hadn't uttered a word. He looked across at her with a slightly embarrassed smile.

'Well, to be a member of the Scottish Parliament, of course. We've just been talking about it, that's all. Of course it's something I would talk through with you, darling – Jack just mentioned it, that's all.' James nodded across to the increasingly uncomfortable Mr Chalmers. 'The Party's looking for people to stand. It's a whole new electoral system, Annie – the Greens should have a chance.'

'But what about the job? I thought you were making a proper go of that?'

'What? Like I haven't made a go of anything else I've done?' She was annoying him. She knew it but she couldn't help it.

Jack obviously sensed the tension. He shifted uncomfortably in his seat before knocking back some of the whisky. 'Sorry, Annie, I didn't mean to suggest he'd leave Evergreen. Oh no, didn't mean that at all. It's just he's got a good head on his shoulders, you know, bright lad. Maybe I shouldn't have suggested anything.' He was starting to bluster.

The bright lad, Annie thought to herself, was nearly fifty-two.

'It's just that he hasn't mentioned it at all, not at all.' She was staring wide-eyed at Jack and avoiding all eye contact with James.

228

'Well, there really wasn't anything to mention, darling. Jack just spoke to me about it today.' James took a slug of his whisky and then got up when he heard the cat at the kitchen door. There was a cat flap but when Ludovic knew someone was at home he steadfastly refused to use it and waited for whichever serf was available to answer his call. They'd been doing it for years and neither cat nor its humans were going to change behaviours now.

'I'm sorry, my dear. Upset things a bit there, haven't I?'

Annie smiled across at him. 'No, it's fine. I just don't always know what's going on in his head.' But Jack did. She was very aware that although he was only fifteen years older than James, Jack was turning into a bit of a surrogate father. How could he need a father figure in his life at his age? Was she not enough of a sounding board, confidante? She put her own misgivings to one side and turned her attention back to their guest.

'Another whisky, Jack? Let's hear a bit more about it when he comes back in from the kitchen.'

And so it came to pass that Annie's Saturday morning routine of run round the park, home, breakfast, shower and shopping in Stockbridge all now had to be planned around attempting to avoid a small stall in the main street manned by James, Gordon and Virginia. They stood handing out leaflets while wearing oversized bright green rosettes. James the candidate, Gordon the election agent and Virginia – well, Annie wasn't sure what Virginia's role was. This particular morning Annie had grabbed her coffee from Costa while on her 'cool down' walk and crossed the road. She stood right at the end of a small cobbled lane and peered round the corner at her friends. The display of neon-green circles reminded her of the gantry above a Formula One starting grid. Cars revved under the circular red lights changing to green to signal a rush towards success and glory. There was little evidence of success and glory here. Stockbridge residents were certainly rushing, for the most part right past her earnest little trio. At one point it looked like Virginia had managed to engage someone in serious political discourse until Annie noticed that she was selling an assortment of knitted items at the end of the stall. Annie smiled – that was Virginia's place in the scheme of things. The sale of knitted tea cosies would bolster campaign funds, no end. She noticed James trying to break into the conversation but his attempts were being rebuffed and she surmised that Virginia was either discussing knitting patterns or the cost of wool with the little white-haired woman who had deigned to stop. Politics would have to wait.

Later in the afternoon, after another clandestine venture negotiating the back streets to the shops, Annie sat down to do some work before James got home. She was concluding the buy-out of Ogilvie's and preparing for press announcements and launch events. Ludovic sat at the window looking out to the garden. *Must be getting old*, thought Annie; this much paper would normally have signalled playtime. As her mind drifted and she followed the cat's gaze, Annie suddenly heard the key in the door. She absorbed the familiar sound of his footsteps and tuneless whistling until she turned towards the lounge door and watched him amble into the room. He walked right up to her, saying nothing, bag of shopping in one hand, brushing past her cheek with the other and slipping his fingers through her hair. Holding the side of her face he bent down to kiss her. He smelt of stone, trees and tweed. She grabbed the sleeve of his well-worn jacket and kissed him back – breathing him in. She pushed him back slightly so she could stand up and started to unbuckle his trousers.

James moved his hand down to hers. 'Think we've got a guest arriving any time soon, darling. Let's keep this till later.' He kissed her forehead and took his shopping through to the kitchen.

You bloody started it, thought Annie.

She followed behind him and watched him unpack olives, heaven-scented bread and three large Portobello mushrooms.

'What am I smelling?'

'I think it's the rosemary from the bread.'

'Mmm, lovely. Will we have some now?'

'Okay. I'll put some coffee on.' He kept his back to her as he opened up the cupboard in front of him and reached for the cafetière. 'Annie?'

Ominous, she thought. 'Yes?'

'How do you feel about moving house? Out to the west, Cramond perhaps or south, Fairmilehead, that sort of area.' Now he was getting cups down from the shelf above. China was clanking as loudly as his words. 'Just think it would be nice to have somewhere a little bigger, detached even, with a proper garden.'

Annie stood dumbstruck, gripped by a sudden feeling of panic. Proper garden? The garden was fine. It had taken her years to get it just right. Well, to be honest it had taken Gordon years to get it just right. She didn't need a different garden, a bigger garden, a garden planted out in a place she didn't really know.

He turned, looking puzzled at the lack of response.

Annie suddenly found her voice. 'Cramond? Fairmilehead?'

'Just suggestions, darling.' He looked shocked, unprepared for the verbal barrage that was about to hit him.

'They're miles away from anything. I mean Fairmilehead is halfway to the Scottish Border for God's sake – might as well move to Cumbria. And I know I love Cramond and all that, but I never gave any hint that I might want to *live* there. It's under the bloody flight path for a start. Did I give you that impression? I mean if I did, well, it's all been a huge mistake, I can assure you. Did I? Did I give you that impression?'

She decided to stop for fear she was starting to sound like a lunatic. Both were perfectly pleasant parts of the city but they weren't for her. And really he should have known that.

'Oh, Annie.' His features relaxed and she could feel the familiar warmth of his smile pulling her in as he stepped towards her, arms outstretched. She hid herself in the crook of his neck, slightly embarrassed at her sudden outburst. His words were muffled but she heard them all the same.

'Of course, darling. I'm sorry. I should have known how important this place is to you. How important *home* is to you. Just forget I said anything.'

Her heart rate returned to normal and she felt able to resume making coffee and buttering herb bread.

James quickly changed the subject and started to talk about preparing the evening meal. Annie's head was still rattling but she joined in – something about marinades. Chicken – rested and soaking up chili, mint, garlic, lemon, olive oil. Rested. Yes, it was important to feel rested.

'You know, Virginia just uses that stall to chat to the world and his wife about anything other than politics. Honestly, she was waffling on about knitting patterns today. I know she means well and she's trying to fill the coffers but I'm not sure it's really helping the campaign.' He was pulling packets of chicken breast from the fridge now.

Another complete change of subject. Good. They were now two subject areas further away from moving house. She could return to the moment and fully engage with the conversation. Virginia, politics and knitting – couldn't be easier.

'Well, you know, darling, there's more than one way to skin a cat. She could speak to anyone, with authority, on renewables – you know that. But she also knows it's not the most scintillating topic for most folk. Gin knows how to make people feel comfortable. She might not have launched right in there on climate change but the people she did speak to will remember that they spoke to a lovely lady who helped them out with their knitting queries – and I'll bet she still managed to give them some campaign info. Might be more of a vote winner than you think.'

'Ha, yes. I hadn't thought of it like that. Imagine what a formidable team we'd be if you joined up as well.'

'Right, that's enough of that.' Annie dragged him off

to the lounge to drink coffee and eat bread before their dinner guest arrived. The moving house conversation was well and truly over.

Bang on seven, the doorbell rang.

'I'll get it.' James shouted. Annie was filling bowls with olives and crisps.

She heard the men's voices in the hall as she rushed through, all the while wiping her hands on the dishtowel. 'Ah, there you are.'

'Here I am, *ma soeur.*' Hugo walked over to his sister and hugged her, lifting her off her feet.

'Oh my. I think you're taller every time I see you. Don't you, James? Don't you think he's getting taller?' She could see James wink at her brother out the corner of her eye as she was dropped back down to the floor.

'Yes, an inch a week I reckon.'

'Right, that's enough. Come and tell me how you're getting on at uni.'

She slipped her arm through Hugo's and marched him into the lounge. As they sat round drinking the champagne James had bought to mark Hugo's arrival in Edinburgh, she couldn't help but study his features, watch every mannerism, listen for the inflections in his voice. He sat forward, leaning his arms on his knees and clasping his hands. His crisp white shirt accentuated the dark sheen of his hair and the olive smoothness of his skin. They might be brother and sister but Annie felt he belonged somewhere on the Mediterranean, in a fishing boat perhaps with the sun beating down on his head. But he wasn't and she was glad. He was in Edinburgh, poring over books in stuffy lecture rooms in cold concrete towers.

'It's good. There is a lot of reading to get through but I am fine with that.'

'And halls? Are you settling in okay there? Are you managing with the cooking and the laundry? Do they have washing machines?'

'Yes, yes, it's all good.' He smiled at her. 'Don't worry. You sound just like my mother, Annie.' And as he smiled she recognised traces of her father. The smile that encouraged, the smile that calmed, the smile that reassured.

'Oh dear, sorry, Hugo. How is your mother?'

'She's fine. She misses me, I know, but we have to grow up and move on. Both of us I think – with our lives.' His smile disappeared.

Céline had travelled over with Hugo when he arrived for freshers' week. Annie had thought she looked terribly gaunt and painfully thin. Her whole life had been devoted to this boy and the parting was clearly going to be a struggle. The night before Céline was due to go back the four of them had gone for a meal to the little French bistro along the road. Céline nervously pushed food round and round her plate, eating very little.

'Well, Annie. It is over to you now. You must take care of my boy now.'

Hugo looked across the table at his mother, his coal dark eyes blazing.

'*Maman, non.*'

Annie was shocked at the sharpness of his rebuke and she could see that James was too. She had known it wasn't going to be easy but suddenly the pleasant little dinner felt incredibly uncomfortable. Was it her fault? Should she have not been so encouraging to Hugo?

Céline's mouth began to quiver and Hugo's fierce gaze suddenly softened. He hung his head, reached out and took his mother's hand.

'*Je m'excuse, Maman. Je m'excuse.*'

Céline had lifted her hand, lifted her head and stroked her son's cheek. Now it was her turn to look fierce. Fiercely proud. '*Mon chéri.*'

Now here they were in Dean Terrace on a warm Saturday night. Annie, James and Hugo were tucking into a meal of stuffed mushrooms, chicken, salad and bread all washed down with Sancerre and Evian. They laughed at Hugo's tales of freshers' week and at his stumbling attempts to understand the more nuanced features of the Edinburgh dialect. They roared with laughter when he described an encounter with one of the university's canteen staff. The concerned woman had served Hugo more than his fair share of pasta as, in her words, he needed 'fattening up'. She explained that he would need to hurry along before her supervisor came back – someone she described as having '*a face that was aye oan the edge o' a battle*'. Hugo had required an immediate translation from a fellow student standing in the queue behind him and the expression had clearly now turned into a bit of a party piece for him. He screwed up his face and repeated the guttural Scots phrase in a warm French accent, which had the effect of making all of its harshness dissipate completely. He sounded both ridiculous and hilarious.

As the evening flew by, Annie considered what good company he was. He had her father's engaging qualities but there was more. He had a confidence about him. She wasn't sure where that came from – Presbyterian Scots didn't like to exude too much of the stuff. *Must be Céline*, she thought as she watched him talk politics with James. *She has brought him up to be a confident young man who has no qualms about stepping beyond his own borders and finding his way in the world. I hope she knows what a good job she's done*, Annie thought to herself.

'I was thinking.' Hugo's demeanour suddenly turned serious. 'Could I work for you, James? On the campaign, I mean? I think it could be good for my studies but perhaps also just for me. The Green Party in Switzerland is starting to make a mark – lots of factions but they are coming together now and starting to make some gains. I think I might be interested in joining them, maybe working for them when I go back.'

James beamed; firstly back at Hugo and then right round to Annie.

Oh Jeez, she thought. *Does everyone I know have a burning need to become politically engaged?* She summoned up a half-hearted smile.

'Well, that sounds wonderful. I'm sure he needs all the help he can get.'

That hadn't come out quite as intended and so she leant across to touch James's arm, hoping to assure him of her unstinting support. On the contrary, he just looked resigned to the fact that Annie might not be fully on board with his political ambitions.

'Well, you know what I mean.'

Hugo laughed, rescuing her from her *faux pas* and they carried on chatting through the rest of the evening – not just about politics, much to Annie's relief.

As the night wore on she found herself studying her

little brother more and more. He seemed so at ease in their company. How strange it was that just a few years ago, she couldn't possibly have contemplated making room for anyone else in her life and now here she was with two men she simply adored. Two men she simply couldn't contemplate living without. And just then it struck her that Hugo was planning to go home. Funny, it hadn't crossed her mind that he would want to go back. Not for good anyway.

*

It was the weekend before Thursday's election and all hands were on deck at Dean Terrace. There were leaflets, badges, rosettes, and envelopes ready for stuffing, placards ready for hoisting. Ludovic sat up on the windowsill looking down at the detritus the humans had tipped up and spread all over his lounge.

Annie politely declined all invitations to help. 'Oh, you don't need me. I'll just get in the way.' James and Jack stood in the hall engaged in an earnest discussion, Virginia and Gordon were tying bits of string to various bits of green cardboard and Hugo had started stuffing envelopes. There was green everywhere, bombarding her senses. She would happily never look at anything green again. Cutting the grass might even set off an adverse reaction.

She headed off to the bedroom to pack a bag having decided to escape to Drummond House for the weekend. The final straw had really come the previous evening as James and Hugo endeavoured to explain proportional representation and transferable voting systems to her. It wasn't anything to do with a lack of comprehension – she understood perfectly what they were telling her but it was beyond tedious. She had been sitting opposite them both, desperately trying to keep her eyelids from crashing shut. Inside she was straining and sweating to hold up the leaden covers until suddenly – boom.

'Are we boring you?' James asked the obvious question. Hugo just looked disappointed.

'No, no. Well, I suppose – yes.' They were prised open now. 'Look, it's great that all that stuff interests you both. Honestly. It's just not my thing.'

She reached out to hold each of their hands and tried to look lovingly at both of them. 'Spoke to Kirsty last night and think I'm going to pop up there at the weekend. Get out of your hair. Why don't you both come up Sunday? Give yourselves a break.'

'Final push, darling. Really can't spare the time.' They both looked earnestly at her.

'Okay.' *All fine*, she thought. *They can have the run of Election Central and I'll go and put my feet up and knock back the gin.*

CHAPTER 15

Annie made good time and by lunchtime was driving up the sweeping driveway to the front of Drummond House. Kirsty had made every effort to soften the stark facade of the gothic mansion with pale pink China rose bushes sweeping over the walls either side of the imposing doorway. A forest of deep pink fuchsias grew at one end of the sheltered border that ran the length of the house while a mass of lavender filled the opposite corner. Marigolds and pansies filled bright blue and terracotta pots, carefully protecting them through the vagaries of a Scottish spring. The scene was filled with colour. It was a welcome sanctuary, made all the more so by the appearance of Kirsty at the front door, grinning widely, arms outstretched.

'Welcome, welcome,' she screeched as she ran out, smothering Annie just as she was about to open up the boot.

'Great to be here, Kirst.' Annie managed to get the words out while clasped to Kirsty's bosom.

'Oh, darling. So lovely that you can spend some time here. It feels like an age since you've been up.' Kirsty grabbed the bags from the boot and marched off. Annie trailed in her wake struggling to pick up what her hostess was saying. There was something about an election-free zone and Johnny being a difficult little shit which left her struggling to frame an adequate response.

'Oh dear, what's the problem?' She wasn't sure she really wanted to know but thought it best to appear interested.

They had marched through the cavernous hall to the kitchen at the back of the house. It still looked like something from the Victorian era, all pale green and cream tiles with a massive range at one end. It looked Victorian but it was state-of-the-art Aga. Kirsty was already reaching up into the cupboard for the gin.

'Could you cut some lemon, darling? It's his name, that's the problem.'

'Johnny, what's wrong with Johnny?'

'Well, they've all started to give each other nicknames at that overpriced school we've sent him to and the other little monsters have decided Johnny's nickname should be "Beef". First Torito, now Beef for God's sake.'

'Beef?' Annie couldn't help but smile.

'I know. Outrageous, isn't it? But that's not the worst part. The worst part is that my little angel has decided he likes the name and is determined not to answer to anything else. Thinks Beef Drummond is like some sort of comic book hero. It's bloody ridiculous. And of course Duncan doesn't help. Thinks it's not a bad name for a future Scotland prop forward.'

And just then, Annie heard the thundering footsteps of the boy they called 'Beef'. As he rushed into the kitchen she thought how much like Hugo he was at that age. She held her arms out and he rushed into them clattering against her pelvis. *Thank God for pilates*, she thought to herself, as she winced slightly.

'Hello darling. It's been ages since I've seen you.' She lifted up his chin to get a good look at him. He was a miniature Duncan for sure – all round and red faced.

'Come into the garden, Annie. I've got a tree house.' She smiled down at him, kissing the slightly damp top of his head. He was all boy smells now; all traces of soft toddler aromas had gone.

'Later, Johnny. Annie's just arrived. Give her some space.'

'It's *Beef*, Mummy, I've told you.' And with that he marched back out again.

'Right. Let's take these out into the garden. You can view the tree house from afar.'

They sat out on two large recliners and Kirsty told Annie about the latest house improvements and new ideas for landscaping at the front of the house. The future of the planet didn't feature at all – just the future of a little corner of Perthshire. Annie listened to it all while watching Johnny clamber up the ladder, scramble through the tree house and fling himself down the chute at the other side. He was on a loop, performing an endless number of circuits, the off button clearly broken.

'Right, Johnny, that's enough. You're going to make yourself sick.'

And then suddenly Duncan's booming voice erupted just to the side of Annie.

'Right, Beef, you heard what your mother said. Down now.'

Thrilled that his father had acknowledged the name

change with no fuss whatsoever, the little boy shot down the chute for the last time. Annie hadn't heard Duncan arrive but she turned to see him standing in his cricket whites, blocking out the sun. He came over and planted a kiss on Annie's right cheek and then moved round to his wife.

Annie could see that Kirsty wasn't best pleased with his intervention but she seemed to decide against opening up the argument there and then.

'So how's things, Annie?' Duncan asked the question as he rushed towards his son, grabbing him under the arms and lifting him high above his head. Johnny squealed with delight.

Annie talked about work for a while, just how stressful the last few weeks had been, but she wasn't really in the mood. The excitement of the buy-out was over and reality was sinking in. They were going to be bigger. Lots of new, thrusting young go-getters would be rushing around, setting up conference calls, holding debriefs and, worst of all, they were going to have to cohabit and move to bigger premises. Probably to some glass-panelled, soulless space, which inevitably meant a move out of the New Town. She hadn't thought through the practical outcomes while she had been immersed in balance sheets and business projections. A move; another move. Why couldn't everybody just stay still?

And then, just as she was beginning to relax into her full-strength gin haze, she couldn't help feeling just a little bit out of things. James was always in her thoughts somewhere and today he was more front brain than back. Annie wondered if she should really have stayed and helped, worried that he might think she wasn't interested in his success. When all the time she was, she really was.

'What's wrong, Annie? You look miles away.' Annie had lost the last few minutes of a discourse on cleaning out the dahlia borders.

'Oh sorry, Kirst, just feeling a bit guilty, sitting here relaxing and they're all out trying to get James elected.'

Kirsty swept her hair back with one hand, pulled it until it stretched the skin from her face and completed the manoeuvre by twisting a band round the mass of hair gathered at the back of her head. She meant business but what kind, Annie couldn't be too sure about. 'Nonsense. You hate politics and anyway, nothing wrong with a bit of downtime. You work bloody hard too – deserve a bit of a break.'

'Yes, well. You know, I don't think I *do* hate politics. Not exactly. Don't get me wrong, I can't be bothered with all the campaigning and stuff. To be honest I'm too scared to knock on other people's doors and I really can't summon up any enthusiasm to stuff leaflets into envelopes – all of that really turns me off. But I think just being with James, understanding him better – it just doesn't all seem so meaningless anymore. I've gone along to a couple of meetings to show willing and when I've heard him – and others, for that matter – speak, well, I think it's really about how we live, the kind of society we want to live in and I guess kind of taking a stand. It's not all about crofting or Virginia banging on about climate change. It's no *one* thing. I mean, I'm not sure about political parties and I'm not sure James is either. But if you want to do something, if you're serious about making a difference you have to have a go at trying to change things, somehow. Don't you think?'

Her own strength of feeling surprised her and she took a moment to compose herself. 'Anyway, I'll head back first thing and see if there's anything I can do to help.'

Kirsty sat back looking as though she was trying her damnedest to process everything she'd just heard.

Duncan leant forward. 'You're right, Annie. You have to try. Everyone has to feel like they belong, that they have rights, that they can do something to make things better. Working with James has shown me that. And I guess we have to vote to, well, as you say, to at least try to make a difference.' His round ruddy face broke into a wide smile and Annie couldn't help but smile right back at him.

Later that evening, after the three friends had polished off a lovely pheasant stew, the illusion of Drummond House as an election-free zone had all but completely evaporated. They were sitting in the massive wood-panelled lounge, a room that brought Annie right back to her suite of Agatha Christie metaphors borne out of her very first visit to Drummond House.

'What actually happens Thursday? Are we having some sort of party?' Duncan was obviously keen to exploit the potential for the democratic process to throw up huge amounts of revelry.

'Well, I'm going to be at the count with James until late. Why don't you both come along if you can make it?' The absolute certainty that she had to be by his side came as a bit of a shock. She hadn't really been sure about what part, if any, she should play in all of this but now she knew.

'Don't we need to be certified or something?' Duncan

was sitting cross-legged in his Chesterfield armchair, large tumbler in hand.

'Yes. I think he needs to get passes for us but if I phone now I'm sure it can all be arranged.'

'What d'you think, Kirst. Shall we park the boy with the olds and shoot down there?'

Kirsty thought for a moment then leaned forward, looking dubiously at them both. 'Not exactly my idea of a grand night out but if you think it might *help*?'

Annie smiled. She couldn't imagine any circumstances, win or lose, where Kirsty and Duncan's presence would, actually, in any material sense, help. But then they were prepared to trail down midweek to suffer the tedium of an election count with no realistic prospect of a Drummond-style social event at the end of it. There would be an awful lot of hanging about and their presence alone might help move the evening along – but more importantly, it would pour just a little bit more cement into their rapidly solidifying friendship with James. *So that's all good*, she thought. And then came the cold sweats. *As long as they behave themselves.*

*

'Oh, Annie, that's a lovely thought, darling, but they probably won't get round to announcing the successful candidates from the list until the following morning. Maybe not till seven or eight. No point dragging the Drummonds down and you'd be out on your feet. No really, I couldn't ask you to do that – what with work the next day.'

She was crestfallen. James's supporting and hopefully victorious troops had been slain before they could even get anywhere near the gates of the citadel.

'Oh, but I so wanted to be there to see your victory. This is an important time for you.' She picked up a green rosette, pouted and started to pull the ribbons apart.

'Careful, darling. We haven't got too many of these left. Being a bit too presumptuous about my victory, aren't you?' He walked across the lounge and put a comforting arm round her. 'Why not invite the Drummonds down anyway? We'll have a lovely supper before I go off to the count. They can stay here and then I'll be back in the morning to let you all know how it went – one way or another.'

'Okay.' She almost said something about how ridiculous it was that the results weren't going to be in before midnight but then the spectre of another lecture on voting systems loomed large. She duly surrendered and nestled back into his warm neck.

It was just like the old times. Annie and James, Kirsty and Duncan, Virginia and Gordon. Hugo was at Jack's – phoning round to make sure supporters, already pledged to the cause, had actually made the journey to the polling station to cast their vote. The six friends sat round after a meal of roast chicken and salad and talked about everything other than the election. Annie surveyed the scene with an air of quiet satisfaction.

Virginia was sitting on Gordon's knee, one hand pulling at his Fair Isle tank top, the other running through his mop of still black hair. Slowly her head descended to rest on his. The line of grey down her centre parting had, over the years, spread out, now engulfing every tightly sprung curl. It was a stark contrast – the unruly grey frizz set against the thick black mop. Gordon shifted uncomfortably in his seat as her hand strayed towards the only piece of flesh on view; two buttons were open at the neck of his shirt and her fingers were getting closer. He smiled albeit a slightly embarrassed smile. Virginia was just a little bit drunk and Gordon clearly wasn't used to this much manhandling in public.

Annie's gaze wandered round to Duncan who was sitting upright and still chatting to everyone at least an hour after they'd finished supper. How times had changed.

Suddenly Kirsty burst forth. 'Are you sure we can't come with, James? I would love to see how it all happens. Do you think there are any shenanigans? I mean there must be a few backhanders going the rounds, don't you think? *"I'll make it worth your while just to lose some votes"* – that kind of thing?'

Annie couldn't tell if she was joking or not while James just looked incredulous.

'It's not Zimbabwe, Kirsty, or Capone's Chicago for that matter. I don't *think* there'll be a big Mafia presence at Meadowbank Sports Centre but you never know. So no, it really will go on all night and I couldn't get everyone in now anyway. All will be clear soon enough.'

Gordon hadn't been drinking and as he held the lofty position of election agent, had taken on the job of driving James to the count. Virginia would be dropped off on the way and no doubt told to get straight to bed with a large glass of water and a couple of ibuprofen. Duncan and Kirsty were going to 'crash at the bolthole' so no need for Annie to make up the spare room.

Before she knew it she was alone. After filling the dishwasher and watching some Westminster political grandees droning on during Scottish Election Special for half an hour, she heaved herself off to bed. Having probably had a couple of glasses more than usual, she quickly fell asleep.

Annie slept like a log and woke at seven. *Bloody hell*, she thought. *Forgot to set the alarm.* After showering and quickly switching on radio and television she dashed between bathroom, bedroom and kitchen trying to pick up snippets of election news as she moved. Something about biggest party, possible coalitions but what about the bloody Greens?

She was standing in the kitchen in bra, pants and pop socks. Her hair, still wet and uncombed, resembled a deserted birds' nest. She was in completely the wrong place. The competing noise from television in the lounge and radio in the bedroom meant she really couldn't hear anything clearly but her immediate need for a quick reviving breakfast had trumped election results. As a consequence, she didn't hear James's key turn in the door and it was this dishevelled sight that greeted him as he walked in. With a mug of coffee in one hand and marmalade-laden toast in the other, Annie stared at him, trying desperately to swallow a large lump of soggy brown bread and gauge his mood, triumphant or otherwise. He wasn't speaking, why wasn't he speaking? And then his eyes softened and he smiled gently.

'So, does your local Member of the Scottish Parliament get a "well done" kiss?'

Annie let out a short sharp yelp, spilled some coffee and wiped toast crumbs from her mouth with the back of her hand.

'Really? Oh absolutely. Well done *you*, James. Really – well done *you*.' As she moved towards him arms outstretched she suddenly realised how ridiculous she must look.

'Good God, look at the state of me.' She looked down at her black nylon socks and felt the tangled mess sitting on top of her head.

'You look just lovely.' And then he kissed her, marmalade residue and all. They started to move in unison towards the bedroom and then just as they got to the foot of the bed, the doorbell rang.

'We could pretend we're not here,' she whispered.

James nodded in agreement and resumed his passionate kissing, pulling at her bra straps. Then suddenly he pulled himself away.

'Ah, wait a minute. Might be something to do with the count. Maybe there's paperwork I forgot to sign or maybe there's something wrong, with the result, I mean.' Flames of desire had been quickly doused. He shook his trousers in an attempt to rearrange and settle the contents and made his way to the front door.

'Bloody hell, James.' After Annie's own ardour had quickly been extinguished, her immediate thought was that this was not the state in which anyone from officialdom should find the partner of a recently elected politician. She ran out and locked herself in the bathroom.

She was trying to untangle her hair when she heard voices at the front door, barely audible at first and now getting louder. She took her towelling robe from behind the door and went out to join them. It was as she had thought. Kirsty and Duncan, Virginia and Gordon, Hugo

250

and Jack. The girls were showering her man in kisses and the men were slapping him and each other on the back. Annie joined the melee just as Duncan produced a bottle of champagne and carton of orange juice. 'Bucks fizz all round?'

'Well, lovely people, some of us have to get to work so I'll pass, thank you.' Annie briefly joined in the kissing and hugging and then quickly extricated herself to finish off her morning prep. She wasn't sure anybody had noticed until, just as she picked up her briefcase and headed for the door, James was suddenly at her side.

'Sorry about all this, darling. They've all got a bit over excited.'

Alcohol and citrus gave him a little rosy glow but he looked tired. Happy but tired. It was his turn to burrow down into her neck.

'It'll just be us tonight – finally.'

Her walk up Gloucester Lane to the offices of Saunders and MacKay was brisk. She couldn't help but feel elated at James's success, and the adrenaline rush that accompanied his news was propelling her up the grey cobbled lane, through the higgledy-piggledy arrangement of mews properties on either side.

She had a nine o'clock with Bryce and had only just made it in time. Simon was waiting to give her a brief 'state of mind' update. It helped Annie no end to understand Bryce's frame of mind before any meeting and this was just another unique, if quirky, little role undertaken by the indispensable Simon.

'Not himself at all today. Not angry or anything, just not himself. Looks like he'd rather be anywhere rather than here right now.' Simon handed her a plastic cup of insipid dark brown liquid. 'Here's your coffee. Hope you can fathom him out.'

He gave her a kind of good luck look and ambled back to his desk. *Not like Bryce, not like him at all*, Annie thought. *He's always so focused*.

She knocked gently and waited for him to invite her in.

'Come in.' He sounded weary, reinforcing Simon's assessment. 'Aah, Annie. Of course. We've got a meeting, haven't we?'

She sat down opposite the large mahogany desk and watched Bryce pull out a number of the drawers on either side and swiftly close them again. Clearly unable to find what he was looking for, he looked up at her and smiled.

'Yes, I've brought my briefing notes. Normal Friday run-through of where we are on key cases?' She looked for some sign of recognition.

'Ah yes, of course. But before we begin I just wanted to speak to you about something.' He cleared his throat noisily before going on.

'We have a couple of options for new premises that I'm going to put to a full meeting of the partners. My recommendation will be Lyon House on Queensferry Road. It's a purpose-built office block, as I'm sure you know, and it can accommodate everyone.'

Bryce looked blankly at her as Annie considered the implication of his words. Neither he nor Annie had worked anywhere other than Moray Place. They would be leaving the grand stone edifice with its cracked ceilings and flaking plaster, unable to cling onto the cornice's ornate carvings. They too could cling on no longer – the open-plan glass box awaited.

'It'll be stifling in the summer – all that glass.' It was an inadequate response but it was all she could muster.

'And the other thing is – I won't be going. I'm going to retire, Annie. It wouldn't be me. I know that and so there's no point trying to lever myself into something that's just not going to feel comfortable. It's a young person's game now. Settlements over lunch are a thing of the past. You could beat someone hands down in the courtroom and a couple of hours later you'd be sitting down to dinner. It was the people I knew, the friendships forged. That kind of thing is gone – and I need to go with it.'

He spoke crisply and curtly but at the same time she thought he looked terribly sad, as though he'd lost someone very dear to him.

'Oh, Bryce. I can't imagine this place without you. You *are* Saunders and MacKay. Can't you just give it a go? It might not be all that bad.' She knew she sounded less than convincing.

He pulled himself up, clasped his hands and set them resolutely on the desk in front of him. The old Bryce was back.

'No, Annie. I've made up my mind.'

Change again, Annie thought. *So much change.*

CHAPTER 16

Over the next few years life seemed to settle down; everyone seemed to stay in the same place and finally take root – everyone that was apart from Hugo. After he had finished his studies, during which time he had worked part time as a researcher for James, he headed back to his homeland before settling in Brussels to work on climate change policy. Much to Annie's delight he had not returned alone. At university Hugo had met a pretty young girl from Glasgow, of Italian heritage, named Sofia, and they were now engaged to be married. She was small in stature, of slim build with long dark hair and huge brown eyes. Annie could see more than a faint resemblance to his mother but James dismissed such notions.

'That's just creepy.' He was listening to Annie, settled into his familiar spot on the sofa, hands clasped and eyes shut.

'Oh, I don't think so. I think it happens a lot.' Annie was reading through case notes for a tribunal hearing the following day. A senior council official's office had been found to contain large quantities of sex toys, pornographic videos and numerous copies of a magazine entitled *Spank*. Annie moved the conversation on by trying to talk to

James about spanking but he claimed not to understand the attraction.

'Must be something. Is it power, dominance or is it just a bum thing?'

'I'm sorry, darling, I really have no idea. It's not something I've ever really thought about.'

'Mmm. Wonder if any of the others might know.' She put her papers down and lifted her glasses up to rest on her head. 'Shall we invite everyone round Saturday or pop up to see the Drummonds?'

'Not if we're going to spend the evening talking about weird sexual fetishes.'

'No, of course not. Just thought it would be nice.' Annie shrugged her shoulders and let out a resigned sigh. Despite the exotic nature of the case she had in front of her, Annie was bored at work and the accompanying negativity was spilling over into home life. Bryce's encouragement to apply for the role of managing partner had failed to persuade her; she knew intrinsically that it wasn't the right fit. Reluctantly she had to admit to herself that she just didn't want the responsibility and was sensible enough to recognise her limitations, or at least that's what she told everybody. The ensuing barrage of objections from friends and colleagues fell on deaf ears. As a result she was, in Simon's words, 'back on the tools' and working for, again in Simon's words, 'a complete tosser' called Logan. It had occurred to her that there must be smart, well-adjusted, kind men who just happened to have a surname for a first name – Annie just hadn't met one yet. She was also acutely aware that she was in danger of joining Kirsty in her condemnation of all such accursed creatures.

The phone rang, jolting her from her moment of introspection. It was Virginia.

'Hello, darling. Just wanted to say Gordon and I are simply overwhelmed at getting the invite. He's such a lovely boy and never in a month of Sundays did we expect this.'

Silence.

'Annie? Are you there?'

Annie was trying to piece together the bits but there were just too many imponderables.

'Sorry, Gin. Invite to what?'

'Hugo's wedding of course.'

Annie was more than a little stunned by the news. Obviously brother and sister had spoken about a wedding – sometime in the future, possibly next year – but she had no idea that firm plans had been made.

'Right, of course, of course. Well, it will be lovely and hopefully the date works for you.'

'Oh yes, don't worry about that. How are we all going to get there though? Kirsty got her invite this morning too and of course they're all excited, as you can imagine.'

'Oh yes, yes. I can imagine. Look, let me just chat to James and we'll see what we're going to do about the travel thing.'

'Oh great, great. I'll just leave it with you. And, Annie?'

'Yes?'

'We *really* are thrilled to be invited.'

'Well, of course you'd be invited. He loves you both.'

'What was that all about?' James was sitting upright, clearly alerted to the note of consternation in Annie's voice and the confused look on her face.

'Hugo's wedding.' She moved slowly to sit back down by his side, mulling over the slightly one-sided conversation.

'Really? When?'

'No idea.'

'Where?'

'Nope. Still no idea.'

The look of consternation slipped seamlessly across to James. 'He seriously hasn't spoken to you about this?'

Annie knew there must be some misunderstanding. Hugo couldn't possibly not invite his own sister to his wedding.

Just as they were discussing ringing him up to clarify, the phone rang. It was Hugo.

'Annie. Have you got an invitation?'

'No, no invitation. But Kirsty and Virginia have theirs.' She tried to sound unfazed by the whole thing.

'Oh God. I am sorry. They were supposed to go out next week but Sofia picked up a few from my desk by mistake and sent them. I'm so sorry. Of course I wanted to discuss with you.'

Tension eased. 'You don't have to discuss anything with me, Hugo, it's your wedding. I'm just happy you've sorted things. So when and where exactly?'

'Well, it's 5th May next year at Craigachie House.'

'Craigachie House, really?' The House was on the Assynt Estate, not that far from the cottage that now belonged to Annie and James, and had recently been restored to something like its former glory.

'Well, we thought about all sorts of venues, countries even, but Assynt means so much to you and James and I think without that, well, I'm not sure I would have found

257

my path in life, my passion. In fact I probably wouldn't have met Sofia.'

He spoke to her in his clipped French accent tinged with Scots from far across the continent. 'It's really because of you two that I've got my career and, I guess, the love of my life. Somehow it feels like it all started there – in Assynt, I mean.'

From far across the continent, he'd never felt closer.

'And, Annie?'

'Yes?'

'I want to ask James to be my best man. Do you think he would be okay with that? Can you hear me? It's not the best connection.'

Now she was choking back the tears. 'I'm sure he would. Let me pass you on to him.' She passed the phone, absolutely sure about the connection.

*

It was a beautiful, simple wedding. The ceremony took place in a light and airy room that had all the hallmarks of a Robert Adams neo-classical interior design project. Pale pastel colours and ornate plasterwork. Alcoves filled with busts of Greek gods and charioteers racing round the ceiling. Annie and her cohort were among the first to arrive; she was without James who had already headed off to meet up with Hugo and so it was Duncan, puffing out his chest and straining to get free of his tartan cummerbund, who proudly escorted her in with Kirsty at his other side. They entered ahead of assorted Scottish, Swiss and Italian guests and suddenly a kaleidoscope of deep reds, greens and blues had shattered the pristine formality of the room. The bride and groom had requested that guests wear something tartan, anything at all, from a mere notion of tartan plaid to full Highland dress. And what an assortment it was: kilts and trews, skirts and sashes. The Highland hordes had descended and the pale Wedgwood tones and white plaster mouldings shrank back into the walls in fright.

Hugo looked dashing. His sleek black hair had grown and was swept back from his face. He had chosen not to wear a jacket but stood proudly next to Sofia in a crisp white shirt and kilt while James, with a nod to formality, was wearing his green Lovat tweed jacket, setting off his tartan perfectly. Annie was sure she'd never seen him look so handsome. Drummond, Anderson, Kerr and other assorted shades and patterns of plaid mingled, swirled and clashed. It was a magnificent sight.

The general din began to subside to allow the ceremony to begin. Annie glanced across to the other side of the room to see the elegantly pristine figure of Céline. She stood perfectly still; quiet and still, wearing a pale pink Chanel suit and matching pillbox hat. White gloves and sharp stilettos completed the mother of the groom ensemble. There was no tartan here. She suddenly turned, smiled and waved and Annie could see she was pressing a small cotton handkerchief with her thumb, hard into the palm of her hand. Annie smiled and waved back – and then suddenly she saw it pinned to the left side of Céline's Parisian creation. A small ribbon of Anderson tartan. Annie blinked back the tiny tear that had filled the corner of her eye, sure that Céline had done likewise.

After the ceremony and reception, Céline was heading back to Edinburgh with family members for some mandatory sightseeing. The happy couple were spending a few days at Annie and James's cottage before spending the rest of their honeymoon in Italy and the New Town friends were heading back to Drummond House for a few days. Annie had overheard James giving Hugo instructions on setting the fire, hot water controls, location of various keys and what could be found in the makeshift garage that he might find useful. Annie smiled. She had left detailed instructions on the table in the lounge and had stocked the kitchen with enough provisions to make their stay more than comfortable. It hadn't occurred to her that there might be something in that garage remotely useful to a couple on their honeymoon but, then again, James knew best. Best man after all.

Duncan's brother Lachlan had brought a small minibus from one of the estates Drummond Enterprises was now managing and they all stumbled in with their assorted cases and shopping bags filled with provisions for a long weekend. Beef, who was now playing rugby for Scotland Schoolboys, plonked himself down opposite Annie. He was only thirteen but he was starting to develop a muscular physique even at that tender age. His round face was covered in freckles and his teeth gleamed at Annie as he regaled her with tales from the playing fields of Perthshire. He was such a gregarious little lad, full of energy and zest for life. She knew it was unlikely to last through adolescence but she enjoyed his vim and vigour for now. Soon he would enter the dark teenage tunnel and so best to appreciate him now.

They were exhausted but still laughing at Duncan's exuberant approach to Scottish country dancing. They were all completely satiated with good Highland fare but, despite numerous protestations, Kirsty and Virginia quickly whipped up some serious doorstopper sandwiches and heated a mountain of sausage rolls in the Aga.

The detritus from Hugo's wedding was spread across the Drummonds' sprawling lounge – tweed and tartan accessories, ties and sashes, wilting buttonholes were all cast aside on tables or draped over the back of chairs. Annie sat with her head on James's shoulder and looked across at Gordon. He was lying flat out, his head in Virginia's lap, one arm outstretched with his hand round a tumbler of malt. His eyes were closed and he was smiling, a strange little crooked smile.

'He doesn't really drink whisky,' Virginia whispered loudly over his head while wrenching the glass from his hand. Duncan had poured out a few good measures of Dalwhinnie for the company and the effects were starting to show. Annie could hardly keep her eyes open.

'My shoulder's still aching, darling. Just about ripped the thing from its socket. And that poor little woman – Céline's sister, I think. She looked positively terrified at Strip the Willow, every time you thundered towards her.' Kirsty was wedged under Duncan's arm and resting her drink on his paunch.

'Well, you shouldn't get up for a fling if you're not prepared to throw yourself into it, I say,' Duncan's dark red cheeks a testament to his physical exertions and overconsumption of the water of life.

Annie wearily lifted her head. 'Right, that's me. I'm off.

Too old for all day celebrations.' She kissed James on the forehead. 'Coming?'

He stretched his arms up behind his shoulders. 'Yup. We've got a mountain to climb tomorrow.'

'You've got a what?'

'The boys are climbing Schiehallion tomorrow,' Duncan boomed.

'Well, climbing is a bit of an exaggeration. It's a pretty well-worn path to the summit. Done it lots of times when I was a lad.' James smiled at her.

'Yes, but look at you all. You're hardly lads now and Gordon looks as though he might struggle to climb into bed never mind a Munro.'

Duncan unceremoniously prised Kirsty from under his arm and staggered towards Gordon. 'Come on, Gordy, look lively. Up early tomorrow to go Munro bagging.' The poor man, rudely roused from his torpor, looked round to see where he was and then fell back into the folds of Virginia's long tartan skirt.

'Oh God, really?' He sounded none too enthused at the prospect.

The next morning, fortified by one of Duncan's legendary fry-ups, the three men stood in the hallway, a tired and slightly bedraggled sight. They wore an assortment of outdoor gear, some of which looked as though it might have survived the Everest expedition with Hillary, while other highly coloured and very shiny pieces of apparel shouted out their newness. Most of James's outfit, courtesy of Helen, fell somewhere in between, although the sheen was coming off some of the more well-worn items. Suddenly the massive front door swung

262

open and there stood Lachlan, looking like Action Man. Annie's view of the expedition had softened slightly once she knew that the athletic and very capable Lachlan was accompanying the motley crew.

'Right, guys, let's go.' Lachlan picked up their rucksacks and headed back out as quickly as he'd come in.

'How long will you be?' Annie looked into James's pale blue eyes and noticed a dullness to them now, their shine tarnished by a day and night of excess. He pulled her into his chest and kissed the top of her head.

'Should be about four hours up and down. See you about teatime.' His lips brushed across the top of her head.

She moved back from him but kept her arms round his waist. He smiled at her and his eyes shone again, just for a moment.

*

At first there were multiple layers of noise. Incessant and varied. Small quiet sobs to loud cries of anguish and everything else in between. Somebody sounded very officious. He was in bright yellow and was talking at her but he was blinding her with his bright yellow. He needed to stand back, far away from her. Some were sitting, others standing right in front of her, beckoning her to sit down. She tried to shut them out but they just wouldn't stop. At the boulder fields near the summit someone was saying. No warning. Crumpled to the ground. Crumpled. She remembered that was how he looked when she first saw him. Crumpled. But then his face, his smile and his eyes, his beautiful eyes. She wanted them all to be quiet so she could just sit down and see him in front of her; the blueness of his eyes. They made so much noise she couldn't hear him. Why wouldn't they be quiet so she could just hear him? Or just stand back, just a bit so she could see him. The blueness of his eyes. His beautiful eyes.

It was Virginia's arm that went round her shoulders. She was starting to shiver and her friend's gesture momentarily made her stop. She stood rigid, unwilling to let herself fall into the comfort of her friends. Someone talked about driving Annie to the hospital. Couldn't be Duncan, he was a mess. Couldn't be Gordon, he was sitting with his head buried in his hands. Kirsty was on the floor crying, retching. Maybe it was Lachlan or was it the policeman? She really didn't know. She just wanted them all to go away. He wasn't there so why drive all the way to the hospital? If they just all went away, taking their crying and loud talking with them, it would be quiet enough. Then he would see her and come back. She knew he would.

*

Finally she answered her phone. It had droned on long enough. Kirsty and Virginia were coming round whether she wanted them to or not and it was probably time to let them in.

Annie had endured the last few weeks in a daze. Céline, Hugo and Sofia had all been there, her brother far more traumatised than she had thought possible. Duncan and Gordon pored over every step of the trek up the hill desperately looking for any sign that they may have missed. It was agony to watch them but nothing she nor

264

Kirsty nor Virginia could say stopped them dissecting and analysing those last few hours. It was nobody's fault. Not theirs, not the hill's. An undetected heart abnormality was the cold clinical explanation. Could have happened with anyone beside him or with no one beside him and at any time in his life.

Heart abnormality. There was nothing abnormal about his heart. Nothing at all.

Everyone rallied round to help her arrange the funeral. A funeral that seemed to belong to someone else, not to her, not to James. There were so many people she didn't know from the worlds of government, publishing and even the crofting communities that he had worked with or spent time with while researching his book. The closed little world that she inhabited with James took up no more than a couple of pews. She knew that hundreds of strange pairs of eyes were trained upon her but her little protective band insulated her from their stares.

In the days afterwards she felt a strange compunction to pull everything out of cupboards, away from walls, out of drawers. Anything that belonged to him, which might smell of him, that might just bring back the sense of him. This was the sight that greeted her friends when they finally gained access to the world she desperately wanted to protect. They said nothing but huddled together on the floor of the lounge and cried unremitting tears. The release was overdue and it left her exhausted and drained. After an age, Virginia heaved herself up and off to the kitchen to make tea.

'Why don't you come with me – today? We can pack a bag and you can come up to Drummond House for a few days. Just to be with people.'

Annie looked at Kirsty's tear-stained face and managed a faint smile but couldn't speak.

'We just don't think it's terribly good for you. Being here, I mean. Some time away and you might feel stronger, more able to deal with all of this.' Kirsty looked at the piles all around covering the floor, the sofa, the tabletops, and then took Annie's hand in hers.

'I can't really, Kirst. Sorry. There's Ludovic and he's so old now – I'm sorry, I just couldn't leave him.'

These were the words but it wasn't what she meant. Not really. How could they ask her to leave? He wouldn't know where to find her. Just when he needed her most, he wouldn't be able to find her. His pain, his agony, made all the worse because she wasn't there. How could she make him suffer like that? How could her friends imagine for a second that she could do that to him?

Kirsty and Virginia left defeated but undeterred. They continued to watch over Annie, hovering on the periphery of her sadness. They waited, kindly, benignly in the wings. There were no grand gestures, no more offers to take her away or move in with her for a period. It was almost as if they knew to wait until she was ready to re-join the world.

She wasn't sure when the transition happened. It took its own time but gradually the solid weight of her sadness began to shift and the desperate need to keep things as they were began to dissipate. She began to think more clearly. A plan was needed, a new course to be charted, but one she would need to steer alone. This time there was no one to help take the tiller. Thoughts began to crystallise, decisions began to take shape.

CHAPTER 17

She chose the cream silk blouse with the tie bow at the front and the black Austin Reed suit with the thin pinstripe. Makeup was carefully applied and her nails painted with her favourite Chanel taupe enamel.

She walked up the sweeping Georgian thoroughfare of Circus Place to the offices of Evergreen in Howe Street. Her appointment was at 2pm and she arrived with one minute to spare. As she opened the pale green outer door into the small vestibule she could see the portly figure of Jack Chalmers through the frosted glass talking to someone, a man perhaps, sitting behind a desk. He turned as she walked in, took one giant step towards her and gave her an almighty bear hug.

'Oh, Annie. It's lovely to see you. How are you?' He let her loose from his embrace and stood holding her hands.

'Well, I don't really know how I am, Jack, not really, but I am starting to think about things now. About trying to move forward.' Even as she said the words, it happened again. The sheer pain of it all ripped through her and she had to stop talking to catch her breath.

'I still can't believe it, my dear. None of us can. Murray

267

here was working with James on final revisions to his book and, well, we're all just devastated.'

She looked round at the young man behind the desk who sat looking up at her with great brown eyes filled with tears. He stood up, walked round the desk and offered his hand in greeting.

'I'm so sorry, Miss Anderson, really sorry. He was a fine man. Inspirational really and I learnt so much from him. We were so close, so close to finishing his book.' He looked down at the floor, his mop of brown hair falling over his eyes.

Annie held on to his hand tightly. 'Thank you, Murray, thank you for that. And please call me Annie.' He looked up at her, blinked a tear and smiled.

Well, there you go. Surnames for first names wasn't such a bad concept after all.

She sat in Jack's office holding a mug of coffee, looking all around her. Books, papers, files covered every surface.

'So, Annie. What can we do for you? As I said on the phone, door's always open if you need anything, you know that.'

'Yes, Jack, thanks. I do. But actually I was wondering if I might be able to do something for you. You see I've resigned from Saunders and MacKay. I hadn't really been happy there for some time – even before James.' Her voice trailed off as she spoke his name, the piercing pain quick to return. Once more she took a deep breath. 'You see, the thing is, I know what makes a business profitable and I know, well, we talked, James and I, about how much Evergreen was struggling just to stay afloat. And then there's the book of course. I would really like to work with you, or perhaps Murray now, to see it finalised and get it published.'

Jack's grey bushy eyebrows raised up as he pursed his lips. Annie couldn't be sure what was about to come next.

'Well, that's grand, Annie, but really I have nothing of any kind of a salaried nature to offer. After James was elected he forewent his salary here, so we could just about stay in business.'

She put down her coffee mug and clasped her hands tightly. 'I know, Jack, but James made me the sole beneficiary of his estate. I'm selling his flat in Great King Street and there's other money, inherited money from his father, that I can invest. If it really doesn't work out I'll go back to plying my trade as a lawyer but I really want to do this and I think I can really make a difference. I know how much Evergreen means to you and how much it meant to James.'

She couldn't remember feeling this sure or confident about anything before in her life and she knew Jack wouldn't be able to resist her offer. They reached an agreement in principle, with Annie promising to submit a more detailed proposal in the next couple of weeks.

The following week she gathered her friends round to Dean Terrace. They were a sombre little band but they managed a few smiles and the odd laugh at Kirsty's tales of 'infiltrating' the local branch of the WI.

'I'm trying to steer them away from the whole jam and chutney thing and get them to focus on what really matters to rural communities. I mean, our little village is suffering death by a thousand cuts. Shops closing down, young people moving away. I want to get the ladies marching, campaigning.'

Annie couldn't believe her ears. Kirsty was suddenly getting all political. But then maybe that's all politics was – using what we have to make the communities we live in, large or small, work and flourish.

Kirsty sat on the floor, leaning against Duncan's chair with her customary large glass of Sauvignon in hand. 'Don't laugh, peeps. I think this is where it's at. People have to care about where they live, how they live – no one else is going to.'

Annie seized her moment. 'Well, in that vein, but on a much smaller scale, I'm going to be moving from Dean Terrace.'

The assembled throng sat bolt upright from their slouching positions and stared at her.

'I think it's time. I've put an offer in for a place down at Cramond. It's lovely, looking out over all the little boats to the Rosebery Estate. I just love the sounds and the smells down there. You know, the clanking masts, the sea.' She looked round at them all but nobody said anything. Annie knew what was going through their minds. She was a New Town girl, what on earth was she thinking?

'I went there a lot with Dad and of course James and I – well, James and I loved it too.' She felt the cat nuzzle into the back of her head as he lay sprawled along the back of the sofa. 'I just think it's time.'

Virginia was sitting beside her and quietly slipped her arm round her friend.

'Well, nights out at the Cramond Inn. Not too shabby, I say.' Duncan held up his glass and beamed across the room at her.

Knowing the vagaries of the Scottish conveyancing

270

system, Annie resolved not to be too disappointed if her offer was rejected. A closing date had been set and they were going to sealed bids. The allotted time of twelve noon came and went and Annie decided that Rose Cottage was not to be. She would just need to keep looking. As she busied herself in the kitchen, the phone rang. She looked up at the clock – it was almost two thirty. Heart racing, she ran through to the lounge and snatched up the receiver. It was Scott from the conveyancing section of Saunders and MacKay.

'Well, Annie, congratulations. You are now the proud owner of a lovely little whitewashed cottage at the mouth of the River Almond.'

Annie's hand tightened around the receiver. She felt relieved rather than elated but also sad – sad that he would never know this place.

'Thank you, Scott, thank you.' She managed to say the words without her voice breaking, replaced the receiver, composed herself and began to think about the next thing.

She laid James's brochures and maps out on the floor. The sun would be shining, there was amazing cuisine on offer and spectacular scenery to behold. She looked at it all but none of it mattered. She might enjoy the company of her fellow travellers and she knew the food would be good but all that mattered was that she got to the gardens at Villa Taranto.

'Seriously, Annie. You're going to go on your own? Why not wait a few weeks and I'll come with you or even better come with me and Duncan out to Portugal.'

She hadn't expected that. Much as she loved them, Annie knew she wasn't ready for a fortnight in the sun with the Drummonds. She was round at Virginia's setting out her plans to the girls and being fortified by herbal brews and homemade cranberry and oatmeal cookies.

'No honestly, Kirst, it's fine. I really want to do this. I can't believe I've never actually travelled abroad on my own before. I mean, not really. When I went to visit Dad he would meet me at the other end and I knew exactly what I was travelling to.' She sat back, feeling the soft crocheted fabric at the back of her head. The room was full of Virginia's knitted creations.

'Well, I think if it's what you need...' Virginia poured out another cup of lemon balm tea.

'What exactly does this stuff do, Gin?' Kirsty lifted up her cup and screwed up her face.

Virginia swept back a few grey ringlets from her face. 'Soothes the soul, Kirst. Soothes the soul.'

*

As the taxi driver drew up to Hotel Gardini, Annie suddenly felt anxious. Small beads of sweat appeared on her top lip and she could feel her heart race. Maybe she could just turn round and go back. The driver would be okay with that, glad of a return fare to the airport. But then suddenly they had stopped and the driver was out, quick as a flash, getting her bag from the boot of the car. She looked out the window and could see the bottom half of a black skirt, black stockings and flat black shoes. The driver opened the door for her and she stepped out, thanking him in Italian. He smiled and she shook his hand, transferring the fare to him at the same time. Madame was waiting with outstretched hands.

'Good afternoon, my dear.' Madame Gardini seemed smaller now, hair greyer, as she stood slightly hunched at the entrance to her dominion. 'How was your journey?'

'It was fine, thank you.' Annie felt the old woman's hands warmly envelope hers and the feelings of panic subsided.

'Come come, we have your lovely room for you, right at the front of the hotel overlooking the lake.'

'Oh, Madame, it's only for two days. A small room at the back would have been fine. It's just me after all.'

'I know but I think you are happier in this room.' She took Annie by the arm and led her through the hotel. 'I think you need to be in this room.'

After unpacking she sat for a while on the balcony looking out over the sharp azure of the lake, mirroring the sky perfectly. Madame Gardini had been right. She felt comfortable, at peace here.

The prospect of dining alone was not something she relished but again the calmness of her surroundings had seemed to do the trick. She walked down to the dining room, comfortable, assured and ready to enjoy her meal. She had been thoughtfully seated right at the front of the little terrace so all she could see was the lake in front of her and a few guests at the extreme periphery of her vision. Perhaps it was the serenity of the place, perhaps it was the effects of the wine but suddenly her heart seemed to fill again and she knew. She had never really lost him. If she needed guidance he would be there for her, taking the tiller even just for a moment. The physical loss was still immense but there would always be something more, something stronger that would hold them together. For the first time since James's death she felt at peace. The maelstrom of thoughts, emotions and pain had settled and finally found a place to rest.

The following morning she boarded the little ferry to Villa Taranto. The hustle and bustle buoyed her. Tourists mingled with little old ladies travelling further up the lake to the weekly market. Old men sat and played cards, gesticulating wildly and arguing fiercely.

As the boat shuddered to its halt at the gangway, she joined the little queue of garden lovers disembarking to the sound of the ferryman calling through his loudhailer, 'Vi – lla Ta – ran – to'.

Annie saw him as soon as she stepped on to dry land. He stood waving, his olive skin set dark against his light blue shirt, navy trousers and tan shoes. Hugo would accompany her on this little part of her pilgrimage.

They hugged before turning to cross the busy road to the gardens' entrance. Hugo took her hand.

'My, you look very Italian today.'

He laughed. 'Okay, so French-Swiss Scottish man living and working in Belgium and now I look Italian!'

'The very embodiment of a modern European man.' She held on to his arm and smiled up at him.

He squeezed her hand as they walked to the little café situated under the shade of century-old trees. They would spend some time here before Hugo drove Annie to Geneva to stay with Céline for a few days.

'How is your mother, Hugo?' She sipped at her lukewarm cappuccino.

'Oh, she's fine. Really looking forward to seeing you and of course very excited about the baby, as you can imagine.'

'Oh yes, it's wonderful news.' She sat back and let the gentle breeze that was fluttering through the trees brush over her face. 'I can't believe I'm going to be an aunty.'

He beamed at her. How incredibly proud he looked. Proud and happy.

'And everything is okay back in Edinburgh, with the business and everything?'

'Yes, it's busy but it's all good. We're so happy that you and Sofia can make the book launch next month. That should be really exciting. And then of course there's the land reform legislation going through Parliament. I know he won't see finished what he started but I feel it's *such* an achievement for him. Funny how I should feel that.'

'Well, of course it is. You are right to be proud of him. We all are.' Hugo gently squeezed her hand before getting up to pay the bill and buy their tickets to the gardens.

'It's funny, James loved this place so much. When you think of Assynt, how barren it is and you compare it to here. It's amazing of course, but then so cultivated, manicured.'

'I know, Hugo, but he loved what men, what anyone, could do with the land in front of them. Whether it's carving out a living in an unforgiving landscape or creating something like this – full of intensity and colour for people to enjoy. It was all beautiful to him.'

'Are we walking to the top of the hill?'

'Yes. But do you mind if I walk up ahead of you? There's a little spot, a bench under a Douglas fir that looks out over the Alps. He loved that spot. I just want to spend some time alone if that's okay. Just for a few minutes.'

He hugged her again. 'Of course not. I'm going to walk

round to see the giant water lilies. They're supposed to be amazing.'

'Lovely, see you in a little while.'

Annie turned to begin her walk.

'I won't be far behind you,' he called.

She smiled as she climbed, walking through the avenue of dahlias that led her up to the top of the hill.